Praise for Fault Lines

In this fun, intrigue-laden space opera, // Jennings gives an intriguing glimpse of a much larger setting. // Fans of found family will love the portrayal of Velocity and her crew of scrappy underdogs.

— *Publishers Weekly*

Kelly [Jennings] has been compared with C. J. Cherryh, and I think deservedly. *Fault Lines* isn't burdened with the awful angst of Cherryh's [] *Cyteen*, but it has the same intensity and conviction.

— Gwyneth Jones, author of the Aleutian trilogy, winner of the World Fantasy, Clarke, Dick, and Tiptree awards

More political intrigue and gamesmanship than a standard space-battle story... // Solid world building, likable characters...nifty plot twists...

— Craig Clark, *Booklist*

A sharp, character-rich space opera packed with angry, capable women and attractive, vulnerable men. Jennings builds a large, politically complex world // but expresses this through an intimate slice...

— Tansy Rayner Roberts, author of the Creature Court trilogy, winner of multiple Ditmar and WSFA Small Press awards

Also by Kelly Jennings:

Broken Slate

Note: the crew of the *Susan Calvin* made its first appearance in "Velocity's Ghost" in *The Other Half of the Sky* (Athena Andreadis editor, Kay Holt co-editor; Candlemark & Gleam 2013).

Fault Lines

Kelly Jennings

Candlemark & Gleam

First edition published 2018

For information, address
Athena Andreadis
Candlemark & Gleam LLC,
38 Rice Street #2, Cambridge, MA 02140
eloi@candlemarkandgleam.com

Library of Congress Cataloguing-in-Publication Data
In Progress

ISBN: 978-1-936460-83-0
eISBN: 978-1-936460-82-3

Cover art by Ciaran Gaffney

Editor: Athena Andreadis

Proofreader: Patti Exster

www.candlemarkandgleam.com

This one is for Cooper,
for everything they've taught me

Chapter 1

Hell in a Bucket, Free Trade Station, The Drift

Y ou're stranded here," the little girl said. "Everyone knows it."
Tipping brandy ostentatiously into her glass, Velocity said,
"Tell it to your nanny."

"I sold my nanny on Bastiat. For ticket money."

Velocity laughed. "Well then, you don't need me. Travel agency, six quats spinward. Big sign, you won't miss it."

Across the tank, a table of miners broke into a noisy quarrel. It ended in laughter, not blows, and Velocity sighed. When she looked back, the child was scowling. Pale as raw silk, her cropped hair dyed brilliant orange, she was so short she had to kneel on the bench to get her elbows on the table. She ought not to have been able to pull off that regal glower. The eyes, Velocity decided. Gengineered agate-blue, they had an entirely unchildlike intensity. Velocity sighed again. "Listen, Bon—Blondy?"

"Brontë," the child snapped.

Velocity paused; but she had no brief to mock anyone's deck name. "Brontë. While it's true I'm for hire, it's more as a troubleshooter, and less as a nanny."

"What is true," Brontë said, with the bright precise vowels of the inner Core, "is that you cannot make your deck fees. Or the fuel costs, or payments on your liens. Those last make your ship subject to seizure at any civilized station." Having stressed the penultimate word, she flattened her small hands on the table. "The truth is you're desperate."

Velocity swirled her brandy. Desperate was the word, she admitted. Maybe not desperate enough to take on jobs minding infants, though.

Brontë leaned forward. "I require transport to Hokkaido Station."

"Ticketing agency. Spinward. Ask for Jens, tell him I said to book you a ship without pirates."

"I'll be traveling with my Security officer."

"Tell it to Jens. Now, I'm working, so—"

"I can pay your dock fees and fuel costs, along with a bonus that lets you clear the back payments on your liens."

Velocity managed to keep her expression from changing. "Well. I see why you need Security. I don't see why you need me. Passage for two to Hockey, on even the best ship out of here, will run you, ah, somewhat less than that." As the best ship out of the Bucket was likely to be a merchant freighter taking passengers as an afterthought, this was a safe calculation.

"I need your expertise," Brontë explained.

"At navigating eight jumps?"

"For certain matters on Hokkaido Station."

Velocity sipped her brandy. "Who needs killing?"

"No one. I need help with my aunt. Torres Ikeda Alonzo. But I don't need her death. Just…your troubleshooting expertise." Brontë scrubbed at her mouth with a closed fist, and added, "Torres has six of my bonded workers. She's refusing to release them."

Velocity grunted. A property dispute. Property dispute resolutions tended to be relatively simple, if a little dull. Also, as an exile from the Combines, she would be more adept at handling their policies than most here on the Bucket, the child was right about that. She found herself tempted. On the other hand, like most exiles, Velocity kept an eye on the politics of the Inner Core. Six months earlier, Ikeda-Verde Combine had weathered a coup—a hostile takeover, as the Combines called such things. The Ikeda House Board had lost its Primary Seat Holder, Dhia Ikeda Hayek, who had only held the Primary Seat for a few years. Dhia had been killed in a perfectly reasonable shuttle accident, along with two heirs to the Seat, and twenty incidental bonded workers. Directly afterwards, several other heirs to the Seat had also died, in various other accidents and illnesses. Last Velocity had heard, inheritance issues and stock prices were shaking out all over the Republic. "You're an Ikeda," Velocity said, making sure.

"Nowhere in the line."

It was a fact that Velocity didn't remember a Brontë Ikeda anywhere along the line to inherit in Ikeda House. Ikeda-Verde Combine was ranked sixth among the top ten Combines currently in power, so its Board Seat members and their direct heirs, particularly the heirs to the Primary Seats, were straight enough in her memory. However, it was also true that every heir to the Ikeda House Primary Seat she knew off-hand was dead now. After a moment, she toggled her inskull uplink and ran an Orly. Torres Ikeda—Torres Umi Alicia Ikeda Alonzo—popped right up. She was in the line to inherit, currently ranked a tentative eleventh for the Primary Seat on the Ikeda House Board—tentative because at least five heirs in front of her were only missing-presumed-dead.

The search for Brontë Ikeda came back null. But given that Brontë was no more this child's register name than Velocity was hers, that meant nothing. Capturing an image of the child, Velocity ran another search. Null again. This also meant nothing. Most Combines kept images and captures of their minor children off-nexus for just this reason—so scrod like Velocity couldn't pirate their images in the public sphere, see who they were, and decide the snatch was worth the stick.

"I don't involve myself in Combine power struggles," Velocity mentioned.

The unnatural blue eyes shifted, taking her measure. "This would be a stupidly indirect way of fighting for a Board Seat, Captain Wrachant."

Velocity grinned. "Good point. Well, tell me what you want. Specifically."

"You'll do it?"

"I didn't say that. Start talking."

$$\text{λ ╫ ⅄ ⅋}$$

Hell's Bucket, a Free Trade concern, was stinking, leaking, and over-crowded, the sort of station where you wore your skinsuit and kept your eye on the nearest e-kits. Velocity had spent more time docked here since leaving Dresden than she liked to remember; and even here—Brontë was right—her credit stood short. Brooding, she took the lift three levels out from the concourse to Station Security.

Security: hah. Thieves, more like. Though berths were cheap on the Bucket, bribes made up for it. Luckily, the current lot were willing to take theirs in trade, skilled techs being rare this side of the Drift. "Your boy's not done," the Station Security officer on the gate said as she came through the hatch. "Another three, four hours' work yet."

Velocity looked at the wallboard behind the gate, though she didn't need external clocks, not with her inskull uplink. "Midwatch. That was our deal."

"Yah, well, he's a lazy bit of ship filth. You didn't tell us that."

"We can re-negotiate more work for more pay. Until then, give up my tech."

The Security argued, which Velocity expected. The Bucket, like most Free Trade space, saw a deal (negotiated, agreed upon, witnessed) as more theory than obligation. Velocity kept her boots firmly on the line. Freeters treated anything like civility as a request to be robbed. The Security was restating his main point a third time, louder, when Rida emerged from the back corridor, slipping the strap of his tool case over his head.

"Captain," he said, walking past the gate.

"Hey! Hey!" The Security rose.

"Your boss has my call sign," Velocity said, her palm on her Vyai short rifle.

The Security bellowed his argument for the fourth time: "You're on our dock, you'll follow our rules!"

As if the Bucket had rules. Rida kept going. Velocity ducked through the hatch, following him. "I hate this place," Rida said, when she caught up.

"He's just making noise."

"Some shift here, you'll come find me impounded. How much noise do you plan to make then?"

Velocity moved a little closer to him, matching her steps to his. "Tai and I wouldn't let that happen." Rida shot her an angry look. "Good news," Velocity said, changing the subject. "We might have a job."

They had come to the lift; Rida leaned on its call panel. "Another plumbing job? Another job chipping rust from some idiot's boards?"

"A real job."

"One that pays in crap or one that pays in shit?"

"Mzala." She cupped the back of his neck, and then squeezed his shoulder. He scowled more darkly. The lift opened, and they got inside. A weeping stationer, skinny and bruised, darted up the corridor, calling for them to hold the lift. Rida hit shut instead. "That wasn't kind," Velocity reproved.

"He just wants to run a con on us," Rida said, "like every other freet on the Bucket."

Since he was probably right, Velocity didn't argue. Instead, she told him about the Hokkaido job—only the outline, since she'd have to repeat it for Tai. She played up the rescue part of the job, how they were being hired to retrieve some bonded labor. The disgruntled expression didn't leave Rida's face. "Retrieve," he said flatly. "Not set free. Get them back so this Combine silk can keep them under contract."

Velocity didn't mind this reaction. Back when Rida had been new to her ship, he would never have let her see his temper, much less argued with her. She much preferred this irascible Rida to the polite, frightened child he had been then. "They're being held as hostages. That can't be pleasant for them. And Brontë seems nice enough."

"A nice enough slaveholder," Rida said.

The dock-level concourse was, as usual, swarming with beggars, buskers, and thieves. A tiny girl sold puppies from a basket; another, rebuilt handhelds from the back of a tuk-tuk. Water dripped from the overhead; the grimy deck was patched with scraps of metal and plastic. As she followed Rida, two little boys tap-dancing in a chalked-out circle called out, "Pesa! Pesa!"

Free Trade stations loved hard money. Velocity dug out a few coins and tossed them over. Even after all these years in the Drift, she had a hard time believing the brass discs were actually worth anything, but the kids scrambled after them.

Their berth was blissfully quiet. Velocity coded open the dock gate and locked it behind them, and they crossed their yard—empty at the moment of any cargo—to the umbilical gate. Both of them ducked into the umbilical. Rida reset its lock behind them. Tai's voice came through the feed: "Meal's ready, but I can hold if you want a scrub first."

Velocity climbed on up to the galley while Rida bathed. Dinner was bean pau, served with sugar melon. Velocity opened a flask of Rustin white, figuring to help the discussion go down better. She explained the job to Tai while she did. Scrubbed and dressed only in clean canvas shorts, Rida climbed through the hatch when she was halfway through the story and her first bowl of wine. "A Combine Security officer?" Tai said doubtfully as she finished.

"A passenger," Velocity said, "who's fetching along her own security."

Tai filled a bowl for Rida. Tall and lanky, with black eyes and brown skin, Tai wore his hair long. On most planets in the Republic, those in the contract labor system had their heads shaved, supposedly to control vermin. Though Tai had been years on the *Susan Calvin*, he'd come up in the system, and maybe never would leave that experience entirely behind. Rida, short, round, and very good looking, his eyes smudged with thick lashes, had different nightmares in his past.

"She's still Combine Security, Captain," Tai said, handing Rida the dish.

"And that's beyond the central point," Rida said. "How the job makes us slavecatchers."

"It does not," Velocity said. Rida snorted, and Velocity added, "Hokkaido is three jumps to the other side of the Drift and it's a nothing job, for which this Combine child will pay us enough to clear our slate. It will give us room to look for legitimate work."

"Blood money," Rida said.

Glumly Velocity poured the last of the wine into her bowl. The alternative was kiting out on their debts. Orleans-Vijo Combine held massive liens against the *Susan Calvin*. A few had come with the ship when Velocity bought her, but others she had been forced to incur over the years, for repairs and refueling. Paying them back had begun to seem impossible. Even keeping up with the interest payments was rough. More and more lately she had considered just running. They could jump further out system, cross the Drift into Pirian space.

Except the problem with *that* was they were not Pirians. If you weren't in the fleet, you were last in line for any job at a Pirian station. Velocity had heard rumors that unaffiliated ships could buy into the fleet—that they could, in effect, become Pirians. She had no idea whether these rumors were true, or what it meant to become part of the Pirian fleet. She suspected, given the Pirian attitude toward owning things, it would mean giving over ownership of her ship. Anyway it didn't matter. She didn't have funds to buy shares in a box of bees these days. "It's a soft job," she repeated. "Basic work, big pay-out."

"Too much payout," Tai pointed out, "considering what we're being hired to do."

Velocity chipped at the rim of her bowl with her thumbnail. She had noticed that herself. "Maybe they're just too green to know the going rate. Rich kid, out here on the edge for the first time." Tai looked doubtful. Rida scowled. "We won't let them bring weapons aboard. Also," Velocity tapped her forehead, just above her left eyebrow, more or less where her inskull uplink was seated, "I can watch them."

Tai took a breath, as if to argue, and then just ran his hands through his hair, which he wore loose here under station weight. The uplink let her access the ship's grid directly—let her monitor every feed in the ship—so she could, theoretically, monitor their passengers non-stop.

Furthermore, almost certainly neither Brontë nor her Security would suspect that Velocity had an uplink. Inskull links were even less common in Republic space than they were here in the Drift—here, they were uncommon due to the expense and because Pirians, who might have afforded them, considered them adaiya—*out of balance, wrongly done.* Only someone who was adaiya, to the Pirian way of thinking, would commit so much in resources for so small a gain. In Republic space, the links were both proscribed and believed to be insanely dangerous. Not without reason, either: medical care and skill in Republic space being what they were, the risk of infection both with the initial surgery and along the port was much higher than it was in Pirian space.

"We're a hundred and twenty watches on the Bucket now," Velocity said. "This is the only serious job offer that's come near us. It's this or I start renting one of you out for real."

Rida flinched, and Tai shot Velocity an exasperated glance. "She's joking, Ridashi. Maybe run a deep Orly first, at least? Rid can do it without tripping flags."

"That's fine. How long will it take?"

Rida gave her the sort of nervous look he used to give her when he was new to the ship. "Maybe," he said, and licked his upper lip, "if I can use premium channels, maybe two watches? Or three. If I have to use basic, three or four."

"Use premium." Velocity squeezed his shoulder, smiling. "Let me know what you find. I'm going to grab some pit."

She looked back from the hatch: Tai had an arm around Rida, murmuring in his ear. Guilt heating her belly, Velocity dropped down into the trail.

In the scrub outside the pit, she woke the dagan via her uplink while pulling off her station gear. Her jih was stuffed in her locker, where she had left it more than six watches back. She sniffed the fabric, shrugged, and pulled the suit on. She did the waistband with the correct thief knot, and then ducked through the flap hatch into the pit.

The dagan was emerging from the gear locker, its flex-skin rippling. The "real" dagan, if you could use the word real for something built of code, lived in a program uploaded to the ship's brain. This mechanical body was only a tool it used, here in the pit. The pit itself was large for a ship's cabin, with several of its planes flattened—it was like being inside a buckyball. Velocity settled to the surface which, under the push of the station, was its deck, and set about stretching. The dagan, its dark face peaceful, mimicked her motions, just as if its muscles were organic, as if they needed warming up. "It's been seven watches since our last session," the dagan noted.

Velocity rolled to her knees and began stretching her shoulders. "I've been busy."

Behind its eyes, the slight flicker that meant the dagan was accessing its link. "You've been in the station bistros."

Velocity had bought the dagan some years back from a Pirian rebuild shop on Surya Station, both because it was cheap and because Indaiyi was supposed to be the best general purpose workout around. Unfortunately, with Pirians you couldn't separate the mystical from the practical. Also the dagan never shut up. Part of its programming, undoubtedly: every Pirian Velocity had ever met was three-fifths amazingly helpful and two-fifths non-stop lecture.

Only much later had Velocity understood that the primary function of the dagan was subversion. When she'd understood this, she'd felt more stupid than betrayed. Of course it was here to subvert her. It was Pirian. Subversion was what they did.

"So you found work," the dagan said now, moving into the first position for First String.

Velocity followed the dagan's lead as they moved through First String and then First Following String. This was one she had trouble with, due to old breaks in the bones of her left forearm and hand. She ignored the pain as they spun through the rolls, just as she ignored the ache of her bones on cold stations.

"Shady work," the dagan added.

"Oh, please," Velocity said. "Who said that?"

"Keep your head up as you turn. You can't see the enemy if you're watching your feet. Combine money?" the dagan added. "Or Free Trade?"

"Why would I mind taking money off some freet?"

They finished the warm-up, and Velocity attacked, choosing Borrasca, a string which worked better with weight. The dagan countered, dropping its center of gravity and turning around that center to catch her and roll with her. Shortly she was pinned beneath it. She smacked the mat, and the dagan slipped away, back into Awarê stance.

Velocity retreated, breathing deeply. *Remember to breathe*: that had been the second lesson. Right after: *Run away if you can*. She put herself into attack stance, thinking what to try next. The dagan waited, its dark eyes calm. "No lecture?" Velocity asked, in a useless attempt at distraction. "Don't I get to hear what a fool I am, to deal with the Combines again?"

"If you know it's dangerous, why do you need to hear it from me?"

Velocity leapt into Fohla. The dagan pivoted, grabbed her elbow and bicep, torqued up on the elbow and down on the bicep, and slammed her forward. Velocity got her shoulder under her in time for a roll and let the momentum spin her to her feet. The dagan gave her a nod of approval. Half of fighting was learning to fall. That had been the third lesson. "How much choice do you think I have?" Velocity insisted, her breathing ragged. "My crew needs food, fuel, and a ship."

"You should consider your other motives in taking this job."

Velocity flung herself into a very sloppy Yu attack. Not bothering with a counter, the dagan slid sidelong, out of the way. *Run away if you can.* Velocity hit the wall with a thump.

"This child is not your sister," the dagan said. "Helping her now won't absolve you of what you did then."

Abruptly, Velocity stood straight. "End session."

She knew it was impossible, but as the dagan shut down and folded itself back into the locker, she thought she saw reproach in its mechanical eyes. Annoyed, mostly with herself, Velocity left the pit and climbed up to the sauna. She set the long cycle going and while it ran made a list via her uplink of everything she needed to get done if they took this job, and then a secondary list, of what she might do if they didn't take the job. The second list was much shorter than the first. She'd run them out of options, or at least the debt on the ship had. Alice, her sister, had nothing to do with it.

The drying cycle started. She shut her eyes while the hot air buffeted her, refusing to think about her sister, or any of that which had happened so long ago.

Chapter 2

Hell in a Bucket, Free Trade Station, The Drift

As usual when Rida had a problem to solve, he went at it non-stop. Tai did pit, made dinner for everyone—taking a bowl up to Rida, since he wouldn't remember to eat otherwise—and then climbed through the ship to their rack.

It occurred to him as he unbuckled their bunk, yawning, to wonder if the Captain had considered the problem of housing their passengers. Exhausted by the double watches he'd served, he spent no time worrying about this. Instead, he fell into sleep almost as soon as he'd strapped into the bunk. Since they were at dock, and under push, he didn't have to strap in. But after all this time on the ship, he slept better when he did.

Some long time later Rida unstrapped the bunk just enough to slide in with him. "Mm," Tai said, only half awake, moving to make room. When Rida had strapped them in again, Tai wrapped himself around him. "You smell awful."

"Too tired to scrub."

Tai nuzzled his shoulder. "What time is it?"

"Afterwatch third." Rida burrowed down into the bunk, fighting for a share of the pillow. Tai let him have it. Rida took his hand and held it against his own chest. "I'm not finding much."

"There's a shock."

Rida grunted. "I need an image of her Security. If I had that, I could hunt her out."

Tai wrapped himself more closely around Rida, the weight and warmth of his rounded muscles easing something deep inside him, as it always did. "You're working too hard," he murmured. "You don't have to work this hard."

"Not like I can sleep anyway. Not with the Captain bringing these silks on ship, to do who knows what to us."

"Hush," Tai said, hugging him close. "Hush now, Ridashi. We'll be fine."

Rida shoved back with an elbow. "You don't know that. You don't know everything will be fine. Not anymore than she does."

Tai pulled him close again, kissing his shoulder. "Did I ever tell you about when I was a kid in the orphanage on Sarat?"

"Is this the story about how you rooked fruit from the bosses' garden or the one about how you'd hide up in the adit, ditch work weeks at a stretch?"

Tai bit his shoulder this time. Rida banged back harder with the elbow. "Mkashi," Tai said. "No, this is the one about how every year or two, the bosses would run a cull."

Under his hands, Rida's muscles went tight. "They what?"

"Sarat didn't fund orphanages all that well. Also, the bosses had to have their cut of the funds. So when the board money ran short, they'd line us up, all of us old enough to stand—they didn't cull the babies—and the boss would go down the line, pulling out jesses. They'd take the culls out to the pit, that was this old shaft that was played out, shoot them, drop the bodies down the pit."

Rida was silent.

"We used to—all of us, in the orphanage—we'd talk and talk, trying to see what it was, how the bosses decide who to cull. What we could do," Tai explained, "so they'd choose someone else, not us. Keep our gear mended. Keep clean. Stand up straight. Look them in the eye. Don't look them in the eye. We watched, we just—we worked *so hard*, love, trying to understand what it was they did wrong. Our brothers. Our bunkmates. Why they'd been culled. What they had done, so we would not do it." Tai hugged Rida tight, all his own muscles hard at the memory. "But they hadn't done anything. They died because the board money was short."

"You're saying there's nothing I can do," Rida said.

"Well, eventually, maybe. Eventually I was in a place where I could do something. But when I was nine? Nothing." Tai shifted, moving even closer to Rida. "Sometimes, when there's nothing you can do, you have to wait until there's something you can do. And fretting yourself sick when you can't do anything, that's not useful."

Rida was quiet. Tai didn't know if this meant he was thinking, or if it meant he was angry, or what it meant. Rida had come up in a tech house on Tija Station, raised up as an apprentice. Up until he ran out on his indenture at sixteen, he'd had a soft life. Or at least it always sounded soft to Tai, no work except tech work, getting fed every day, never mind no one with a gun to his neck. "Captain's meeting them again, Midwatch next," Tai offered. "Go with. Get an image of the Security then."

Rida turned in his arms and reached up to cup his face. "If I'd been in that orphanage with you," he said, "we'd have figured out something to do."

Tai smiled. "I'm glad you weren't," he said, and kissed the sweet place next to his eye. With a dozy murmur, Rida relaxed entirely, falling to sleep. Tai lay drowsing beside him for some time, trying to fall back to sleep himself. Eventually he unbuckled the bunk and slid out.

He was thinking of an hour or two of pit, followed by a session in the scrub, his usual remedy for these dark angry moods, but when he emerged from their rack, he saw the galley lights were up. Climbing up through the trail, he peered through the galley hatch: the Captain, tucked into the booth with her legs folded under her, drinking coffee and working via her uplink, to judge by how her eyes were flickering.

In her leather leggings and a long-sleeved undershirt, she looked the same she always did to Tai: long, lean, and tasty.

He climbed into the galley, and headed for the coffee. The Captain always made it too strong, but he filled a bowl for himself anyway. Hunting out the tube of condensed milk, he squeezed in thirty or forty milliliters. "Are we running short of biscuits?" he asked, settling in the booth across from the Captain. She shot him a distracted glance, and he moved his chin at her. "Is that what that face means?"

"Oh." She grimaced, and then twitched her left eye, shutting down her uplink. The angular, crooked bones of her face settled into a disgruntled scowl. "Just running data on Ikeda-Verde Combine. Their boards and history."

Tai didn't know much about IVC specifically. Taveri-Bowers had held the mines on Sarat. "Good people, are they?"

"I hate this," the Captain said, brooding. "It's why I left Dresden, to get away from crap like this."

"I thought you left because you didn't want to die for a Board Seat."

She turned her bowl of coffee like a top, setting it spinning on the table. "Well, keeping my head on my neck, that was *some* of it," she agreed. He laughed at her and smiling faintly she spun the coffee again. "Machiavellian pirates," she said. "To read their history, you'd think they spent their time building wonders instead of plotting how best to cut each other's throats."

"What does Ikeda-Verde do?" Tai asked. "Besides cut throats, I mean."

She spun the bowl once again. "Science, mostly. They're the Combine that works up most of the nanotrope protocols for the settlement planets."

"Or not," Tai said, thinking of Sarat, which had been minimally 'troped. Speculation in the barracks had given any number of reasons why this had been so—why TBC had settled a planet and then never rebuilt it—but in fact, he knew, as with the bosses at his orphanage, the simplest explanation was the best. Cheaper to let jesses die young from the hostile environment than to pay what this IVC wanted for the rebuild.

"Or not," the Captain agreed. Her eyes were distant, turned inward, lost in some memory. "These two will be like that," she added. "Funds before everything. I'm like that half the time, if you notice."

Tai stayed silent, politely. The Captain reached out and caught the bowl, stopping it mid-spin. "You don't have to put up with it, from them," she said. "If this Combine child starts treating you like she's got your contract, or the Security does, you let me know. You don't have to stand for that. Not on this ship."

"Rida fell asleep," Tai said. Confused by this sudden swerve, the Captain squinted. "Right in the middle of my very best allurements," he added, and gave her a wickedly smutty look through his lashes. "What about you?"

"What about me? Are you asking if I can stay awake through your best allurements?"

Tai laughed again. "A challenge," he said, and picking up her bowl took both it and his to the sterilizer. When he turned, she was studying him, the disgruntled, unhappy look gone. Most of what he had been after, he had to admit. He took her hand and pulled her toward her cabin.

𝒦 ♯ 𝒳 𝒮

Four watches after their first meeting, Velocity met with Brontë again. Rida accompanied her. He was sullen as they were prepping to leave the ship. Velocity knew what was bothering him. She almost always did. Like when she'd had him rented to the cop shop: Rida hated being around Security, he hated being left on his own on a Free Trade Station, he hated when anyone—but especially Security—started shouting. Not hard to see why he'd been ill-tempered then. This time, she knew, it was the job. He didn't like any aspect of this job, and he especially didn't like that they were taking Combine holders aboard the ship.

This second meeting with the Combine child was set for a teashop spinward in the stockholder's quat. Unlike Velocity's usual tank, the teashop was shiny clean, with bamboo deck covers and interesting art on the bulkheads. Brontë awaited them in a private booth, eating sherbet with ferocious concentration. On the bench next to her, the Security. Tall, with shorn hair, gray eyes, and thin pale lips, she wore a fancy Combine skinsuit, black on black, her muscles outlined crisp through its fabric. Brontë wore the same grimy swat she'd worn in the bistro.

Velocity got right to the point: "Dock and fuel fees up front, and half of the bonus. You provide that, we have a deal."

Sucking on her straw, Brontë squinted. "You expect the bonus up front."

Velocity shrugged. "Good faith payment."

"I'll pay a third up front."

This was more than Velocity had expected to get, frankly. "I'll also need data tags for everyone taking passage," she added, at which Brontë scowled. "It's a standard request."

"If our funds clear, that should be all the data you need."

"That might be true in the Core," Velocity said, though she knew better. "Not out here."

Disgruntled, Brontë scooped out a bit of glacé fruit and chewed on it. At length, her expression still discontented, she said, "Sabra, do you have our tags?"

"I'm afraid not," the Security said. "We can get them to you by next watch."

Velocity smiled. "Also, you'll bring no weapons aboard my ship." This time, the Security reacted, her chin lifting, her mouth flattening. "Will that be an issue?"

"I have weapons," Sabra said. "Yes."

"And you don't wish to leave them behind."

Sabra pulled an immense short rifle from her hip holster and laid it precisely on the table. "No," she said. "I do not."

Rida had drawn back. Velocity gave the Security a steady look. "A Lopaka, yes? But I don't know that model."

"It's new," Sabra said. "Lopaka TAC-20 Plasma short range. Developed for close use on stations and ships. Fifty bolts per minute. Precise within twenty meters. Three hundred bolts per magazine. And it travels with me."

Velocity smiled again. "Not on my ship."

Sabra stared at her. Velocity stared straight back. Beside her, Rida was stone-still. "Perhaps," Sabra said eventually, "we can reach a compromise position."

The compromise was that Sabra would send her weapons in a crate beforehand and Velocity would lock them in the ship's armory. No one was happy about this. On the other hand, during Afterwatch Second the local debt enforcers had come by their gate, wondering with less civility than usual when Velocity would make payment on her deck fees. And this wasn't Pirian space, either, where if you didn't make your payments everyone got together and worked out a nice civilized solution.

At breakfast, Tai had pointed out another issue—berthing. The *Susan Calvin*, a merchant ship requiring minimal crew, had minimal living space. Finding berths for two more, even if one of them massed under 40 kilos, was a tricky proposition. (Rida had suggested locking the passengers in the brig. Velocity was almost certain he was joking.) The sole empty cabin was too small to house two passengers. Its single bunk, when deployed, nearly filled the available space, and it had only one tiny locker. Also, because it was near the hull, it had much less overhead than any of the other cabins.

Velocity and Tai debated logistics at length—it was like one of those riddles with a snake, a mouse, and a bucket of corn—before finally deciding that Tai and Rida would move into the smaller cabin and let their passengers bunk in their (slightly larger) cabin. Velocity imagined that, for the amount she was paying out, their Combine child would think as little of this solution as her Security did of leaving her weapons in Velocity's armory during their trip.

Moving Tai and Rida meant packing up and storing most of their gear, since there was no room for it in the small cabin. Since Rida was still running the search for Brontë's identity, as well as packing the code for their jump out of Bucket, this task fell to Velocity and Tai. There wasn't much to move—neither Tai nor Rida had a great deal of personal property—but it still made six respectable bundles before they were done. "Storing them in the brig sounds better every minute," Tai said, as they dragged the first bundles through the trail.

"Also, then we could keep them locked up," Velocity said.

"Exactly."

"They're passengers, not prisoners."

"They're Core," Tai said. "Worse, they're Combine. Pirates, not passengers." He used the Pirian word for pirate, *gadro*, which everywhere in the Drift, even among the Free Traders, half of whom *were* pirates, was a vile insult. Velocity glanced at him, and then shoved her bundle through the hatch into the hold, and climbed down after it.

It was dusky down here, the chill air scented with industrial solvent as well as the crates of spices in the cargo they'd hauled here to Hell in a Bucket. Ten or twelve of these crates remained, unsold among the new cargo they had loaded: web-packed Pirian-manufactured medicals, fifteen crates of wine, bundles of Pirian silk. These should all fetch prime prices over the line in Republic Space.

The brig sat in the center of the hold—'brig' being a fancy name for a strap-iron cage bolted to the deck of the hold, with only a suction tube for waste and no scrub at all. Right now it was packed full with some of their more fragile cargo. Velocity regarded it while Tai was strapping the bundles into cargo netting. "I get that I'm from the Core," she said, "but what you're forgetting is that I'm from the Core. I grew up in a Combine. I survived that, and I've survived years in the Drift and in Free Trade space. I might be silk, but I'm not a fool."

Tai smiled, the crooked, half-broken smile she had thought was long gone from his face. He moved close to her, reaching to straighten the collar on her shirt. "I know we have to do this," he said. "Rida knows it too."

"But."

He smiled again. "But it's still Combine Security, not to mention a Combine holder."

Velocity bit down on her first hard answer. He was right. This was a bad decision, a bad risk. That it was their best choice didn't make the risk any less. *You do what you have to do.* "I won't let anything happen to you," she said. "Either of you."

His smile went a little more crooked. "I know you won't, Captain," he said, and turned back to work.

$$\text{𝕂 ✝ 𝕏 𝕊}$$

"That's the Security?" Tai stood restless by the umbilical hatch. He wore a loose jersey over green and orange Pirian silk-knit leggings. His hair fell down his back in about fifty braids, liberally decorated with multi-colored beads. He and Rida had been bored. A tuk-tuk powered by two barefoot boys stopped by their gate. Brontë Ikeda climbed from it, scowling. A second tuk-tuk came rattling through the crowd; Sabra got out, reaching back to haul baggage onto the dock.

"Captain Sabra Walker," Velocity said. "She's got wonderful manners."

Tai grunted. "You could barely tell those tags she shipped us were forged."

Sabra paid the boy peddling her tuk-tuk, and went to pay the other two as well, leaving the baggage unguarded. Of course a kid from the concourse darted in to make a grab for it. Brontë, who had not seemed to be paying any mind, whirled and kicked the thief's feet out from under him. Sabra shouted; the thief's crew scattered into the crowd. Brontë, knee planted on the thief's neck, snarled. Sabra gathered up the baggage. Only then did Brontë let the thief go, rising to her feet and backing away. The thief bolted. Brontë stood watching him go.

"Huh," Tai said. Velocity grunted agreement. Brontë and Sabra came toward the *Calvin*, Sabra lugging all the baggage. Velocity pushed the gate open.

Their passengers made no objection to the shared cabin, nor to Tai's announcement concerning housekeeping. "We handle maintenance," he said. "But no one's going to clean up after you. Also, the only meal served is at Mainwatch Third. You're on your own otherwise."

"Mainwatch?" Brontë said with delicate contempt. Sabra's lashes lowered.

"Tai will give you a brief on shiptime later," Velocity said. "Hours and minutes are universal time. It's Midwatch First now. Rid, how are we with station break?"

"Sawa sawa," Rida said. He and Tai climbed into the com.

Velocity stayed in the galley another moment. "We're breaking dock in," she checked her uplink, "half an hour UT. Heading out toward the jump point at a quarter push. That'll give us about point three gee, here on the ship. Six hours to jump at that push. I don't expect you to stay in your cabin that entire time. But pit is locked down, as is the galley. Cold meals only, and I'd prefer passengers in skinsuits." She paused, eying Brontë. "You do have suits?"

"Yes, Captain," Brontë said.

"I'll issue sedatives if anyone needs them." Some people were bothered by jump, and preferred to sleep through it.

"We'll be fine," Brontë said.

Velocity glanced past her, at Sabra, and just nodded again. "We'll talk after jump," she said, and climbed up into the com.

Chapter 3

The *Susan Calvin*, in Transit to Chernyi Point

T his Security," Tai said.

Rida, so exhausted he could barely move, stood stripped in the tiny facility off their cabin, bracing himself in place with his knees and heels while he washed with a wet scrub. They had stacked the first three jumps, because of some payments the Captain hadn't quite gotten around to making on the Bucket, and were now pushing toward Chernyi Point. Scrubbing under his arms, Rida asked, "What about her?"

"I'm to keep watch on them. The cargo. Like the Captain said." Tai, already in their bunk, his hands tucked behind his head, watched the line of Rida's spine and his dark hair, growing out just now from its usual close crop, floating loose around his skull. "The silk keeps dodging. I don't know if that's intentional."

Rida yawned, scrubbing the back of his neck. Tai had scars everywhere, some from beatings, some from the mines. Rida's fine brown skin was barely marked. Most of his scars were internal. "I can pack up a code," Rida said. "Track her. See if she's playing you."

"Meh. If you have time. She's probably just being a kid. My *point* is, this Security, she's dogging my ass round the spin. *Talking* to me."

Rida dumped the grimy cloth in the laundry bin and propelled himself into the cabin, rattling the hatch shut behind him. Hunting through their shared locker, he gave Tai a squinting frown. "You think the Combine Security is trying to seduce you."

"If she is, she's terrible at it. Charming as a toaster." Tai shifted to his side, making room on the bunk for Rida. "But nothing she's doing makes sense otherwise. I mean, asking questions she has to know the answers to. Like, we're in the Exchange, she asked what it's for, does it help with the environmentals, why I'm running pH tests. Like that."

Thinking this through, Rida pulled on the undershirt he slept in, a ragged faded rose-red one. "Well," he said. "If she's never shipped out anywhere, maybe..." He yawned, rubbing his wrist over his eyes. "Why's a Security want to bunk you?"

Tai kicked his ribs, not that gently, sending him spinning in the low gee.

"Oof." Rida caught himself against the overhead, pushed off, and tumbled down to the bunk. Laughing, he caught Tai and pinned him against the mattress. "Well, you are ugly," he said, tugging at Tai's braids. "And cranky."

"And mean." Tai pulled Rida closer. "Don't forget how mean I am."

"And skinny." Rida licked his throat. "And not at all tasty."

"So you won't mind when I let her have me." Pushing back a loose strand of hair, Tai nuzzled his ear.

"Just don't bring her here."

"Why? Ain't you like tall muscly blondes?"

"Security?" Rida murmured. "Rather bunk a toaster."

Tai laughed and began kissing down his belly.

𝄞 ✝ ⅄ ⸱

Making a jump required much tedious work, mainly packing code and running error checks. Plus, there was a certain amount of danger, although Velocity's anxiety level over the jumps had dropped off markedly since she had taken Rida aboard. She was all right with math, but he had a feel for it she couldn't match. Post-jump you ran analysis, also a lot of work. In other words, after they'd stacked the first three jumps across the Drift, both she and Rida had been working very nearly round the spin.

After the third jump, Velocity slept all through Midwatch and most of Afterwatch. Waking, she washed, and then climbed through the trail toward the galley. The ship was at push again, after several watches at zero-gee. Velocity liked microgravity, especially after time on stations, where the gravity was often near standard. Also, keeping the ship at push meant higher fuel costs. But the plants in the Exchange did better with some gee, as did the bones and muscles of her crew. It was a trade-off—the expense of the fuel against the benefits of gravity. Though fuel costs usually won, on this trip the Ikedas were buying. She'd had Rida plot a course that kept the ship at a nearly a third standard gravity most of the way.

In the galley, she found Tai in the booth with the Combine Security officer, Sabra. "Captain," he said brightly. "Come eat. Rida cooked, so it's not terrible."

"It is quite good," Sabra said. Though in fact the bowl in front of her, filled with fish and salsa, remained almost untouched. Hiding her amusement, Velocity went to tap some coffee into a bowl. Another benefit to burning fuel for gravity—it made eating and drinking much easier.

"So." Velocity sipped the coffee—strong and dark, which meant Rida had made this too. Tai liked his coffee sweet and light. "Twenty-seven watches until the Hokkaido jump. Plenty of time to run the trouble list."

"Dibs on scrubbing the water tanks," Tai said.

"Isn't that fortunate," Velocity said. "That's precisely the item I meant to assign you."

He made a rude gesture with his thumb and went back to eating. The 'water' tanks were actually recycling tanks, through which all their recycled water went—including the tank which held their waste water. Scrubbing and sterilizing these tanks was one of the more unpleasant tasks on the ship, and volunteering for the job—while not entirely beyond the realm of Tai's character—was unexpected enough to cause Velocity to regard him skeptically.

"I'll be happy to help," Sabra said.

Now Velocity studied her. "Help scrub tanks?"

"If Tai doesn't mind." Sabra smiled at him. Velocity felt her eyebrows twitch together.

"Oh," Tai said, "I'd love that, Sabra." He got up from the booth, taking his dishes to the sterilizer. "You'll want to take off that pretty uniform, though," he added, giving her his best charming smile. "Come on, I'll find you some work gear."

They left through the aft hatch, Sabra letting Tai take the lead. Velocity settled into the booth and wound her ankles around the stabilizing bar in the booth—handy for when the ship was at microgravity. She blinked up her inskull link and opened the trouble list. But she kept thinking about the Security's behavior, and Tai's, for that matter. So she shut down the list and accessed the ship's feeds, hunting first for Brontë—in the passenger cabin, viewing something on a handheld—and then for Rida, in the Exchange. Velocity recycled the last of the coffee and went up to join him.

Aside from standard maintenance, there wasn't much to do between jumps on the *Calvin*, at least for her crew. This was one reason she saved maintenance for when they were en route—you needed some distraction on these two hundred to seven hundred hour cruises through space, when anything could go wrong and mostly nothing did. Space travel was the most boring way to be terrified that Velocity knew of. If they'd been running cargo instead of passengers, her crew would have gotten involved in some new interactive, or got caught up on animates—Rida always updated their bank while they were docked. Velocity had known passengers would complicate the journey. Just how much, though, she hadn't guessed.

"He wants to let her run," Rida said, in the Exchange. "See what she's playing at."

Rida was running chem tests; she was cleaning filters. Around them were fig trees and wide-leaved pumpkin vines, bamboo, yams, blackberries and dates, watercress and carrots, lilies and the acrid stink of tomato vines. Bees buzzed, ladybirds bumbled. Velocity gave a filter a last rinse and held it out to Rida, who touched his wand to it, ran a screen on his handheld, and nodded.She followed the tube down to the next filter box and began working the filter into its bracket. Water was pulled from the tube into these boxes, where it ran through the screens before returning back to the water running through the tube below. The filters were supposed to be interchangeable, every filter fitting every bracket, but as usual actual hit up against ideal. As she joggled and coaxed, fish slid through the tube: trout, whitefish, a fat slow catfish, its whiskers moseying the roots tangling around him. Fish were happier when the ship had push, too.

"It's not that she couldn't be interested in him, obviously," Rida said, moving down to the mums. "Only she's not."

Remembering the transparently fake manner in which the Security had smiled at Tai in the galley, Velocity agreed with this assessment. "That's...interesting."

"It's one more reason to believe they're running a con on us," Rida said.

The filter slid in finally. Velocity went to pull the next. "Let's flip the con."

Rida said nothing. She glanced over her shoulder, but he was expressionless. Climbing back past the tangle of squash vines, she set about worrying the next filter into the sterilizer. She raised her voice over the racket of the scrub as it cycled: "Tai goes along with it," she explained. "Gets them to trust him. The poor jess," she said, shifting into a more pronounced Combine accent, "so mistreated and oppressed by his Captain. He'd do anything for their help."

Rida eyed her. "What's anything, exactly?"

"Nothing he doesn't want to do." Velocity hit the steam cycle, glancing up at the black currants, which were coming ripe again. She was on dinner this Mainwatch. She wondered if she could get away with a nice fruit salad one more time. "He's good at this. Running people. You know he is."

Over by the lab bench, Rida said nothing, pointedly. Velocity pulled the filter from the scrub and held it out to be checked. "If you handle dinner this watch, I'll do your laundry shift next two watches running." He gave her a wary, startled glance. "Three watches?"

"What if I teach you to cook?" he said, putting the wand to her filter.

She pretended to consider. "Will I still have to do your laundry?" she asked, and Rida snorted. Velocity grinned. "All right. But only two watches for one."

After they had finished maintenance, Rida carried off the figs, tomatoes, and other fresh harvest from the Exchange to stow it in the galley keeper. Velocity went down the Exchange to her favorite place, a patch of mint under the fig trees, and brought up her uplink. She hunted the feed until she found Sabra, now with Brontë in the pit. Velocity widened the screen at the corner of her vision until it covered most of her left eye.

Sabra had loaded neither the dagan nor any other program—she was training the Combine child herself. Nor was she using any regime Velocity recognized. Whatever this was, it was more aggressive than the Kendo she and Alice had studied when they were young, and far more aggressive than Pirian Indaiyi. Every attack went to kill; every defense assumed the aggressor was an assassin. Velocity watched the attacks and parries, remembering hiding in the walnut tree in the garden after her childhood lessons, her muscles light with exhaustion, her bruises stinging, sick at heart because she could not, *could not* get the sword-throw right. Her Kendo coach, Malachi, had never said anything during these sessions, but she knew his thoughts: *This one is dead the minute she leaves the habitat.*

Alice had been better at Kendo. But Velocity didn't lie to herself: her sister hadn't been that much better. Even at sixteen, Velocity had known that.

Sabra drove a vertical strike to Brontë's temple, and the child slid sidelong, her forearm coming up in a block, spun neat as a top and drove her other fist into Sabra's heart—or where Sabra's heart would have been, if Sabra hadn't turned around her strike, caught the collar of Brontë's jacket, and yanked her backwards.

Velocity bit her lip; but Brontë rolled, kicking up at Sabra's face. Connected, too, a solid thump of her small bare heel on Sabra's chin, knocking the woman back. Sabra landed on her feet, launching herself immediately at Brontë, who was crouched, ready for her.

It went *on* like that. By the time she had watched a few rounds, Velocity's muscles were twitching from sympathetic shock. She broke the feed right after Brontë elbowed Sabra in the mouth, sending a gout of blood in fat blobs through the pit air.

Unsettled, Velocity shut down the link and wandered the Exchange, running her hand along the glossy leaves of the lime trees and the snowdrop flowers of the new pear trees (just added two ports ago). After a bit, she opened her link again, to hunt for Tai. He was down in the underdeck, running viability checks on the e-supplies and lifepods. She started for decom—if she hurried she could brace him before dinner.

𝄢 ✝ Ⴆ 𝄢

𝐀 watch and a half after the Captain had floated her plan, and after he'd had two separate fights with Rida about it, Tai went down to the hold to retrieve a shirt he had stowed which he hadn't expected to want. When he cracked the hatch, he found Brontë there before him. She was messing about in the great cavernous space—climbing on the cargo netting and in among the struts and girders, swinging by her hands and flinging herself across open space to catch hold of another girder. It was true the ship had only light push for the next six or eight watches, but even so—

Thinking of the Captain's plan, Tai whistled through his teeth.

The pup jumped. "What are you doing in here?"

Silence. Then Brontë swung out by her hands, flung herself out into the air, did a somersault on the way down, and landed with her feet braced. "Nothing," she said, staring straight at him.

Tai had used that trick himself more than once—look right into someone's eyes while you lie—and he was not impressed. "Good," he said. "Come do laundry."

He expected objections, or whining; but instead, when he looked back through the hatch from lower deck, there she was, her small round face tipped up toward him as she climbed, pale and expressionless in the dusk of the hold.

The laundry was at the aft end of lower deck, next to the sauna. Everyone was supposed to fetch their bins here as they filled up, and sometimes they even did. Just now, three packed bins were piled up around the laundry press. Which meant two of those aboard had not gotten their bins to the laundry. Tai shrugged—he wasn't running from cabin to cabin hunting out dirty gear. You fetched your bin or you did without clean gear until next rota, that was his philosophy on the matter. "Now eyes up," he told the Combine child, opening the laundry machine, "because I'm only running one demo. The first essential thing is not to overload the basket."

He showed her how to load baskets and run the various cycles, microwaving and then blasting the laundry with gusts of steam, and drying it with a roar of heated air. While the first cycle ran he taught her to sort bins. There was some gagging.

"Why not just use disposables?" Brontë demanded. "Jettison the...the...these at least," she said, at the scrub wipes. "That's what *we* do. On our ships."

"This ain't the Combine. Out here in the Drift, sometimes we're a long way from port. What happens when you run out of disposables?" Brontë frowned, considering this, and Tai added, "When it's done, clean goes in these bins here. Ship's crew picks up their own laundry. That applies to you and your Security as well."

"We do our share," Brontë said. "Who says we haven't?"

Tai gave her his most charming smile. "You've been great," he said. "I was telling the Captain, maybe we should rebate some of your fee, you've worked so."

In fact, while Brontë did her assigned chores, she never strayed beyond these. She didn't seem to notice when something needed doing, and would leave her used dishes on the table, or her towels and grimy scrubs in the sauna. Sabra did more work, but Tai suspected that was only because she wanted an excuse to dog his heels.

"This has a twenty minute cycle," Tai told the child. "While it runs, come up to the galley. It's my turn on dinner, you can teach me to make that soup."

"With the fish?" Brontë locked the laundry and set the cycle running. "That's Sabr—Captain Walker's recipe. She knows it better than I do." But she followed him willingly enough, and her eyes were lit with interest, rather than wary and guarded as they usually were. Tai kept his satisfaction to himself.

⁊ � ⅄ ⱡ

Afterwatch second, Velocity opened the pit. It was her first time in the pit since she had shut the dagan off mid-session, but the dagan said nothing. They did two hours of straight Indaiyi, and then another hour of assault tactics. Toward the end, they ran disarming techniques— what Velocity ought to do when attacked by an armed opponent, if she couldn't run away, or surrender.

The dagan aimed the weapon at her. A mock-up of a Vyai short rifle, it was one of the dagan's many props. Velocity went to her knees, a motion as elaborate as a dance—trained into her muscles *like* a dance, in fact. The dagan shouted, the way an enemy might shout, lunging toward her, and she slapped up and sideways with her forearm, knocking the plasma rifle off line, kicking herself upward at the same time as she drove her other fist into the dagan's throat.

The Vyai flashed light past her ear; she flinched, but followed through with the punch. Her other arm knocked the rifle loose while she flung herself at him. For once, she was fast enough. Wrapping herself around him, one arm locked around his neck and the other to his wrist, she drove him to the deck. The plasma rifle skittered across the mats.

The dagan slapped the bulkhead, and Velocity let go. Her heart was thumping as it often did during these exercises, even though she knew they were simulations. She rubbed the ear the plasma shot had flashed past. "Am I dead?" she asked.

The dagan knelt by the smart pads and drew a circle, opening a window. Velocity settled facing it, the non-smart mats rough on her knees. The dagan downloaded data from the pit feeds, and captures of the exercise they had just done appeared in the window. It ran through captures from several angles. In all of them it was clear that the plasma bolt—the bright line that represented the bolt—had missed Velocity's skull, though not by much. "The corona would have taken my ear off," she said. "And most of my face."

The dagan tipped its hand palm up. "Attacking a superior force is always a last resort."

She chewed her lip, watching the capture play from another angle. "Run away," she muttered.

"Yes," the dagan agreed.

"What?" They both looked up. Brontë peered at them from the hatch. "*What* did you say?" she demanded.

The dagan sat back on its heels. "Come join us, mzala."

Brontë scowled. "I don't have proper clothing."

"Not necessary," the dagan told her, its tone much friendlier than it ever was for Velocity. "Not for first lessons. Come. We've been needing a third."

Brontë slipped through the hatch and came slowly toward them. "This isn't Shtai."

"It is not," the dagan agreed. "This is Indaiyi. The Pirian way."

Brontë crouched like a little frog on the mat. Her eyes narrowed. "Pirian."

Velocity hid her amusement. Those in the Core didn't know much about Pirians, but they knew they were evil—the demons in the dark, just waiting for their chance to rush the barricades and eat Combine babies whole. Velocity laid odds with herself on how long it would take this child to run for the exit.

"We begin," the dagan said, "with warming strings."

With three in the star, the dagan was much happier—they could arrange themselves in something *like* a circle. All Pirian activities were meant to be practiced in a circle. They worked through the warming strings, rolling and spinning, the dagan running through some of the strings two or three times for Brontë's sake. Velocity, seeing the clumsiness of the child, was reminded of her own early days learning Indaiyi. Finally, they advanced to the first Morning string.

"Do what?" Brontë demanded furiously.

The dagan stared at her from calm black eyes. Velocity, kneeling, said nothing. She'd had the same reaction. "Tokalu," it said. "The first lesson. Run away if you can."

"*Run away?*"

"If you can," the dagan agreed. Brontë stared, frowning. Quick as a striking snake, it slapped her ear. She yelped, knocked sideways by the blow. Catching herself against the bulkhead, she glared. "Tokalu," the dagan said. "Get out of the way."

Velocity kept still. Brontë rubbed her ear, her face squinted up with anger. After a long moment, the child returned to position in the circle, eying the dagan warily. When it struck at her again, she drove her arm up, attempting to grab its wrist—trying, no doubt, one of the moves that Sabra had been teaching her in Shtai. Catching her forearm, the dagan rolled backwards, spinning the child through the air and slamming her into the far bulkhead.

It ended facing her, waiting to see what she would do. Brontë had rolled deftly to her feet and now launched herself like a missile right

for the dagan. The dagan moved itself from her path. Brontë shot
past it to hit the bulkhead. The dagan had turned and was waiting.
Brontë bared her teeth, turned and launched again. The dagan moved
aside again. Ready this time, she rolled, kicking sideways like a piston.
It caught her bare heel and rolled with her. They tumbled through
the pit. Velocity got out of the way. Using the bulkhead and Brontë's
weight for leverage, the dagan spun them down and pinned her against
the deck. The child struggled grimly.

"You have to slap the mat to show you surrender," Velocity told
her.

"I *don't* surrender," Brontë snapped.

Carefully, the dagan increased pressure, bending her arm back.
She cried out, bit her lip. The dagan bent her arm back a fraction
more. Going pale, Brontë bit her lip harder.

"Dagan," Velocity said. "Override." The dagan let her go, sitting
back on its heels.

Flushed, Brontë scrambled to her feet. She shot Velocity a furious
look. "*I don't surrender!*"

Velocity said nothing. Resting on her heels, she watched the child
expressionlessly. After a second, Brontë whirled and bolted through
the exit.

"That was longer than I thought she would last," Velocity said.

"Those who hurry seldom arrive," the dagan said peacefully.
Used to this sort of Pirian yap, Velocity made a face and turned back
to the session.

$$\text{Ҡ ☂ Ⴢ ⱥ}$$

Midwatch third, a hundred and ten hours from Chernyi Point. The
Combine Security officer had the silk in the pit, for the once-a-spin
training session they did. Free of her for once, Tai went hunting Rida.
He was in the com, in his saddle, his ankles wrapped around the post
and his headset loose around his neck. His screen was covered with

simulated trajectories and the attendant math. The Captain sprawled in the com saddle, one foot braced against the edge of the console, her expression disgruntled. "Where's your milk pudding?" Rida asked Tai.

Milk pudding was what Rida had taken to calling the Security. Tai had no idea why—anything less like a pudding would have been hard to find. He climbed into the tac saddle. "Did you run that program?"

Lazily, Rida reached over and keyed something into his port. The math vanished and a bright pink folder appeared on the main wallboard, spun, and flung itself open, disgorging its data: a chart, a text file, and a capture. Rida tapped open the chart, which revealed itself to be a graphic of the ship, with little red lines and blue circles filling it. He enlarged the graphic by two hundred, and then three hundred percent. The lines went all over the ship. The circles were all over as well: in the Exchange, in the hold, in the laundry, in the galley, down in the umbilical. The only place with no circles and no lines was the Captain's quarters. "What am I looking at?" the Captain asked.

Tai explained. "We noticed Brontë showing up in places on the ship she had no real need to be. Rida put a tracer on her." He moved his chin at the board. "She's gone everywhere, looks like. This is over the past six watches, Rida?"

"This is the first ten watches she was on board. Well, I didn't track her most of the first watch. But after that. She's eased up lately."

"Huh," the Captain said. Then she said, "She is a kid. They do get into things."

"If that's not running reconnaissance," Tai said, "it's a fat imitation." The Captain sat up straight to peer closer at the board. "We've only got their word for it that this job is about retrieving their missing bonded workers."

"They paid us buckets up front," the Captain said, still squinting at the board. "Way too much for it to be bait."

"It doesn't have to be they're pirates," Rida argued. "Not Drift pirates, anyway. It could be a setup for something else." The Captain scowled darker, and Rida added, "Plus, this story, that they want your help getting these workers back, why pay you so much to do a job they could do on their own? Station Security would give this Brontë whatever she asks, if she's who she says she is."

"Also," Tai said, "the forged tags. I was thinking it was to hide who they were from Ikeda-Verde Combine, but what if it's not? What if it's to hide who they are from *us*?"

The Captain shoved at her hair, making it stand on end even further. "What do we have that's worth all that work? A ship that's in debt for more than twice her worth, and a hold half full of cargo? And anyway Brontë does need help getting her bonded labor back. If she's a minor child low in the Combine ranks, someone not in line to inherit, she *will* need help. That's especially true if Torres Ikeda Alonzo has possession of that bonded labor. She's high in the line now. And once the Combines are involved, Station Security won't interfere. Too big a risk and no reward."

"This silk *claims* she's not in the line of inheritance," Rida said.

"And your search checks that story," Tai said.

"My search only found what's on the nexus. What was on the nexus that I could find from the Drift." Still brooding at the screen, Rida shook his head. "Brontë's in the line. She has to be. Why else lie about her name? Not to mention the Security officer."

"I thought that was standard for Combine Houses," Tai said. "Lying about the names of their babies."

"It's not lying." The Captain was still intent on the screen. "They're like nicknames. Milk names, they're called. It's to keep Combine children anonymous, even to other children. Brontë would have a milk name whether she was in the line or not. On the other hand, her whole name is a lie. And an obvious lie at that."

Tai had been there when Rida was running the forged tags Sabra had sent them. The name on Brontë's tags, Brontë Elizabeth Leonardo Ikeda Vijo, had seemed a typical Combine name to him. "What's obvious?" he asked, curiously.

"House names have content," the Captain said. "You can read someone's history, to some extent, by the names they're given. It's how we know Brontë is a milk name—no Combine child would be given a name like that. And Ikeda Vijo isn't likely either."

"What's wrong with Ikeda Vijo?"

"House names tell people who your parent houses are. Your first House name comes from your mother—Combine Houses reckon descent from the mother, so that's your more important name. The second House name gives the secondary line of inheritance. That name comes from the secondary parent, usually the father. Ikeda House and Vijo House have been enemies for centuries. No Ikeda is going to let a Vijo into their line."

"Huh," Tai said. "Well, maybe they weren't expecting scrods out in the Drift to be able to read House names. Or maybe her parents were romantics. Or maybe they're really are just terrible liars."

"That's well past terrible," the Captain said. "In any case, lying about her name, even badly, doesn't have to mean she's high in the line."

"She's a low-level silk who travels with her own Security officer? How likely is that?" Rida shook his head. "They're lying, and maybe they're lying so we'll take her into the Core, so she can run a stealth attack on the Combine. Maybe we're diving into a box of bees."

"That doesn't fit the data, either," the Captain pointed out. "Even now, after the shake-out, Torres Ikeda Alonzo is only eleventh in the line to inherit, and that's only if some of those in front of her are really dead. If Brontë is high in the line, why would she need to target someone low in the line?"

"If she's not high in the line, she wouldn't have dedicated Security," Rida insisted.

"She might," the Captain said, and abruptly changed the subject. "What about Sabra? How's that running?"

Tai waggled his head back and forth. "Maybe? She's spinning me dust and dreams now, how her Combine could buy me out. Set me free."

Rida snorted. "Did you tell her you already freed yourself? Anyway, what is she, but contract labor?"

"She's bonded labor," Tai corrected.

"What's the difference?"

Tai shrugged. He didn't know that exactly himself. But bonded labor squalled and shrieked if you called them jesses, so he knew it must be some difference. "Whatever she wants, or whatever her little silk wants, they haven't come out with it yet."

The Captain grunted. "Show me this new approach to the jump point," she told Rida, "and tell me again why you think it's the best one."

$$\text{𝒜 ✝ ✗ 𝒮}$$

She and Rida were up in the dorsal air shaft, a shallow spine that ran along the ship between the hull and the com deck and hold bulkheads; interspersed along this spine were the particulate-silica-zeolite panels, uptake filters which, along with the Exchange, scrubbed CO_2 and toxins from the air, keeping the mix on the *Calvin* breathable, "at least so far," as Velocity liked to add. Internal sensors monitored when any of these needed changing. Fifteen PSZ filters along this spine were functioning at less than twenty percent, which was as low as Velocity liked to let them get. The ship's other six spines, ventral, port and starboard, were reading similarly, so this watch she and Rida were bent on changing them all out. And what else did they have to do, anyway, with eighty more hours to jump?

"You could do Indaiyi with me," Velocity suggested. "That would make the dagan happy. Well, happier."

"True joy lies in action," Rida said, mocking the dagan's Pirian accent.

"*In*action," Velocity corrected. "Please. Far better to do nothing than something stupid. And most actions are stupid actions." She added, "If you did Indaiyi with me, you'd know that."

Rida laughed, which was what Velocity had been after. Having snapped in the new PSZ panel, he slid down the spine. She floated after him—they were back at microgravity for the next three watches, which made this particular job a bit easier, due to the narrow confines of the spines. Microgravity felt wonderful. Her bones hardly ached at all.

As they skimmed through the small space, she watched for red lights on the sensor grid. The serial numbers were listed in her uplink, and they could have searched for suboptimals that way; but hunting via the sensors was faster.

"Here's an idea," Rida said. "What if you lock just the Security up? The kid we can probably handle. Probably."

"*In*action. Remember?"

"Well, the Security can't act if she's in the cage. Especially if we drug her food."

"And when we get to Hokkaido, and this Combine Security and her charge swear out a complaint against us for unlawful imprisonment? Never mind getting paid."

"It's not unlawful imprisonment. You're Captain, this is your ship, what you say is lawful is lawful."

"Good luck getting that to fly in a Republic court."

Rida shot her an annoyed look. *Another reason to avoid Republic space*, that look meant. Velocity had to admit he had a point. She spotted a red light, and kicked herself to a stop. Rida, his shoulders braced against the spine's overhead and his feet against its base, pulled the worn PSZ panel. Just as he was handing it to her to stow in the carry-all, an alarm began to racket through the ship: three short blaring bursts, a pause, and three more.

Collision alert.

Velocity's heart stuttered. She and Rida stared at one another. Then she eeled around and launched herself through the spine toward the ship's bow, scrambling past struts and flanges. She heard Rida flying after her. The collision alert wailed in steady blaring rhythm, too fast for it to be a drill. She hadn't scheduled a drill in any case. Reaching out through her uplink, she jumped to the exterior boards. Nothing. Clear. She ran the boards again—still nothing—as she hit the hatch to the berth-deck trail, and burst through it.

All along the trail, e-lights flashed red. She shot down the trail, and flung herself into the com, filling her lungs to shout: "*Tai!*"

Rida tumbled after her, yanking the aft locker open. He tossed Velocity her skinsuit and began pulling on his own. "Tai!" she shouted, fighting the suit, most of her attention still on her uplink. The boards were clear—nothing. "Rida, nothing's on the boards. *TAI!*"

Rida sealed his skinsuit and shoved himself down into his saddle, snapping shut the safety gear, slapping up his data feed. He didn't have an inskull link. Velocity kept meaning to get inskulls for him and Tai, but so far they'd never had the funds to spare. Reaching up, he hauled down his aux-port and slapped on the wallboards. Helmet still in one fist, Velocity linked to the ship channel. "This is the Captain," she said, her voice echoing around her. "We've got collision alert. Repeat, collision alert. Passengers into skinsuits, and seal yourself in your cabin. Tai, report—"

"That won't be necessary."

Velocity spun in midair. Sabra was braced in the hatch from the galley, her face rigid. "What?" Velocity said. "*What?*"

Sabra answered something; Velocity never did hear what, because she got hit hard between the shoulders. Her helmet was knocked from her grip; she spun, tumbling, and her head slammed into the bulkhead. Lights burst. *Meteor*, she thought. Rida yelled; noise crashed around her. The deck slapped her hard. She couldn't breathe. *Hull breach.*

The dagan gazed at her clear-eyed: *Get out of the way, mzala.*

Rida shouted her name.

Darkness.

Chapter 4

The *Susan Calvin*, in Transit to Chernyi Hub

Velocity woke in the hold, in the brig cage. Though she was still wearing her skinsuit, she was cold. They were under push again, she realized. Serious push, too, what felt like full thrust. Alarmed, she tried to straighten, and found she was in restraints, the kind used by Combine Security. These were heavy canvas-covered metal-flex wrist bands, with a built-in snub, a stout metal cord that could be used to bind the restrained person to something. She was bound to the strap-iron of the cage wall.

In the dusk, a shadow stirred. Rida. "Captain?"

She scooted toward him. "Are you hurt?"

He flinched away. He was in restraints too, she saw, snubbed like her to the cage wall. Both his eyes were bruised; his upper lip cut and scabbed. Scabs of dried blood lay dark under his nose and along his neck, and a raw swollen scrape marred his right temple.

"Did we get boarded?" Velocity asked. Her inskull link was undamaged. She linked up, reaching for feeds. "Where's Tai? Is it— it's pirates? Or…the Navy?" She said the last dubiously. The Republic Navy did not generally venture this far into the Drift. Rida looked away, his eyes lowered.

"Rida?" She spoke with only part of her attention; she was linking through the ship grid, running the boards, checking feeds. Every feed was wide open. Nothing blocked. Whoever had boarded them had taken away Rida's handheld, probably, but had not guessed she had an inskull uplink. The ship was at full push, she saw from com boards. That had been nowhere in Rida's flight plan, and she wondered what new trajectory they were on, where they were headed. But when she accessed that, the trajectory, it showed the same destination, Chernyi hub. The new flight plan looked on point, but since the math hadn't been logged with it, she couldn't be sure.

She accessed other feeds: Sabra in the com, sitting at Rida's saddle, her long legs wound around its anchor; Brontë in the pit, running resistance weights. She opened the feed to her cabin and stopped in surprised. Tai lay there, on his back in her bunk. He was entirely unrestrained. She muttered a curse under her breath; Rida flinched. Harried, Velocity shot him a glance and finished running the feeds. No one else appeared to be anywhere on the ship. "Rida?"

"We weren't boarded," Rida muttered.

She returned to her cabin feed. Tai, his arms wrapped around his face. She checked the hatch of her cabin—locked. There were feeds all through this hold, and three in the cage itself. With great care, she reached through the uplink and began lowering the volume on each of them. Her first thought was to shut them down; but that would get noticed. Low volume might not. "What happened?" she asked, as quietly as possible.

Rida, huddled against the cage wall, told what he knew: how Brontë had hit Velocity from behind, and gotten a drug patch on her neck; how Sabra had a weapon, a tiny Lopaka stun gun. "She made me put you in restraints. Put another set on me. She wouldn't say where Tai was. She wouldn't say why they were doing this." His head down, Rida added, softly, "I tried to fight. When that Brontë came at me, I…was going to use her as a hostage. But," he shook his head, "a kid."

"Never mind now," Velocity said.

He shot her an angry look. "A *kid* beat me up." Velocity checked the feed to her cabin again. Tai was moving toward the facility. "They wouldn't tell me where Tai was," Rida repeated, huddled up.

"They've got him locked in my cabin." Velocity watched Tai stop in the hatch of the facility, his head bent, his fists braced on the jambs. "He seems all right. No damage I can see."

Rida made an inarticulate noise. She focused on him. He was frightened as well as angry, she saw. Grimacing, Velocity moved closer. "Ridashi," she said gently, Tai's pet name for him.

He huddled tighter. "They'll sell us."

She got as close as she could. He was shivering. The hold was kept some degrees colder than the rest of the ship. "We won't let that happen," she promised.

"They're taking us into Republic space." His fists wrapped around the metal cord of the restraints. "They'll sell us into the system, make us contract labor." He shivered harder, convulsively. "Shit, they won't—Tai's delinquent, they won't even have to lie. They'll get a bounty for him." He was gasping before he finished the sentence, panic making him breathless.

Velocity threaded her bound arms around him. "Ridashi. That won't happen. I won't let that happen." She held him close. Behind her eyes, in her head, shadows flickered and formed: Sabra on the bridge; the empty bower of the Exchange; the feed from the boards; Tai in her cabin, his angular face mute with misery.

$$\text{%} \quad \text{✝} \quad \text{Ɂ} \quad \text{§}$$

The cargo had been removed from the cage, and shipmeals as well as bins of water added in, secured in a net in one corner. Counting up the meals, Velocity reckoned no one would need to come near them for sixty watches; more, if skinny prisoners were no objection. Trying to think up some way to fashion a lock skip, Velocity reviewed what was within that range from Chernyi. As a hub, Chernyi was a jump-point that could link to several systems. Something out of this hub must be Sabra's true aim in hiring them at the Bucket.

Security restraints throughout Republic Space opened with a universal key. The official versions of these keys, legally possessed only by Security officers, were metal. As Tai had told Velocity—and demonstrated, during one bored cargo run—most contract labor could fashion restraint keys using nothing more than a stiff bit of plastic; but these skips, as he called them, were highly illegal bits of contraband. Getting caught with one meant a beating, or worse.

Pirian shipmeals came packed in biofiber, a stiff material meant to be used either as fuel or compost. Tough, constructed to shed water, it was nowhere near as stiff as Republic plastics, plus all Velocity had to cut with was her teeth and one edge of metal jutting from a badly welded place on the cage wall. She had worked a square of biofiber into more or less the proper shape to be a skip, and was now trying to bite its edge into the correct configuration, which she then planned to refine using the metal edge on the cage.

Rida was politely withholding his skepticism about the likelihood of any skip manufactured under such circumstances being functional. Also, toward what end? What if they managed to get their restraints off? There they would be, unrestrained in a cage with a hard lock.

"Are we still heading for Hokkaido?" Rida asked, watching her doggedly working to cut the correct narrow notch along the skip edge.

She grunted. She had tried to infiltrate the ship's system, via her uplink, and take the ship back that way. These Combine pirates weren't quite stupid enough, though. One of them, probably Sabra, had installed their own security system, and she hadn't been able to get through its shieldwall yet. At this point, her access was read-only. They were having trouble with Rida's shieldwalls, too, she had been glad to learn.

"Captain? Are we? Heading for Hokkaido?"

"Brontë is packing code for some other jump," she admitted.

Rida twitched. He lifted his head, his eyes wide. "Captain."

"She might not be able to load it. They can't get past your walls into nav. And we've got—at this speed—just over twenty hours to

Chernyi. But they're talking about Zaidya." That was a hub two jumps beyond Chernyi.

"*Captain.*"

"I know."

"Never mind entering new code, I wasn't anywhere near done with the code for making the jump through Chernyi! I haven't even run checks on it!"

"I know."

"And—that Brontë, she's a kid! She can't be more than twelve years old! She can't possibly have the math!"

"I *know*," Velocity snapped.

Because making a jump was dangerous. The computer helped some, but in the end, the computer only did what the pilot's math told it to do. If that math was wrong, the computer might jump you through to who knew where, to a place so far from human space you would never return; it might (in theory) jump you to the center of a star, or into no-space. Theoretically. In actual fact, some ships just never turned up once they entered jump, and no one knew why. Bad coding, everyone said sagely, and hoped fervently that was the truth.

Rida hunched his shoulders. After a long pause, he added miserably, "Plus we didn't finish changing out the z-packs. Did they run those?"

Velocity didn't answer. So far as she could tell, these Combine pirates were doing nothing but riding her ship fast and hard straight toward a jump an uneducated child was packing code on, which coding *no one*—she had checked this twice—was bothering to run for errors.

She lifted her head. "What?" Rida asked.

"Ha." She had been spot-monitoring the ship's feeds, all the eyes through all the ship, and what she had been waiting for had finally happened: Sabra was taking Brontë into the pit for their training session. Unmoving in the cage, Velocity watched the ghosty screen floating just above the corner of her eye, watched them scrub and dress; watched them begin their warming routine.

"What?" Rida demanded.

She waved him silent, and then, focusing, wound carefully through the connections of the ship's channel. When she thought she had it right, she spoke: "Tai."

In her cabin, she saw Tai jump. He sat up on the bunk. "Captain?"

She had split her screen and was watching the pit as well as him. Controlling the path of her voice carefully, she said, "Quiet, now."

"Where are you?" Tai whispered. "Is Rida with you? Is he all right?"

"We're in the cage." She bit at the skip, thinking hard. They had Tai locked up separately for a reason. Did they think he had bought their attempts to subvert him? "Have they said anything to you? Asked you to do anything?"

"Sabra said they were only locking me up until they had the ship secure, and until they had time enough to explain. She said the offer still stood. The one about clearing my contract, she meant." Tai clenched his fists around the metal rim of the bunk. "They think I'll side with them, Captain. That's clear."

"Let them think it," Velocity said. Tai glanced toward one of the feeds—not the one she was using—his face gone expressionless. "Do everything you can to make them believe you're siding with them. Everything except actually giving them any useful information. Yes?" Tai squinted, clearly dubious. Well, so was she. "Meanwhile," she added, "we'll be working the problem from this side."

"From the cage," Tai said, still squinting. "How?"

Velocity hesitated, and Rida said, "The Exchange." She shot him a glance. "And those z-packs we didn't finish changing out. These silks never ran a ship. They buy jesses to do that for them. They won't know what's critical maintenance and what's not. We can use that."

"Or you could just unlock this hatch here," Tai said. "And the armory. Lock them in, wherever they are, let me out, I'll get the guns, and..." He shut up, his expression guarded again. No doubt thinking what it would be like to go up against combat-trained Combine Security.

Velocity brought up the feed from the pit, zooming in for a closer look, mostly to check her memory. She'd already noticed that they were both strapped: Sabra had the TAC-20; Brontë a Lopaka short rifle. If she did this—and she could, the pit didn't have a hatch that locked, but she could seal the e-hatches on the lop deck, the one in the trail between the pit and the armory, and the one at the bow-end of the deck. Box them in. They'd be between Tai and the hold, blocking his path to them here in the cage, but he could come around widdershins, get to the armory, and get armed. But if she did this, he'd have to shoot Sabra—outshoot Sabra—and if he survived that, he'd probably have to shoot Brontë as well. Shoot a child. Even a Combine child.

In her cabin, Tai chewed his lip. "Cut the air to their part of the ship," he said, only barely aloud. "Put them out before I go in."

"If it comes to it," Velocity said, "I'll do that." Tai said nothing. "I will, Tai. They're pirates, and we owe them nothing." In her cabin, alone, Tai nodded, his shoulders hunched miserably. "Or we can wait until they're in the Exchange. Or the galley." Some other place that could be sealed off. Both of them in the same place together. Or even just Sabra alone in that place—would Brontë fight without her? "But right now," she said, "Rida's got a different idea."

𝑅 ✝ ℓ ℜ

Watching Sabra come through the dusk of the hold toward them, Velocity tried to stand straight, which was difficult, since she had to pull against the restraint snub. The Security wore her skinsuit, everything except the helmet. The Lopaka TAC-20 was in its hip holster, strapped at the thigh.

Rida stayed in his corner of the cage, his bound fists between his knees. Velocity moved as close to the door of the cage as her snub would allow. Her muscles ached, from tension and the unaccustomed weight of all this push, not to mention having to sleep on the strap-iron of the cage deck. The cage had no bunks, since generally the

Calvin ran at micro or low push. Sabra stopped some distance away. "Captain."

"You are aware," Velocity said, "that if you continue to burn our juice at this rate, you'll run us dry long before we reach Hokkaido Station?"

Sabra paused, her chin lifting faintly. "I'm not here to discuss our itinerary."

"Well, you should be." Velocity moved at the cage door; the snub cord caught her up short. "Do you have the first idea how space flight works?"

"No."

Velocity, about to excoriate further, shut up. "What?"

"I have no idea how this ship works," Sabra said. "I understand that there are maintenance routines we should be running?"

"Planet-bred," Velocity sneered. "Born into free air. Never had to worry about your next breath. Ignorant as the dirt under your feet."

"You can shout at me, or you could keep us alive."

Velocity laughed savagely. "Shouting? Shouting, you gadro? Pirate my ship, beat up my crew, do who knows what to Tai, and whine about *shouting*?"

Sabra retreated two steps. She stood staring through the iron slats at Velocity, who, after a moment, growled and turned away. "Tai has not been harmed," Sabra said. Velocity said nothing, her shoulder to the Security. "We're using him as a consultant. That is all."

"Lie some more, pirate."

Sabra was silent. Then she said, "Tai says it would be dangerous to go through the jump without running our code through an error check. He also says we should be running maintenance. He says you have programs for this."

"Right. Well, those are all listed in ship's menu. Dig them out. Better hurry, though. You must be close to jump."

"Your ship locked when we tried to log on. Brontë has not been able to get your programs to recognize us." When Velocity just bared her teeth in a grin, Sabra added, "Tai says we must ask you. I am asking. Either you help us, or we go through this jump with the code we have, the ship not speaking to us, and maintenance undone. From what Tai tells us, this would be unwise."

"Unwise is one word for it."

Sabra stared at her. Velocity sneered. Next to her, Rida said. "I'll help you."

Velocity wheeled. "What?"

Moving past her, Rida got unsteadily to his feet. "I'll help you," he told Sabra. "I pack the code for this ship. I do most of the maintenance too. I know all the keys—"

Velocity shoved him. "Shut up! What are you doing!"

He staggered out of range. "Let me out. Let me out and I'll help you."

𝓩 ✝ 𝒷 𝕾

It felt colder in the cage, though Velocity knew it wasn't—one of her feeds monitored parameters like temperature and air mix, radiation, mold level, six or eight other ship vitals. She knew everything was optimal. The cold was her own anxiety making itself manifest. Lying on her back, three of the blankets folded under her and the fourth wrapped around her, she watched her uplink screens, all four of them open, the total filling her left eye's vision:

- **The com:** Rida worked with Brontë, a jump chart open on the wall-board. This wasn't a real jump chart. It was a tutorial used in Pirian open universities. Velocity recognized the perky animation and annoying music. Rida paused the program to let Brontë ask a question. While Velocity watched, Rida smiled at something the Combine child said.

- **The Exchange:** Tai working with Sabra, cutting back the pumpkin vines which grew so well in the abundant artificial light. While they worked, they talked. Velocity eavesdropped awhile. Sabra was telling him stories about growing up as bonded labor in the Combine. This was probably an attempt to gain his empathy, by making him believe they had the same sad lot. Tai was playing along, just as she had told him to.

- **The galley:** Signs of a meal in progress on the kit. Kettle on the hub. Scrub running. The cleaning mice scurried in their busy patterns, scrubbing the already clean deck.
- **The pit:** Empty and silent. Keeping the audio on the feeds up high, she traced her connections carefully from the mainframe through the links across to the dagan, peaceful in standby. She triggered it alert. In its dark cabinet, it eyes opened. Velocity arrowed down into its controls and lowered its volume, cycling it all the way down. *Your orders*, she said, speaking to it directly through the feed. *Use my codes. Break through their shieldwall. Infiltrate the ship's system. Once there, monitor these gadro. Crash their programs. Lock up the system. Harry and harass them. Understood?* She watched the dagan through the single feed in its locker, an incomplete, warped view. After a bare second, it replied: *Harass and harry. Should I also subvert?* Alone in the chill hold, Velocity grinned fiercely. *Oh, yes*, she sent back. *Please do.*

$$\text{𝑘 𝜏 𝑏 𝑅}$$

A watch and a half later, her body aching miserably, Velocity shifted to a new position, hunting some way to lie on the strap iron deck that did not hurt her bones. As she shifted a third time, thinking of getting up and refolding the blankets, the hatch from the conduit opened, spilling light across the dusk.

She rolled to stand, reaching for feeds: multiple angles of Sabra in the conduit, checking the load and the safety of her Lopaka TAC-20; Tai, off to her port. Widening her reach, Velocity found Brontë in the pit with the dagan, and Rida in the galley, slicing radishes. She muted the sound from everywhere except the hold, to eliminate distractions.

Her pulse thumped hard.

Sabra came down the hold ladder and crossed towards the cage, Tai just behind her. Velocity stood straight. "Captain," Sabra said.

Velocity glanced at Sabra, and then looked past her at Tai. "Are you injured?"

He blinked, surprised. "Captain?"

"Has this gadro hurt you? Or Rida?"

"Oh." He glanced at Sabra, whose well-kept Combine skin had flushed. "No, we're fine."

"Captain," Sabra said, more firmly. "We are still having maintenance problems."

"And we're how far from jump?" Velocity asked, as if she didn't know.

"Rida gave us codes," Sabra said. "These worked for a time, and then your ship system locked up again." Sabra peered at her through the dusk of the hold. "Rida believes you must have hidden bugs. Sub-routines, to crash the system."

Velocity smiled. "Want to surrender?"

Sabra shifted the barrel of the TAC-20 toward Tai, who stepped forward to unlock the cage. "You will come up to the bridge," Sabra said, "and remove whatever you have done to the ship's programming. If you do not do this, before the end of this watch, I'll shoot Tai. After that, I'll shoot Rida. Then I'll shoot you." Tai opened the cage. Velocity looked past him at Sabra, whose grey eyes were steady. "Is that clear?" Sabra said.

Velocity held up her hands, rattling the restraints dramatically. Sabra grimaced, and Velocity saw she had forgotten this—forgotten that she had left her chained up like a dog. After only a brief hesitation, the Security circled the cage, the rifle still in her hand, and reached through the strap iron to unlock the snub from the cage wall. Then she started back around the cage, to put the rifle back on Tai.

Velocity moved slowly, emerging from the cage as Sabra came around it, timing it so that she was between Sabra and Tai, pacing herself so that she never moved fast. She kept all her gestures slow, non-threatening. The dagan would have been pleased.

Sabra was combat-trained Security, though. Velocity saw from the edge of her eyes the tension ripple through her. The rifle, aimed at Tai, swung, moving toward Velocity. Velocity had already taken a wide loop of the metal cord in her fists. Now she swung it up in a short sidelong slap, at the same time dropping herself flat.

Sabra did not fire the rifle. This, Velocity had not been expecting—in their training sessions, the dagan *always* fired. The rifle knocked sideways, and Sabra at once caught it back towards Velocity, who kept moving, as she had been trained, swinging her stiffened legs to kick Sabra's feet out from under her—only Sabra jumped over them, shouted something Velocity didn't understand, and shoved the rifle into Velocity's face.

Velocity, sprawled flat on the deck, lay gulping air. "Shoot me. Do it, you fucking gadro."

Sabra, teeth bared, pushed the rifle barrel against her chest and then caught her by the upper arm, jerking her to her feet. "I won't," she said. "I'll shoot him, instead." She aimed the rifle at Tai. "How's that?"

Tai, his eyes wide, shook his head. "She won't, Captain."

"I will," Sabra snapped.

Tai shook his head again. Stepping forward, he put his hand on the rifle, pushing it aside. "You don't have to do this."

"Don't," Sabra said. "Don't you—don't—"

"She's out of the Combines," Tai said. Confused, Velocity saw that he was speaking to Sabra, not to her. "She's a Combine heir. Or she used to be. It's true. But she's not like that." Gently, carefully, Tai eased the rifle from Sabra's grip. "Let's just listen to each other."

$$\text{ᘉ ᛏ ᗽ ᛝ}$$

When they reached the galley, Rida was still there, doing prep. He turned, his eyes going wide. Two seconds after Velocity slipped through the galley hatch, Brontë clambered through it, still wearing her pit gear, her face flushed, though whether that was from anger or exercise or something the dagan had said, who knew. Tai went to Rida, slipping an arm around his neck. Ignoring all this, as well as the TAC-20, which Sabra had taken back from Tai and now had gripped in both hands again, Velocity went over to switch the kettle on. "I'm listening. You have two minutes."

No one spoke. Moving with elaborate patience, Velocity pulled out the Brun, checked the filter, and loaded in a coffee packet. When the kettle squealed, she shunted the water through to the flask. Then she faced the galley. Sabra was staring at the deck. "*Now*," Velocity snapped.

Rida jumped. Tai's grip tightened around him. Sabra, on the other hand, took a deep breath. "Captain," she said. "I would like to surrender."

"No!" Brontë yelped.

Sabra held out the rifle, flat, in both hands. Velocity pointed at it. "Tai." Tai went to take it. "Accepted," Velocity said. "Now start talking."

Chapter 5

Zob Kbeer Mountains, Ikeda-Verde Arcology, Planet of Waikato, the Core (Sixteen Months Earlier)

E lena Kora Hodaya Ikeda Verde, who preferred to be called her milk name, Brontë, had lived in Ikeda House all her life, and knew every shortcut through its manifold levels and corridors. However, unlike Tully, her usual morning Security, Sabra didn't let the smallest rule slip. "You shouldn't be on this level, miss," Sabra said.

Brontë jammed her boot expertly in the lift door to keep it open for Sabra's exit, then jumped out herself and ran along the corridor. This was the level for the bonded labor dorms. Brontë knew from visiting Tully down here that the quarters were tiny, their links and bunks all in the same space. Tully said it was lovely, that out in the squats they'd lived six to a room, shitter down the alley, bathing with the street pipe. Shitter meant facility. Brontë had no idea what a street pipe was, or how you would bathe in one.

"Slow down!" Sabra called. Stopping at the intersection of two corridors, Brontë hopped in place, waiting. Adults were so slow. "Do you even know where we're going?"

"Yes, yes, yes, this way." Brontë took off again.

"Elena Kora Hodaya Ikeda Verde!"

Sabra only used Brontë's register name when she was serious. Brontë skidded to a halt, though in her opinion Sabra's caution was ridiculous. Who would take her here in the House? Not to mention she hadn't passed her prelims yet, so who even knew if she was fit to inherit? Brontë said none of this, not wanting another lecture from Sabra. Instead, she slowed to a deliberate dawdle, placing one boot in front of the other along a woven helix that ran through the rough carpet of this level, blue and black and grey.

The helix made her think of Dr. Hegel, who in Genetics Seminar had set them engineering problems. The problems required them to gengineer sets of zygotes on their boards, place them in pre-built populations, and then work different genetics problems with these model populations. Theo, her older cousin, heir presumptive to the Primary Seat, bored with such elementary work, had ignored the lecture that went with these exercises, rolling links with Eté instead. Dr. Hegel had zeroed in on this inattention. "Theo. Do you have a question?"

Unhurried, undisturbed, Theo straightened in his chair and closed the link on his screen, the one he and Eté had been laughing over. "Not a question about your lesson."

Hegel didn't take offense. Or at least he didn't appear to take offense. Once or twice Brontë had seen a look around Hegel's eyes when he thought no one was watching which made her wonder just what Hegel really thought about the imperious attitude of the young citizens in his care. All Hegel said, though, was, "A question concerning an earlier seminar?"

"A more general question." Theo braced one foot on the window sill. "A *global* question."

Hegel linked his hands behind his back, standing straighter. Though born outside the House walls, Hegel had bonded in young, so he didn't have the crooked bones or bad teeth of those who came to House late, or their rough manners either. He waited for Theo's question in polite silence.

"This is a seminar in practical genetics," Theo said. "So why aren't we getting any practice?"

Hegel frowned. Behind him, the program he had started kept on running, its animated images flickering silently over the cream-colored wallboard. Brontë glanced through her lashes, and then covertly brought up a new program on her screen. "We are doing practical work, Mr. Ikeda," Hegel said. "That's the point of the exercises. Practice."

"Models." Theo snapped one finger against his own screen. "Games. We should be working with live subjects."

"Lab work will be available once you've qualified. If you're truly interested."

"No one can learn this way. Either give us lab work, or don't pretend to be teaching us anything."

Shutting out Theo's rant, Brontë worked through her own program. It was one Sabra had linked her—Sabra was her tutor. Like Theo, like everyone in the line to inherit, Brontë got extra lessons in science and math, as well as in history. This program went with Sabra's recent genetics lesson, which had covered most of the same information Hegel's seminar did, but had added more math and emphasized aspects of the process that his seminars had not.

As with the problem set Hegel had given them, Sabra's program had her build sample zygotes and then run them through a developing population. But the possible variations in this program were much more interesting. Just now, for instance, the program was running her through variations having to do with genetic drift. Hegel had defined genetic drift for them, but hadn't discussed it as a factor in the genetics of populations.

In this game, various events occurred—natural disasters; or deliberate decisions by those in power; or wars—and then the game would pause, and make her work out the math of what this would mean for a certain trait shared by this percentage of the population. What percentage would have that trait in two further generations? What if thirty percent of the population emigrated, and by chance half of those who had this trait went with them—what percentage of the population who still had that trait would remain six generations later? Now what if an epidemic hit, one with a sixty percent mortality rate, and only those with this trait had immunity? Once Brontë entered the answers, the game would give her a new scenario, sometimes with the same population, sometimes taking her back to her base population and starting fresh.

"No, it's worse than useless." Theo was still baiting Hegel. "Learning this way actively teaches us incorrect information." Over by the seminar wall, the Security officers, Tully among them, stood at attention, their expressions schooled to blank masks. Hegel had flushed red with restrained temper. Brontë winced, expecting an uproar like the one the term before which had ended with Theo doing lessons in his room for ten days, and their math instructor being formally cited for contempt toward a citizen (which lost her two months' pay, Tully said); but luckily just then the seminar door opened. Sabra stepped through.

"Captain Anador," Hegel addressed her rigidly. All the bonded labor called one another by their titles. *Captain* Anador, *Doctor* Hegel, *Officer* Tolliver. Tully said that when you didn't have anything else, rank got really important. "May we help you?"

Sabra was there to retrieve Brontë. But surveying the seminar room swiftly, she stayed a moment longer than she might have, talking idly with Hegel—cooling him down, and giving Theo time to cool himself. When they left, Hegel was taking up the interrupted lesson. Theo had retreated back into flirting with Eté.

Sabra was there to take her to medical, for yet another upgrade. This year, just like every year since she'd turned six, Brontë had missed almost more seminars than she attended, due to all the upgrades her mother authorized. Most of these upgrades were standard—a boost to her immune system, another to her metabolism—but a few, such as the upgrades to her musculoskeletal system, had kept her off-planet for weeks at a time, up on Waikato's orbiting medical station, first getting the upgrade, then adjusting to the changes to her body as it took effect.

That one had happened three years ago, before she'd been old enough to notice that most children in Ikeda House weren't getting so many upgrades, or at least not these sorts. Almost everyone got the metabolic upgrade—no one wanted fat kids, after all. She'd asked her mother why she needed so much work, and her mother explained it was due to her status. Heirs high in the line of succession always got extra work, her mother said. And it was true, Brontë noticed, that Theo got nearly as many upgrades as she did. His little sister, Marie, second in the line to inherit, didn't get nearly as many, though.

Brontë herself was only seventh in line. So why would she need more work than Marie? It was a puzzle. Brontë had wondered for a while if Marie was going to be pulled from the line. Maybe Marie's mother knew Marie would recuse herself, the way Brontë's mother had. If that was the case, Brontë hypothesized, she might not want the trouble of all the upgrades.

The medical work *was* annoying, and sometimes painful. Mostly it was boring. Sabra always went up to the station with her, to act both as Security and as tutor. Brontë liked that part, getting all her lessons from Sabra. Rather than the simple-minded Combine Child's version of genetics, or history, or Shtai, Sabra always taught her the real version of everything. Sabra taught her what was right, and not what was proper. Also, Sabra gave her access to files that Brontë was 110% sure no one on her level was supposed to be reading. No one on Sabra's level either.

Sabra hadn't told her to keep quiet about it, either. This had started a steady warmth in Brontë's center that had never quite gone out. She knew her mother loved her; but no one had ever trusted her, not before Sabra.

Now, following the double-helix pattern in the rug, Brontë frowned. Did Theo have someone teaching him the truth, too? Was that why he was so bored in seminars?

Sabra caught up to her. "This corridor leads to Training."

"Down these stairs," Brontë agreed. She bolted ahead, shoved the door open, and went down the steps two at a jump. Sabra shouted for her to wait. Brontë whirled down both flights of stairs and burst through the broad double doors at their bottom.

Here, the floors were polished wood. The ceilings glowed with light. Down a center aisle ran a walkway, with arches marking boundaries between training areas. She ran down this aisle to the far end, where Coach Jasper sat on the bottom step of the loft stairway watching the cadets training in the junior-most room. "Kuchling," Coach Jasper said. "Where's your keeper?"

Brontë climbed the steps to straddle the railing above him. From there, she had a fine view of six juniors: three boys, three girls, all wearing training hakama. According to their contracts, they were almost exactly her age. Thanks to her MSK upgrade, they were not as tall as she was; but they shone with health, their dark hair clipped close to their skulls, hard muscles showing on their bare arms. They were very good at Shtai—maybe even better than she was, even though she'd been studying it two hours a day since she started school, not to mention Sabra's private tutoring sessions.

Sabra came striding down the aisle. "Miss Ikeda Verde!"

Uh-oh. That was worse than *Elena Kora Hodaya Ikeda Verde*. Brontë slid through the railing, dropping deftly to the dojo floor. "Sabra. Look." Sabra, her stern face tensed, came at her, and Brontë spoke louder, pointing, "Look!" And because Sabra was a good Security officer, even though she was angry, she looked—and kept looking, frowning.

Three boys, three girls, each as light-skinned as Sabra was, each with her narrow chin and broad cheekbones. Her clear grey eyes. Her lean frame. Her wiry muscles, her neat way of moving, perfectly efficient, perfectly lethal. "I heard my mother talking," Brontë said. "She said the Ikan16 may prove the best the House has ever produced."

After overhearing her mother, Brontë had been curious, and used her hack into her mother's data bank to find their provenance. The name Ikan meant they were the product of *Ik*eda House plus a donor named *An*-something. Ikeda plus Anador. The 16 meant they were the first set from this donor, and that there were six of them.

Brontë looked up at Sabra to see if she understood. Sabra had gone pale. Under her left eye, a muscle trembled. Brontë moved to stand beside her. After a moment, she took her hand.

𝄞 ✝ 𝄢 𝄇

First Day and Fifteenth Day, their Seminar spent in Gardens. Not Theo or the others who were getting close to prelims: these had special prep sessions. But the rest of them took the lift all the way to the roof level, which is where the ecosystems were built. Brontë liked Gardens. Some of the other kids didn't, like Ross, he was afraid of all the open space, and Katya kept screeching about bugs if any got near her. But no bug in the Ikeda-Verde Arcology would hurt you. Tully said.

And Gardens were wonderful. That day they had Forest: trees so tall Brontë nearly fell over trying to see their tops, rich-smelling soil bright with green moss, feathery plants and great craggy rocks. The air was bright and cold, and icy water tumbled through the streams. They climbed rocks, they ran on paths through the trees, they came to meadows where bored deer bounded lazily out of their reach. Chipmunks sat on stumps, trout swam the creeks, bright blue skinks scuttled in the brush. When it was time for lunch, it awaited them in a tiny room made of trees in the middle of Forest. A Little House, Dr. Hegel said. He said that once people had lived in these—*nuclear families*, surviving all on their own in woods just like these. This lecture had confused Brontë when she was little, since she thought *nuclear* was a kind of weapon.

"And if trouble came," Dr. Hegel said, "and they were not prepared, they died. Only the strong, only those with sufficient foresight, survived to pass on their g-set." He handed around a box of jackfruit chips. The children grabbed fistfuls, not listening. They had heard this lecture too often. "This was before the failed social experiments that led to the Collapse," Hegel continued, "before the old social order began protecting the weak and thoughtless from their mistakes, and allowing the defective to survive."

"I gotta wee," Tiare whined. "Dr. Hegel, I gotta wee!"

"You will have to wait," Dr. Hegel said. "It will be good discipline."

Tiare began to wail. Irritated, Hegel snapped his finger at Ginger, Tiare's Security, who led the child toward the facilities at the entrance.

"I'm done," Brontë announced. "Can I go over to Waterfalls?"

Dhruv, Fiona, and Anya went with her. Waterfalls was a high Garden. From its summit, if you climbed to the very top of its highest rock, you could see past all the trees in Forest, and past Grasslands, the next Garden over, and Beaches after that, clear to the edge of the House, beyond which were the immense rising mountains of the world. The other children stripped to their shorts and leapt over the cliff into the deep pool below, shrieking as they plummeted; but Brontë lingered, watching the world outside the House, thinking of stories Tully told, of the scraps Sabra let slip. The sun was high, blazing on the fat white clouds and the fat banks of snow lying heavy on the high distant slopes of the mountains.

Tully's stories were different from Sabra's—Tully told about going with her cousins to dig cockles along the river; or about climbing up the duropass bridge during winters to drop chunks of ice onto the T, aiming for the glass-domed observation cars, which made a lovely smash—how when Security came to chase them away, they had to bunk it quick. How, during power cut, she and Em, the cousin who was her best friend, would sneak into the lumberyard through a gap in the fence and kip scraps for her aunt to burn in the cooking oven they rigged on their stoop. When Brontë asked what "power cut" meant Tully laughed and laughed.

What Sabra told wasn't stories, really, and wasn't funny either. Kids eating coal tar off the sides of their squats, because they were hungry. City Security hunting a runner, and beating a kid nearly dead before noticing they'd capped the wrong boy. Parents who just didn't feed their newest. Rolled it up tight in its blanket, tucked it in its box, left it be until—finally, finally, finally, Sabra said—it stopped crying.

"But why?" Brontë whispered. This was after the birth of her youngest cousin, Josef Spencer Hideki Ikeda Walker, and she could not imagine doing such to that soft fragrant flesh and puzzled eyes. Sabra looked away, but not before Brontë saw her usually placid mouth harden. "Sabra?" she had insisted. "*Why?*"

"Don't you mind," Tully told her when Sabra got this way. "She in't even from the squats. Lived up here in this House all her days. All *she* knows, she got told."

Today Tully hunkered under the tall pines with the other House Security, their Lopaka short rifles across their backs, laughing at something one of their number had said. Brontë shaded her eyes with both hands, looking toward the Garden lifts. There was Dr. Hegel with the younger kids, herding them into the meadow. Bounding down the rocks, Brontë caught Tully by the sleeve and dragged her up the path along the waterfall. Tully followed, obliging as always. "What are we about, miss?" she asked, once they had reached the redwoods.

"Practice levels," Brontë veered onto the path toward the service lift.

"Oh, miss," Tully slowed. "Captain Anador racked me proper on taking you to that level this last once. She said, 'Officer Tolliver, for such a sharp bit you got the biggest wish to eat the bullet I have *ever* —'"

Brontë pounded the call panel. "I'm Brontë Ikeda, I'm your holder, and I'm telling you we're going down, so you just say that to her."

Tully grimaced. "Sometimes it's like you never *met* Captain Anador, Miss Brontë."

The lift arrived and Brontë hopped into it. As it rushed them downward—she hit override express—she instructed Tully: "We're going to tell Coach Jasper I'm considering a req. It's not a lie, because I am. We'll bring them up here, to Gardens, but not to Forest. Because of Hegel. I don't want to have to argue with him." Tully made a mournful noise. "We'll take them to Rivers, that's always fun." Brontë spun in place. "It's interesting that they're sextets, you know? Instead of quads or octs?"

"Yes, miss." Tully's voice was flat now, not merry or teasing or any of her usual tones. Brontë knew that the Ikan16s had almost certainly originally been an octet. Probably two of the zygotes had been destroyed for quality control issues. But she didn't see why Tully would be angry about that. Defective zygotes were always destroyed.

Anyway, she reasoned, leading Tully through the corridors, it didn't have to be a quality control issue. Sometimes zygotes were frozen for later use, or used in other ways. It didn't have to mean the Ikan16 g-set was defective. And she hadn't *said* that they were, anyway.

Coach Jasper was on the main floor of the training level, doing katana work with David Ikeda Ito. Brontë knelt at the edge of the mat to wait. David was good at katana, nearly as good as the coach, and the match was interesting to watch, with both of them moving with grace and the economy of skill. Everyone in the House knew David, though he was far down the line—seventeenth, at the last audit. Besides his skill at almost everything, he was both beautiful and friendly, speaking to everyone, even scrubs and bonded labor, and listening with true interest to anything anyone said. Brontë liked him, too. But whenever she saw him, she thought of his wedding.

She had been little then, five or six years old. It had been a frosty party up in Gardens. She remembered sitting under a table decorated with silver and blue gilt stars, crunching spun-sugar flowers between her teeth and listening to him talk with her mother and her Aunt Noya about raising tariffs on the export of bonded labor. When David had left, her mother had said, quietly, to Aunt Noya, "That one has ambitions."

Brontë had always remembered it because of how her mother had said it. She hadn't thought, before that evening, that ambitions could be something bad.

Coach Jasper forced David to the left, off-balance, and then slid past him, bringing the katana around to thump the side of his head soundly. David laughed and stepped back, bowing. That was another thing Brontë always remembered about David: how easily he treated losing, as if to lose was just another event he rose up from, as strong as ever.

David stripped off his padded helmet, and Coach Jasper spent a few moments walking him through what he should have done when Jasper had crowded him. David promised to practice the move. Then, his helmet under his arm, he came off the floor, pausing to smile at Brontë. "Look at you," he said. "So tall. A new upgrade, yes?"

Brontë rose to her feet, smiling back. They talked about the MSK upgrade, and how much it made their bones ache while it was installing. "Six years of growing pains in six weeks!" David said, smiling. "How's your mother? She's back from Durbin, I hear."

"Yesterday afternoon," Brontë agreed.

"I hear she's asking for a sabbatical. Maybe she'll be able to come to Gagarin this year."

This was the first Brontë had heard about any sabbatical, but she didn't admit that. Instead, she and David talked about the upcoming holiday to Gagarin, and about the ice sailing there. Then he went off toward the changing rooms, and Brontë turned to Coach Jasper. He had already stripped off his armored vest and was stowing it and his other gear in the floor locker. "Here for extra training, kuchling?" he asked, his attention still on arranging the gear properly.

Brontë smiled at him. Coach Jasper came up to Residential every Prime afternoon for their training sessions. "No, Coach. I'm here for a trial req."

Coach Jasper's eyebrows tipped upwards. "Ah." He glanced past her at Tully, and dried the sweat off his forehead with his sleeve. "Is that's why you've been cluttering my dojo?"

"I know the ones I want," Brontë went on, making her voice like her mother's when she spoke to bonded labor: straightforward, firm. "If it's not a big problem with their schedule, I'll take them up to Gardens for a few hours. Run them through their paces."

Coach Jasper shot Tully another glance. "Which set are you thinking of, now?"

"The Ikan16s."

Coach Jasper's customary faint smile vanished. His gaze locked on her. "They are a bit junior for req."

"That's my concern," Brontë said: one of her mother's favorite phrases.

Another deep pause. Then the coach bowed, stepped backwards, turned, and went to fetch the set. Brontë felt her muscles relax, which was interesting. She hadn't realized she was worried. Tully shifted her weight, and Brontë glanced toward her, and then past her. David was still in the doorway to the changing rooms, standing fiddling with the clasp on his vest. When he saw her watching, he smiled and waved, and then went on inside, his vest still on, and still fastened for that matter.

That one has ambitions, her mother spoke in her memory. Brontë narrowed her eyes, and then as the Ikans came from their practice room turned away again, David slipping from her mind as she watched the six cadets move toward her.

ᛉ ᛏ ᛦ ᛣ

Brontë knew the Ikans were identical genetically—well, except for their sex chromosomes—yet even from the first she had no trouble picking one from the others. Nora was like Tully, always laughing; Wolf and Maggie, the two shortest (not by much, just a few centimeters), were always together, each always seeming to know what the other was thinking; Ruçar, the tallest of the three boys, was always moving, jumping up on things, or doing handstands or cartwheels or wrestling with Ian. And Adder, the most direct of them all—Adder was their leader.

She took the cadets up to River Garden, at the far end of the roof, and led them down the trail along the rocky riparian bank, where the river ran clear over broad flat stones. Above them, tall trees arched, and off the trail hummingbirds darted and dragonflies hovered on the sun-spotted air. Ruçar and Ian ran ahead, scrambling and bounding from rock to rock; the others waded the shallows; but Adder stayed near Brontë, watching her closely.

"You know I'm lying," Brontë said, and when Adder glanced at her, added, "About this being a trial session. About bringing you up here so I can consider acquiring your contracts."

They had reached the steep rock path. Adder stayed silent while they climbed. "Feinting," she said, once they were at the top.

"What?" Brontë frowned, having heard this as *fainting*.

"Not a lie. You're prepping a feint." Adder didn't call her miss, not even there at the beginning. Brontë always remembered that later.

At the center of the Garden, River Trail opened into a lovely meadow surrounded by tall trees spreading their leafy shadows over the grass. The other Ikans, having reached the meadow well before Adder and Brontë, were out in the sunny bit, organizing a game of Assassin. Brontë veered left, going up towards her favorite pavilion, a small round one with a red tile roof. It had wooden seats inside, but she and Adder sat on the steps.

"Coach knows it's a feint," Adder told her. "He has to. You can't have the funding to acquire us, really."

Oh. Good point. Brontë hunched her shoulders, thinking this over. "Maybe I'm going to ask my mother to get you for my prelim gift."

"You're at least two years from prelims."

"Three," Brontë admitted. She brightened. "But maybe I want to train with you. So we'll know how to work together when you're my Security crew."

Adder grinned a little. "Maybe you can get Coach to pretend to believe that."

Out in the meadow, the game sped up. They played Assassin differently than Brontë's Seminar did. In Seminar, you stood in pairs or triplets, bowed to one another, and then tensed, hands out from your sides, waiting. Your job was to hit your opponent, or one of your opponents, either in the shoulder, hand, or elbow, before they hit *your* shoulder, hand, or elbow. Getting hit anywhere else did not count as a kill. It was harder in triplets than in pairs, but more fun, too.

The Ikans played all at once—all five could attack any other of the five—and while they started in a tight circle, they did not stay there, but moved anywhere they liked, dodging, leaping, retreating— Nora did a backflip at one point, avoiding a lunge from Wolf. They were also a lot faster and more graceful than anyone in her Seminar. It was more like a dance than a game, their Assassin. And they were so serious while they played, but laughing, too, under that seriousness, the whole time. When Wolf got tagged, he rolled over in a triple back somersault and lay flat on the grass, wailing in despair. The others just kept right on playing.

"Why did you bring us up here?" Adder asked. That was the other thing Brontë would always remember about Adder, later: how direct she always was.

"I know your mother," Brontë said.

Adder turned to look at her. The grey of her eyes was clear as river ice, winters when the rivers in River Garden frozen solid. Sabra's eyes. "We don't have a mother," Adder said. "We're artifacts."

Brontë shook her head. Then she shook it again. She didn't know, then, why she was disagreeing, because—then, that day, that afternoon—she believed what Adder was saying. She believed, then, when she was eleven years old, that there were differences among people and that these differences were self-evident. It was obvious to her then that Tully didn't need the sort of education that she, Brontë, did—Tully wouldn't even want it. Or the same sort of housing, or food, or clothing. Imagine Tully having to wear Brontë's trousers, her linens, her jacket! Or having to do the mountains of prep Brontë did for Seminar.

Looking away from Adder, out at Maggie, who had just tripped Nora and leapt over her falling body, she said, "Your mother's name is Sabra Anador. She's been Captain of my Security team since I was six years old."

Adder said nothing. Brontë took her handheld from her satchel and brought up her captures, finding the one from last House Day. In the capture, everyone was in fancy dress; Security wore their dress uniforms. Sabra looked lovely and sleek in hers, deep black with dark blue piping. She also looked remarkably like Wolf, especially when she laughed, as she did at something Brontë said to her on the capture. "Do you see?" she said, and glanced at Adder, and then tapped the screen, bringing the focus in on Sabra even more sharply: on her features, the bones of her face, her short dark hair, the shape—and shade—of her eyes. Adder said nothing, but her already pale skin went an alarming ice white.

"I heard my mother say it." Brontë moved to another capture, this one of Sabra with Brontë and Theo at party at their aunt's flat. "She didn't know I was listening."

"Your—" Adder paused. "Your mum said this Security was our mother."

Her mother hadn't said any such thing, obviously. She hadn't mentioned Sabra at all. Brontë moved to another capture, Sabra trying to teach Mia the proper block for a head strike. "She said…" Brontë bit her lip.

Adder looked away. "I know what she said. You don't have to say."

"She said your set was the best we've gotten from Sabra's line," Brontë said, though in fact her mother had said *this source*, not Sabra. "That she's been receiving bids on your contracts for two years now. That we're starting another set in the spring."

Adder gazed out at her set-mates in the field. Then she shook her head, expressionless as any bonded worker. "That doesn't make her our mother. That makes her a donor." She paused, and added deliberately, "Just another donor. Every House has hundreds of them."

"Sabra doesn't think that," Brontë said. Adder said nothing. "Sabra doesn't think she's just a donor," Brontë said, more loudly.

"She does." Adder shook her head. "Even if she doesn't, so what? We belong to your house. Same as your boots and your toys." She slapped at the handheld in Brontë's hands. "What do you think my *mother* can do about any of that?"

She got to her feet and whistled through her teeth. All the Ikans in the garden wheeled to face her. She pointed toward the path, and they went toward it at a trot. Adder turned to Brontë. "You're sacking about in matters you don't understand. You should mind your own."

Tully, who had come nearer when Adder struck the handheld, said, "Hey, now, you. Mind that mouth." Adder shot her a glare, and went to join the other Ikans, waiting at the trailhead. They all vanished down trail together, off toward the Gardens' entrance.

Chapter 6

The *Susan Calvin*, in Transit to Chernyi Hub

Velocity sat on the prep counter, drinking her third bowl of coffee. Brontë had climbed into the booth about halfway through Sabra's recitation and sat huddled there now. Velocity kept wary watch on her.

"I gave up the eggs." Sabra was still standing, rigidly straight, by the trail hatch. "I did it of my own will. Ikeda House isn't like some in the Combines. They might own us, but when it comes to such matters, they ask."

"And you can say no," Velocity said.

Sabra licked her lips, dry from all the talking she had been doing. Tai, in the booth with Rida, got up, filled a bowl of coffee, and took it to her. She stared at him, and then took it, using both hands. Bending her head, she inhaled the scent coming off the bowl. Her eyes shut, she said, "When I saw them," and then, without changing her tone in the least, "Dr. Ikeda took me from the training floors when I was six years old. She had me trained for her own Security team. She made certain I had the best food, the best teachers, the best medical. The best of everything."

Velocity made herself stay silent.

"When Ikeda House asked for my eggs," Sabra said, and shook her head. She drank coffee thirstily. "I didn't mind. Why would I? My body threw eggs away every month. How was this different? But when I saw the children." She opened her eyes, looking not at Velocity, or Tai or Rida, or anything in the galley, but at some other scene, distant, interior, far in the past.

"Nothing she could do about it." Tai took the empty bowl from Sabra. He brought it over to the kit. "You know that," he told Velocity. "She came up in a House," he told Sabra. "She knows."

Velocity grimaced and held her bowl out for Tai to refill along with Sabra's. "So who *did* you sell on Bastiat?" she asked.

"My cousin," Brontë said.

Velocity jumped. She had forgotten to pay attention to Brontë. "Your, ah…" She lifted an eyebrow. "Who?"

Brontë, wearing the pegged trousers and the worn swat Velocity had first seen her in back on the Bucket, was clay-pale. Muddy shadows showed under her eyes. She folded her arms on the booth table and braced her chin on her wrists. "I sold my oldest cousin. Theo. Heir-presumptive to the Primary Seat on our Board. We took him hostage when we ran. Used his tag to buy tickets as far as we could go, which was Bastiat. Sold him there and came on to your station." She paused. Sabra moved, as if to speak; but then just stood still again. Brontë swallowed, and said, "When we reached Hell in a Bucket, we heard from Torres."

"Torres Ikeda Alonzo, who is on Hokkaido Station," Velocity said, when Brontë did not go on. "Torres Ikeda, who has nothing to do with your coup."

Brontë didn't startle. At the most, she grew a bit more still. "Yes," she said, after a pause. In the booth across from her, Rida made a noise, not quite a laugh. Brontë shot him a glance and hunched her shoulders. "What we told you back on the Bucket wasn't entirely true."

"Was any of it true?" Velocity asked politely. "For instance, are you in line to inherit the Primary Seat? Or I suppose I should ask: *where* are you in the line to inherit?"

Brontë wet her lips, and then said, "I haven't taken my prelims. But if I passed, I would have been seventh in line for the Primary Seat on the Ikeda House Board, and fourteenth for the Primary Seat on the Verde House Board."

"There have been changes in the line rankings," Sabra added.

"So there have," Velocity said drily. "Is Torres trying for the Primary Seat?"

"She does not have the support of the Ikeda Board," Sabra said. "As she surely knows."

"Is she on Hokkaido?" Velocity asked, meaning, *Is any part of your story true?*

Brontë paled further, something Velocity would not have thought possible. But she met Velocity's eyes. "No," she said. "She's on Woodlands." Velocity put down her bowl of coffee. "I know it's further into Republic space than we represented."

"It's twenty jumps from the Core!" Velocity shut her teeth together, fighting for control. Brontë stared right at her, her young back straight, her shoulders square. "Nearly sixty..." Velocity paused, glancing at Rida.

"Fifty-seven," he said.

"Fifty-seven jumps from here. Never mind pirating my ship, where did you think you'd get the fuel?"

"We have funding. And a way...to get more funding." There was some hesitation, as if Brontë wasn't certain about this last point. "But given what Torres might be planning, this looks like it could be a trap. So we need to come in undercover. And we would like your help. That part was true."

Velocity laughed. "So you pirate my ship? Assault my crew? Lock me up? These are tactics you think will make me willing to help you?"

Brontë hunched her shoulders tighter. "We hoped to persuade you during the journey."

"Because you're an idiot or because you're an absolute idiot?" Velocity slid to her feet. "Tell me why I shouldn't lock all of you in that cage, go back to the Bucket, and dump you on the dock."

"Because you'll be no better off if you do," Brontë said. "Because we need you. Because at this point I may well be the presumptive heir to a Primary Seat. And because, because if I am, if I reach Ikeda House and am confirmed, I will be able to pay you enough that you will own this ship, free and clear, with enough money left over to keep you going for years."

"If," Velocity said. "If, if, if."

"Because even if I am not the heir, I can pay you enough to settle your outstanding debts." Brontë glanced, probably involuntarily, toward Tai.

Heat flared burning under Velocity's skin. She stared down at the little Combine crumb. Then, deliberately, she switched her attention to Tai. "Lock them up," she said. "Do it now."

Chapter 7

Zob Kbeer Mountains, Ikeda-Verde Arcology, Planet of Waikato, the Core (Fifteen Months Earlier)

Brontë's mother, Isra Te Ao Caitriona Ikeda Lopaka, was not ranked in either the Ikeda or Verde lines, having filed for scholarly recusal in her twenty-fourth year. She kept residence in Ikeda House, though, and worked for IVC as a Forensic Accountant. She also sat on several advisory boards, including Education, Research & Development, and Genetics & Engineering. In addition, she held membership in six of the most influential inter-Combine societies. All of this kept her occupied when she was on Waikato, as she often was not. Her work with Finance involved frequent journeys out to the settlement planets on which Ikeda-Verde Combine held trade leases.

After Brontë left the nursery, Isra used to leave her at school while she was off-planet. This was not uncommon for Ikeda House—even children whose parents didn't work tended to board their children until they were old enough to care for themselves. Isra had brought Brontë home earlier than most, in fact, five years ago, just before she turned seven. These days, Brontë had a suite in Isra's quarters, and her own Security team, headed by Sabra, who also had charge of her, more or less, when Isra was away. Brontë didn't really need looking after, Isra said, which Brontë agreed with, even if, sometimes, in the darkest points of night, her rooms did seem scarily quiet.

Just now, having recently returned from a job on a settlement planet named Durbin, her mother was still at the point where she was spending a wealth of time on Brontë—sharing meals with her, asking about her studies, even listening to her answers. Brontë knew all this would last only a week or so before Isra, caught up in her own work, would leave her to Sabra again.

Tonight, though, they ate dinner together, and when Isra asked about her seminar work, Brontë mentioned, deliberately, the economics problem sets she had been assigned. Economics being her mother's favored field, Isra sharpened with interest. They talked the problems over, and after dinner Isra came into her study and they worked them together, having such a good time that Brontë felt some residual guilt over the success of her plot. Squashing it firmly, she said, as they worked through the last set, "Isra…"

"Oh, here it comes," Isra said, but she said it fondly.

"Odds are, I'll hold the Primary Seat. Maybe sooner rather than later."

They both knew this; Isra brushed back her hair, her eyes narrowing inquisitively. Because she spent so much time in space, Isra wore her hair short. It feathered around her skull in soft dark waves, not quite curls. Brontë's own crow-black hair was straight as pine needles. "Does this have to do with your visits to the Training Level?" Isra asked. "What are you plotting, little Mach?"

Isra called her this sometimes. It was short for Machiavelli. Brontë grinned. "I was wondering if you might assign the Ikan16s to me."

"The Ikans." So far, her mother sounded more interested than anything else.

"For two reasons. First, I want a dedicated Security team, one that's entirely loyal to me. Working with these cadets—raising them up as my own—that's one path toward that goal."

"And the other reason?"

"I'll probably inherit the Seat," Brontë said. "But maybe not for years. Until then, I'll need a field. I'm thinking of genetics." Isra had said more than once that genetic engineers did the real work of running the Combine Houses. "Their g-set is the best in the House. I studied their data, what's in open access. Their set and their history. It's fascinating." Brontë hesitated. "I know they're valuable. If it's too much, I can work with some other set."

Isra shook her head. "Their value is not the issue. This is a GX set."

Brontë frowned, surprised. That information hadn't been in the files. Isra was watching her narrowly. "That's—isn't that prohibited?" Brontë asked.

In one sense, every child born to the House was genetically engineered. All sets, even those of Combine citizens, underwent somatic engineering, both at the zygote level and during their childhood. In the Combines, somatic genetic engineering was called "selecting for the better genotype"; or, in the case of more extensive work, such as the upgrades Isra had arranged for Brontë—giving her better reflexes and stronger bones, a better immune system—that was just called "proper health care."

But GX was something more. Having GX on your set meant the engineering had been done at the germline level, which was against Republic laws. Brontë couldn't imagine it being done in Ikeda House, not to a g-set living unrestrained in Ikeda House—maybe somewhere in some Combine laboratory somewhere, locked up behind quarantine protocols.

"Subject to certain controls," her mother said, "we've been running selective experimental sets for years." While Brontë was grappling with what *that* meant, exactly, her mother added, "Why this interest in genetics? The last I heard, you were thinking of studying to become an advocate."

Brontë felt her skin heat. She had never been interested in advocacy. She had only pretended an interest, briefly, in order to gain access to her mother's legal bank. "Oh," she said now, trying to sound airy, "I don't think I'm a good fit for the academy."

"Just for finding ways around import laws?"

"Ah. Um." She shot a panicked look at Isra, who didn't look upset. "Well. I didn't *do* it, anyway. In the end."

"You nearly earned a visit from Customs Security all the same. Nanotropic products designed for human use are proscribed for a reason. And," her mother added, as Brontë started to object, "if any product like that did exist, and was safe for human use, it wouldn't be a toffee that made someone who ate it smarter."

Brontë smirked. "The informational was very convincing," she argued. "Also, the Pirians have done things like that with their 'tropes."

Isra focused on her abruptly. "What do you know about the Pirians?"

"I...nothing. Only that they use nanotropes to rebuild their kids." Her mother kept that dark gaze fixed on her, and Brontë found herself continuing: "They rebuild their kids with nanotropes so that they can live in space. To keep their muscles and bones from deteriorating, to protect them against radiation, to improve their brain function. And other things. Somatic rebuilding," she said, because of the way Isra was staring at her. When Isra kept staring, Brontë added uneasily, "I just saw this animate. And read some things."

"From the House bank?" Isra asked. Brontë bit at her lip. In fact, she had borrowed Tully's handheld, as she did when she wanted to read anything not in the Ikeda House bank. Isra shook her head. "Information from outside the House isn't reliable. It hasn't been vetted. Most of it is sensationalist trash. Stick to our feed. When you're older and more grounded in science and history, when you know enough to evaluate evidence, you'll learn more about the Pirians. For now, keep in mind that whatever you saw was almost certainly propaganda, created by someone with a minimal understanding of science. There are good reasons for not allowing the use of nanotropes to edit human genetic material, and very good reasons for proceeding carefully with genetic engineering of humans at all, whether it is done on the germline or otherwise. I know Sabra has done some work on this with you. And it should have come up in your Genetics Seminar."

Her eyes lowered, Brontë nodded.

"The Pirians are living in a different environment than we are—a very different, and a much more hostile environment. Furthermore, when they left old Earth right after the Devastations, they took a relatively small number of people with them—less than nine thousand, by some counts. You've studied the Founder Effect, and what that does to a population? Yes. Well, all of this has caused them to make very different choices, ones that a less desperate people would not need to make. The costs they will bear for the choices they have made—those are still in play." Isra paused. "Almost no one here, on the Core planets, has ever seen a Pirian."

Brontë studied her mother, who had been out to the Drift. "Have you?" she ventured. "What are they like?"

"There are good reasons to protect our genetic bank. And good reasons not to believe every shoddy piece of propaganda you read off some street-side feed." Brontë opened her mouth to ask more questions, and Isra interrupted: "Now. Do you want to study genetics for the same reason you wanted to study law? I warn you, if this is another scam, Mach, you're not eight years old now. Security won't let you off their hook, not these days."

"It's not."

"You're actually interested in genetics."

"I am. Or...I might be." She shifted in her seat. "How will I know until I try it?"

"Hm." Her mother watched her, apparently thinking. "All right," she said, at length. "I'll let you have their contract for six months, renewable for another six if you're still interested." She pulled her screen over and started running the contract. As she worked, she added, "And keep your feed in-House from now on."

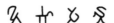

Everyone in the First Class had gone off to Hayek for the three-month qualification process that preceded their prelims—well, everyone sitting prelims. Eliot Verde Alonzo had not gone, for instance. The official reason given was that he had broken his leg on the climbing wall this past summer, and wouldn't pass the physical. Seminar was telling different stories. "Physical, ha," Riku said. "You've seen how he does with maths. Not to mention any other subject that requires a functional IQ. He'd never convince the Qualification Board he had a set worth passing on."

"Pretty green eyes, though," Sophia mentioned.

"My cat has pretty eyes," Leander said. "I wouldn't Board Certify it either."

"Mental instability," Dhruv said. "That's what I hear."

"I hear he didn't *fall* off that wall," Zadik said.

Brontë, three years out from her own qualifications and entirely uninterested in adding to the House's genebank anyway, did not take part in these conversations. She had acquired the contracts for the Ikan16s two days before; yesterday had been spent in making the final preparations of the suite next to hers, which they would share, and laying in last-minute gear for them. Today, she planned to spend the half-holiday—Seminar had half-holidays all through the months that First Class was gone—up in Gardens with them.

Sabra was not pleased. Sabra was not pleased by any of this, Tully had confided. "Captain Anador, she in't say so, but she thinks, oh, that child's baking up schemes." Since this was the level truth, Brontë did not dispute it. "Captain thinks you might get us in it deep," Tully added.

"You can't be blamed," Brontë said. "Not for following my orders."

Today's seminar, covering the collapse of civil governments in a specific area of Earth—a place called Oceania, as well as another place called Japan—and how this led to the rise of the Republic of Sovereign Worlds, might have been interesting, at some other time. Today, Brontë spent the entire seminar reading the files on her

Ikan16s, and scowling impatiently at the guest-lecturer, a bonded labor historian from the Academy. When the discussion was finished, Brontë rushed through the required essay, submitted it, and bolted from the room so quickly Tully had to scramble to catch up.

When they reached home, Sabra was in the koban with Torres Ikeda Alonzo. Sabra was standing not-quite in front of the door that led to Isra's study. Torres was near the entrance, her square face set in determined blandness. "Captain?" Tully said, having taken in this diorama.

"You're off-duty," Sabra said, not looking away from Torres. Tully saluted and went off toward the kitchen.

Brontë lingered, interested. She knew Torres, or at least knew who she was. All through Ikeda House, the love story of Torres and Anja Ikeda Nowak was famous—how they'd met as children in nursery; how they'd qualified together; how their families had forbidden the relationship; how they had run off together and spent months in some primitive farming commune on Earth, coming home finally skinny and scarred by the sun and still fantastically in love. How their families gave in and approved the marriage. It had been the scandal of the House for the past seven years. In the Combines, no one married for love. Marriage was an alliance. It was currency, to bind Houses together, or to strengthen those bonds. So marrying someone within the House—as Torres and Anja had done—while not actually prohibited, was almost never done.

Though Brontë knew all the reasons why their marriage was a bad idea, nevertheless part of her couldn't help admiring what the women had managed to do. But when she said this to Isra, her mother snorted. "They *managed* to make decisions with their adolescent hormones. They gave up any chance of doing anything worthwhile in this Combine, in exchange for sex and someone to eat dinner with. Psh!"

"Did you need something, miss?" Sabra said pointedly, and Brontë twitched. Sabra only called her *miss* when she was trying to make a point.

"Ah," Brontë said. "No. I was just—maybe you'd like some tea?"

All of Torres's attention was focused on Sabra, or rather on the door behind Sabra. It took her a moment to realize Brontë's question was directed at her. When she did, she focused on Brontë. Her expression stayed non-committal for a moment, but then she smiled. It was a kind, merry smile that transformed her face from nothing much to real beauty. Helpless and smitten, Brontë smiled back.

"Thank you," Torres said. "But I'm sure we won't be much longer."

We. Brontë looked past Sabra to the door. *We* meant Anja was in there—talking to her mother? But why?

"Miss," Sabra said, even more pointedly. Brontë smiled at Torres again, and started for her suite. As she reached its corridor, however, she heard the door to her mother's study open. Pausing just inside her corridor, she looked back. Anja Ikeda Nowak came out, turning to say something final to Isra. Tall, slender, elegant, Anja looked severe, almost angry. Torres stood straighter, but Anja did not greet her, simply jerked her chin toward the front door. The two of them left, and Sabra shut the door behind them, and then went into Isra's study.

Brontë considered attempting to eavesdrop. The door was open. She'd be able to hear anything said inside. On the other hand, from that angle, unless she was very careful, her mother or Sabra or both would be able to see her, in the mirror hanging across the way, on the koban wall. It occurred to her for the first time that her mother had placed the mirror there for that very reason. *Huh*, she thought, intrigued, and then turned to go down the hall to her own study.

In the study, she found the Ikans grouped around the worktable going through a unit on dividing polynomials together. It was funny to think they had to do lessons just like she did; and reassuring to see that she was ahead of them in something, even if was just basic math. "Are you close to finishing that?" Brontë asked them. "I'd like to get in a training session."

"Lunch," Adder said, meaning the Ikans hadn't had theirs. Neither had Brontë.

"I'll order a box," Brontë said, just the way her mother would have said it, and strode on down the corridor to her bedroom to change into more suitable clothing.

She took them up to Mountains, where a brisk wind roared through the pines. Both Sabra and Tully came along, since Sabra ruled that one Security was not enough for seven of them—the Ikans, apparently, did not count as Security. Since they didn't argue, Brontë didn't either, but she did feel miffed on their account.

Leading the way, Brontë took them up the switchback trail, and then off it—trail-cutting, which was strictly forbidden—through the loblolly pines to a high plateau she had found long ago, among the barren crags at the peaks on the far edge of the Mountains. "I don't think we're meant to be here," Sabra said, after a brief reconnaissance of the plateau.

"You mean there aren't any feeds," Brontë said. "That's what makes it the best place."

"Adder." Sabra jerked her chin. The Ikan came over at once, her spine straight, her shoulders square. "Run the set through Eel and Leaf."

"Yes, Captain." Adder wheeled and whistled through her teeth at the Ikans, who bounded into practice formation, every motion in sync as they swept into the movements of the Sixth Defensive blocks of Shtai.

Fascinated by their flow of movement, lovely as a dance, Brontë didn't notice Sabra reaching for her collar until she was nearly yanked off her feet. "Hey!" she protested.

Sabra ignored this, hauling her to the edge of the precipice. The wind was strong here, ripping across the city and the sea and the world. Sabra kept her fist clenched in Brontë's collar, dragging her up close to speak in a harsh whisper. "You tell me what you're planning."

Pulling free, Brontë ran both hands through her hair. Her heart hammered, more from astonishment than outrage—Security might lay hands on you to move you out of the way of an assault. But

Security *itself* assaulting you was so outside the bounds that Brontë only half-believed it had even happened.

Sabra leaned forward, her eyes dangerously slitted, and Brontë retreated. She glanced behind her at the precipice, and moved away from it. "Well," she said. "You know I'm thinking of doing gengineering for my field. To do that, I'll have to study at the University in Franklin. On Hayek."

Sabra folded her arms, her hard mouth twisting at one corner. Brontë spread her hands. "I'll have to take Security. You're in charge of my Security. You'll assign who goes with me. You can make sure that the team includes you. And the Ikans, well, by then I'll have worked out a research plan that includes them." She smiled what she hoped was a confident smile. Sabra's eyes narrowed further. "You know how my mother loves genetic engineering. She loves that I'm interested in the field. If I play this right, she'll let me have them."

"I hope you're as clever as you think you are."

"What did Anja want?" Brontë asked, and when Sabra narrowed her eyes, smiled brightly. "I didn't even try to spy on you two. Don't you think such restraint should be awarded?"

Sabra grunted, turning away. "Your cadets are waiting for you."

Chapter 8

The *Fido*, In Transit to Gagarin, the Core
(Seven Months Earlier)

The First Class returned triumphant from their prelims, and most of Ikeda House packed up their children, their bonded servants, and their Security and set out for the annual holiday, which this year was six weeks in the mountains of Gagarin. Isra had planned to come along this year—an anomaly for her; she almost never had time for the holiday trips. But at the last minute some crisis interfered. She said she would try to come later, perhaps in a week or two.

Meanwhile, she sent Sabra, Tully, and one other Security officer with Brontë. Adder and Wolf were also coming along. Brontë wanted to bring all six of her Ikans, but her mother dismissed this idea out of hand. *Too expensive,* she said; and besides, the long voyage would interrupt their training. *Choose two,* she said. *More than enough.* Brontë considered arguing—she really did want the whole team with her— but her mother was already in a rough temper, and she was afraid she might end up with no Ikans.

Six different passenger ships were carrying those from Ikeda House out to Gagarin, along with a few private cruisers. Isra had booked Brontë a stateroom on the *Fido*. Once onboard, she and the Ikans explored the stateroom, with its master suite, sitting room, and separate bedrooms for staff and Security. There were data ports in every cabin, and fully stocked pantry, tea, and liquor cabinets. "Don't even consider it," Sabra said when Brontë and Adder discovered this last.

"Captain." Adder spread her hands. "How will we learn from experience if you never let us have any experience?"

The ship, owned by Nikau Verde Takano, a member of Verde Combine not in the line, was really named the *We Are Faithful Unto Death*, but everyone called her *Fido*, a nickname Brontë understood only because she had done Classics for her Special Topics. You had to study Dead Languages for Classics. She'd done Russian, Latin, and English. Fido was a word from Latin. It was another way to say Faithful. "A joke, then," Adder said.

"Right," Brontë agreed.

"Not a funny one."

Brontë grinned. "It's a shibboleth joke. If you get it, you're one of us. If you don't, we know you're not. Ha ha ha. Look." She tipped the screen toward Adder. "Gagarin has acceptable universities. They're doing good work with g-sets, according to this. Plus, they're further out than Hayek. Maybe while we're onplanet, we'll visit a few schools."

"Better than dodging your cousins," Adder said.

Shutting down her port, Brontë rolled off her bunk. "Let's explore the ship. Sign up for a game room. Or a gym."

Eleven Ikeda families were riding the *Fido* to Gagarin. Use of the more popular rooms would be at a premium. Brontë, knowing this from previous years, explained it to Adder and Wolf as they headed out. As they passed Security's cabins, Sabra spoke, not pausing from stowing away her amazing array of weapons. "Miss Brontë! Where are you going?"

"I'm taking Adder. And Wolf."

"Take Officer Tolliver." Huffing in exasperation, Brontë went back to fetch Tully.

Out in the corridors, ship's crew hurried about, finishing their shakedown. The *Fido* was building push on its drive toward Pickering Point. It would take just over thirty-three hours to get there—more commonly, ships took over four hundred hours to cover the distance, but that was for those willing to trade months of their lives in travel time to save fuel costs. Brontë dodged the crew, ignoring Tully's calls for her to wait, and slapped open a service hatch. This earned her a yelp from one of the crew. Passengers (which she technically was, even if her Combine owned the ship) weren't supposed to use service routes. Ignoring this as well, she plummeted inside, Adder and Wolf on her heels.

The service corridors of the *Fido* were nothing so fancy as the rest of the ship—skinny unlined metal alleys twisting through the decks, filled with electrical, water, sewer pipes, and other such hardware, and the metal grid plates that protected these. Every six or eight meters a fan enclosed in a metal cage jutted down, spinning lazily. Ducking under these slowed Brontë's pell-mell progress somewhat, as did the frequent splits in the path. Tully caught up at one of these intersections. Grabbing Adder, she bashed her into a grid plate. "You shitting cull," she said breathlessly. "Captain Anador will take your ears off! *And* mine!"

"Hey!" Brontë objected. "My Security did nothing wrong!"

Adder's face was blank. Tully released her and stood straight, or as straight as she could, given the constraints of the alleyway. "Miss Ikeda. We have our orders. And we all know them." She spat this last sentence at Adder, who did not react.

Brontë looked back and forth between them, frowning. "Tully?" she said. Tully retreated, slipping her hands behind her back. Her expression was one Brontë had seen before—it was the way Tully and the other bonded workers often looked, standing along the wall in Dr. Hegel's class.

"What's wrong?" Brontë asked. "What orders?" The stubborn muscles around her mouth standing out hard, Tully said nothing. Brontë rubbed her neck. She would get it out of Adder later, she decided, and turned back to the corridor intersection. "I think the game room is this way."

"It's down two decks and aft, miss," Tully said. "That way."

Brontë hid her smirk. "Thanks, Tully."

A few meters in that direction was a ladder, going straight down through the ship. Brontë had started to swing herself onto it when Wolf's arm shot out, blocking her path. She stepped back, surprised, her mouth opening. Adder touched two fingers to her lips, the signal for silence. Directly down the well of ladder, clear as winter light, came a whispered conversation. Two young men, Brontë was certain. More than that, she did not know. Their Public was good—better than Tully's, not as good as Sabra's. She did not think they were from Waikato.

"—the jump?"

"No, after. At the hub."

"That's sixty watches away, why I gotta decide right now standing on one boot?" There was a strange noise, crisp, almost, and a choked sound. "Mehcoma, Kev, did I say no? I ain't say no!"

"In or out, tzayin."

"In! In!"

A thump, and another choked sound. "You weasel on us…"

"I won't. I won't."

"Stop whining, cook's boy. Now. Your access to menus. Let's hear it."

Adder tugged Tully up corridor. In a bare whisper she said they should capture the speakers. Tully indicated disagreement. Wolf and Adder stared at one another. "Officer Tolliver can take Brontë back to the cabin," Adder proposed. "We'll go alone."

When Tully argued, insisting they should all go back, Adder leapt at the ladder, Wolf on her heels. Tully, baring her teeth in a snarl, followed. Brontë scrambled after them. Their climb was nearly silent—but nearly isn't total. Though they went all the way to the hull, they found nothing but empty service corridors, stretching as far as they saw in any direction.

Tully dragged Adder back to the passenger level, and their quarters, where she took her into the suite Sabra and Tully were sharing, and shut its hatch. Brontë stood in the sitting room, chewing her lip, thinking whether she should interfere. Adder was her Security after all. On the other hand, she was also a junior officer under Sabra's command, and under Tully's command. And she had disobeyed a direct order. Everything was so complicated.

As she turned to go into her own suite, she saw Wolf in the hatch of the cabin he shared with Adder. Interest flickered alert in her stomach. She went to stand opposite him. He had grown lately, and was exactly her height. She could look right into his eyes. "Tell me what orders Sabra gave you," she said.

It was odd. Brontë would have sworn Wolf had already been standing straight. The Ikans always stood straight, alert, ready to spring. Yet after she spoke, slowly Wolf stood straighter, until he was as upright as a spear, his clear grey eyes meeting hers.

"I have your contract," Brontë reminded him. "That means I'm your commander."

"No, miss. We're assigned to your Security team. Captain Anador is our commander."

Miss. Wolf never called her that. None of the Ikans did. But she had never before pulled rank on them either. "All right," she said, lounging against the other side of the hatch, deliberately making herself shorter, "don't tell me because I'm your commander. Or because I've got your contract, either. Tell me because we can make better plans if we share data."

Wolf twisted up his mouth. "Oh. You bring data to this trade?"

Brontë grinned. "Not as unlikely as it sounds. C'mon. What order did she give you?"

Wolf exhaled. Then he told her what Sabra had said they were not to reveal—that they were supposed to keep hard watch on Brontë at all times, because intelligence had come down warning of a possible hostile takeover of the Ikeda Board. "But Captain Anador says it's unconfirmed."

Brontë chewed at her lip, thinking which heirs and spares were aboard the *Fido*, thinking what exactly that crew in the service corridor had said. "Just the Ikeda Board? Not the Verde?" Wolf nodded. "No hint who's behind the coup?"

"The Captain didn't show us the intelligence report."

Brontë went past him to her cabin, and pulled out her port. She opened her X-Box—the part of her system that had no connections to any nexus—and brought up the file on the Ikeda family, though in fact she scarcely needed it. While it loaded, she thought through who could be eliminated from suspicion. Direct heirs to the Seat, obviously, and those who were high in the line—they had no need to stage a hostile takeover. Theo, then. His little sister. Yvette Ikeda Kadir.

As she went through the file, sorting out names, she realized, with a chill, that six of the top ten heirs to Ikeda's Primary Seat were aboard the *Fido*. Yvette, second in line of inheritance, was not; her father was taking her to Gagarin on the ship their family owned, the *Tonbo*. The *Tonbo* wouldn't leave port for another day or two, she thought. She couldn't remember exactly. And Vidmar Ikeda Walker was aboard the *Azov*, which had left yesterday. She didn't know which heirs were aboard which other ships, or when they were leaving. But Theo, as the primary heir, would clearly be the main target. "Not that I like Theo, especially," she muttered. "On the other hand, given we're sharing the same ship right now…"

"Theo?" Adder said from the hatchway. "What about Theo?"

Brontë shifted on the sofa, making room, and meanwhile giving Adder a hasty once-over. No visible bruising. "Did you get it bad?"

"What about Theo?" Adder tugged the port over to share the screen. Wolf climbed up to sit on the opposite arm of the sofa. Brontë outlined what she was doing, eliminating candidates unlikely to be behind the coup. "If we can get it down to four or five names," she explained, "or even fewer, it makes our research much simpler."

Wolf and Adder looked at one another, and Adder said skeptically,

"You think we can *research* who is behind the takeover?"

"We need a manageable pool of candidates. We'll narrow down over-conservatively, with a subgroup of marginal candidates we can return to if our prime candidates don't develop." She was swiping through lines as she spoke, changing colors to code the levels of elimination—first level white, second yellow, third orange, all the way down to her top choices, outlined in red. Five candidates, and their direct families. It was a place to start.

"We don't have access," Adder said. "Not to the levels we need."

Brontë put her finger on one of the names: David Raphael Navarro Ikeda Ito. "Our main contender."

Adder took the port from her and tapped the name to access David's history. He was seventeenth in line for the Ikeda seat, with his daughter—Talia Alisa Navarro Verde Ikeda—thirtieth. "Nothing about Mr. David seems suspicious," Adder noted.

Brontë slid down through the files. Remembering all the times David had smiled at her and asked after the small details of her life, she knew why Adder was reluctant to believe he could be behind the coup. But it was that very factor—his ability to make everyone like him—which made him so likely to be behind the coup.

"We should tell Captain Anador," Adder said. "Especially if you think this is true. Also, we don't have access. You think we can do this research, but we don't have the access at the level we'd need. I'm pointing that out one more time. And if you think you're good enough to jump those walls without tripping alarms..." She shook her head.

"First, I am. And second, I don't have to be." Adder scowled, and Brontë explained, "Because I borrowed my mother's keys before we left the House."

Adder looked at Wolf, who shut his eyes. "Borrowed."

"Borrowed is such a pretty word," Brontë said with her most innocent smile. "My mother has Board Level clearance. No holds, no trace, no bars. We can go anywhere."

"You're going to get us all shot," Wolf said.

"We should tell Captain Anador," Adder repeated, without any conviction at all.

"Why?" Wolf said, his eyes still shut. "So she can get shot too?"

"You can say I made you do it," Brontë explained.

"Oh, yes," Adder said. "That will work *perfectly*."

Chapter 9

The *Susan Calvin*, Chernyi Hub, The Drift

Velocity drifted weightless in her cabin, her eyes shut, her attention on the multiple feeds her uplink cast against her eyelid.

Though Tai had made a few noises about solitary being cruel, neither he nor Rida had protested much when she ordered Sabra and Brontë locked up separately—Sabra in the brig, and Brontë in the pit, leashed to a cleat inside the dagan's locker. This necessitated leaving the locker cover open. For the past four and a half watches, Brontë had done nothing about that. Taken no advantage. Made no move. Acted as though the dagan did not exist.

Velocity wasn't only watching Brontë. One feed showed her Rida at work in the com; another showed her Tai floating in the Exchange among the blueberry bushes; the last showed her Sabra, who had managed to create, out of her restraints and a ripped and braided blanket, a kind of resistance exercise set, and was doing pull-ups between two walls of the cage. Having stripped off the outer shell of her skinsuit, she was exercising in her undershirt and briefs, her muscles crisp under her fair skin.

Tai had talked to Sabra—or tried to talk to her—and he had tried to talk to Brontë. Both conversations had followed, essentially, the same track. *Conversations*, well. More like monologues.

Tai: We need to find a road out of this. A road that's not you and that child being junked on the next port the Captain crosses.

Tai: Because that's where this is headed.

Tai: It's not impossible that our interests might align, is all I'm saying.

Sabra: …

Tai: I'm saying maybe. Maybe that's the case. And maybe we can find a path out of this.

Tai: But this. What you're doing now. This won't work. Captain ain't an idiot. She knows your little Combine princess is lying her highborn ass off.

Sabra: …

Tai: Listen. Tell me what you want. Never mind if it's possible. Tell me what, best case, you want to be the end of this. Then I'll talk to the Captain. Sabra?

Sabra: …

His attempt with Brontë had been much the same, except with cussing instead of silence from Brontë's side. Drifting in her cabin, Velocity bumped against the bulkhead by her facility. She nudged off with her elbow and started the slow drift in the other direction. Opening her Get-Done list, she read through it, swiped away the tasks they had completed, along with two or three she had put on the speculation side which were no longer in play (5. Go down to station medical—does anyone need fast transport to station with Pirian physicians? 8. Go to Port Control, try to get on the list for in-system cargo hauls. 13. Biohazardous transport? (Only if pay is high)), and then read through what was left. The air filters were almost due to be changed. She could do that.

Impatient, exasperated, she reached through the ship's system to wake the dagan. From the dark of her cabin, she watched as the dagan integrated itself into the form it always used for Brontë—a form somewhat different from the lean, angular, asexual face and body the dagan used with her. For Brontë, the dagan had lush eyelashes, rounded cheeks, a wide mouth; it had thick limbs and a suggestion of a potbelly. Velocity watched the pit feeds as the dagan slid from its locker and turned to Brontë. "Mzala," it said gravely. "This seems an unfortunate turn of events."

Brontë snarled. Delicately, the dagan pushed off the pit wall, caught itself on the locker frame, and anchored itself in the hatchway. "Can I help?"

"I'm not an infant," Brontë spat. "I know you're part of *her ship*. Part of the *mainframe*."

The dagan nestled down further in the locker doorway, getting its eyes level with hers. "That's not precisely how I'm arranged," it said. Brontë scoffed. The dagan spread its hands, endearingly helpless. "It can't be pleasant to be chained up like this. My menu has limits, but I'll help you in any way I can."

"Good. Help me gut your Captain like a dog."

The dagan lowered its hands, curving its mouth into a frown. "Mzala."

"Robot," Brontë sneered.

"You're behaving badly," the dagan observed. "Are you hungry?"

"Maybe because your *Captain* isn't feeding us. Not until we answer her questions, *truthfully*. What *she* considers truth."

The dagan curled more snugly into the hatch. "Well, speaking of truth. *That's* not true, now, is it?" it asked. "The Captain has flaws. Mistreating prisoners isn't one of them."

"What would you know? Robot."

The dagan watched the Combine child with its dark eyes. Alone in her cabin, Velocity, who knew this tactic, made a face. The dagan, when it thought you had said something obviously stupid or wrong, would shut up and let you listen to that answer for as long as you could bear to.

In the pit, Brontë made a face very like the one Velocity had just made, and then kicked off the wall of the pit, shooting away as far as the leash of the restraints would let her. The wire snub snubbed her hard, yanking her back, and she kicked off again, even harder. She did this over and over. The dagan watched her peacefully.

Exhaling hard, Velocity rolled into a tight ball and then unrolled, kicking toward the hatch. She wiggled through it and went down the trail to the galley, where she started putting together a meal—Brontë's complaint, though not strictly factual, had reminded her that the prisoners were overdue to be fed. As she worked, she mulled over whether to have Tai or Rida take the food in. Rida was better with people, but Tai was way better at lies and manipulation. Lying and manipulation, Velocity reckoned, might well be what was called for in this particular situation.

It had been one of the first things she had noticed about Tai back then on Sarat, his skill at manipulation. This had been early in her years captaining the *Susan Calvin*—her first real cargo run, no more than two months after buying the ship. In those days, Velocity had still been trying to make a go of running a merchant ship, moving cargo between Free Trade planets and stations in the Drift to the settlement planets and stations in Republic space. Sarat was one of these planets—a mining planet, mostly, though it also did some agriculture.

Velocity had talked to Free Traders, and to Pirians. She did her homework. Before she made the jump, she packed the hold of her ship with agricultural chemicals, proscribed drugs, and about a dozen other items not manufactured in the Republic but in high demand on the Settlement planets. Trading these on Sarat ought to have meant a profit, especially since the deckhand she had hired to run the ship with her was working for passage only—he wanted a ride to Sarat, but didn't have the funds to buy a berth.

Unfortunately, trading goods at any station which was Combine held—as Sarat was—required her to obtain a Combine Trade license, which she had known but not really appreciated until she had her boots on the concourse of Sarat Station. In theory, obtaining a trade license just meant paying taxes and tariffs. In fact, as she soon discovered, on these stations out here at the dusty end of the Republic, it meant bribing the right people. This meant hours and hours of delicate work spent in discovering precisely who those people were, without accidentally bribing the wrong people and ending up arrested and sold into contract labor. It would also cut significantly into her profit margins.

As Velocity would learn in her short stint as a merchant captain, and her longer one as a troubleshooter, Republic settlement worlds were horrible. Sarat was more horrible than most. Though the planet had been licensed for agriculture, the Combine that held it, Taveri-Bowers Combine, was putting its funds into stripping the planet of its mineral resources. Among other minerals, TBC was mining bauxite, silver, and molybdenum, while doing none of the necessary nanotroping which would transform the land into something that could support human life. Even now, eleven hundred years after the first human outpost on Sarat, the entire population still lived in domes and arcologies, and average life expectancy, even if you excluded contract labor in the mines, was less than fifty years.

The planet needed Velocity's cargo, in other words, to refurbish the soil in the greenhouses and domes which grew most of their food supply. It also needed the Pirian-manufactured medical supplies she carried. And as desperately as the population needed her cargo, Velocity needed to sell that cargo even more. But unless she could find her way through the maze of corrupt bureaucracy that was standard on a Combine-held Settlement station, both she and the people of Sarat were out of luck.

Her ninth watch on the station, she was stewing over these problems at a station bistro, drinking a mildly narcotic local tea and calculating whether the *Susan Calvin* had enough fuel to make the jump back to the Drift, where she could offload her cargo at a significantly lower profit to some planet not held by a Combine when Tai slid into her booth. She hadn't known him then, of course. She just saw a young man, well under twenty, so lean his bones showed stark under his dark skin, the tension around his eyes and in his muscles belying the easy smile on his lovely mouth. "You have cargo you can't move," Tai said. "I'm your kwaii."

Velocity studied him. "Kwaii." He widened the smile and showed her two crossed fingers. She shook her head. "Where I'm from, that means *hold on, I've got to sneeze*. I'm guessing it means something else here?"

Tai looked at his fingers, and then at her. His smile widened to an actual grin. Then he sat back in the booth and used the fingers to wave at the kid serving the tea.

"You paying this time, Tai?" the kid asked, taking his time coming to the table.

Tai slid his dark gaze toward Velocity, twitching an eyebrow, his smile now mischievously smutty. Amused despite herself, she tapped the table. "Put it on mine," she said. "And bring some cakes."

Once Tai had tea and two spice cakes inside him, Velocity nudged: "Well?"

He gulped more tea and refilled his bowl from the common pot. "My boss buys cargo under the deck," he said. "Not full price. But she will pay."

Velocity considered this.

"She's a facilitator," Tai explained. "A service she does for those new to the station, such as you, Captain. For a small fee, nothing that's a burden. Hardly notice it. And as a bonus, you get my services." He gave her a smile even smuttier than the previous smile had been. "*Full* services," he added, and Velocity couldn't help laughing. "I can take you to meet my boss, if you like." Tai wiped tea from his mouth with the sleeve of his shirt. "She's usually in-office now."

Velocity considered the fuel calculations she had been making (they kept returning her dismayingly clear answers, no matter how she jacked the numbers—*no, no, and no possible way, are you high?*) while simultaneously studying Tai. For no reason at all, and even though she knew he was using his considerable charm to fox her, she found herself trusting him. Even as young as she was then, she knew what a foolish decision this was. He was contract labor: it was clear in his dress and language and every motion. Being in the system did not make someone more trustworthy. Quite the opposite.

Yet even then there was an intelligence, a humor, in him that Velocity responded to. So she followed him off the dock concourse into the service corridors, narrow, dim, and ill-ventilated—also filthy—and frequented only by other contract labor. They greeted Tai, speaking in the quick fluid language of those in the system, made more complex by the accent and vocabulary of Sarat; Velocity didn't have a chance of following it. Tai responded in kind, though when he spoke to her, he used the more common Public Standard used on most stations in the Republic, with only a faint accent and the occasional odd phrase.

He led her out along the cross-corridors, through three levels to the industrial docks—docks for mining barges coming in from the asteroids, and tech barges coming in from the outlying print shops, and fresh shipments of contract laborers from the Core and elsewhere. As in most stations, industrial docks was a working level. Its deck plates were painted with rust sealant, its bulkheads decorated only with signage. The air was bitter with hydrocarbons and oils, the stink of old sweat and over-worked environmental filters.

Tai took her through the huge open cavern of the docks—loaders hauled cargo from the ships; dockhands hauled immense battered ore hoppers, their big metal wheels twice as tall as any of them, along tram railings from the barges to the sorters; baggage handlers shifted crated cargo stacked high onto flat carts. The contract labor workers— hundreds of them, more than Velocity could focus on—wore only trousers, and sometimes even these were cut off at the knees. No boots. No gloves. Their wiry scrawny muscles gleamed in the dim light of the docks. They worked in teams, guarded by squads of Labor Security officers armed with both plasma rifles and short heavy sticks.

Velocity only caught a glimpse of all this, though, because Tai caught her sleeve and tugged her into another corridor, only marginally less nasty than the service corridors. This held offices, each hatch marked with a tidy metal label. Accounts Manager. Quality Inspector. Dock Security. Labor Agent: Discipline and Contact Management.

Tai took her into a door labeled Elise Salo, Logistics. Inside, a claustrophobic front office, narrow and short. It held two worktables, one to each side of the door—no one at either. Across from the front hatch was an even narrower corridor, hardly wide enough for one person to walk through without turning sideways. Four hatches opened off this corridor. Walking with his head bent against the low overhead, Tai went to the last of these, on the port. Velocity followed him. "Kas Salo," Tai said, as Velocity entered the rear office. "Mem to see you."

This cabin was tiny, its deck plate bare. Its walls held hardcopy prints of docking schedules and work schedules, several of these covering older, out-of-date schedules and even older, more out-of-date ones. These were all marked up with varicolored inks: arrows and underlining and great violent X's slashed through entire blocks of dates. Incongruously, there was also an adorable capture posted, just behind Elise Salo: some sort of fluffy nestling bird, long-necked, wide-eyed, peering quizzically at the feed of whoever had done the capture. It was standing on an empty broken eggshell. Underneath, in bold blue letters: ACT INNOCENT AND EAT THE EVIDENCE.

Elise Salo, at a worktable that held not one but three separate ports, all up and active, leaned back in her chair to study Velocity while Tai explained who she was, and that she had cargo to sell. As short and stocky as Tai was tall and lean, Salo had dark skin and hair worn in many small tight braids. She focused past Tai, meeting Velocity's eyes steadily. "I told her you might can help," Tai finished, "sharp how you are to match those with cargo to willing clients."

Salo gave Velocity a theatrically shrewd stare. Velocity looked back, unimpressed. If Salo's data banks did not, at this very moment, contain a fat file filled with research on Velocity Wrachant and her ship and what its hold was filled with—including its worth down to the last gram of phosphates—she'd eat her own bootlaces. "Did you explain the arrangements?" Salo asked.

"A bit," Tai said.

"I'll get less selling to you than I would selling to a TBC agent," Velocity said. "He explained that, yes. That's fine. It doesn't mean I'll let you rob me, though. You understand that."

Salo's lips thinned into a shape meant to be a smile. "It sounds as though we can bargain," she said. "Tai. Why don't you fetch tea."

Go watch the door, Velocity knew this meant. Tai left, shutting the hatch behind him.

When Velocity emerged from Salo's cabin more than an hour later, their deal hammered out, Tai sat on his heels by the front hatch, talking to a woman at one of the worktables. He stood expectantly at Velocity's approach. "You're to take me to someone named Dwa," Velocity said.

Tai brightened. "Oh, good. C'mon, she'll be heading to dinner soon."

Dwa had an office further out toward the rim, in a warren of twisty work stations and bureaucratic offices where mid-level clerks did the work of regulating not just the docks but the entire station. Dwa was a warehouse clerk for the civilian dock, Tai explained as they rode the service lift in. She was in charge of storage allocation, as well as of assigning the dockworkers to move cargo. She and Salo had a side arrangement—Tai didn't say this part, but why else would they be on their way out to her office?

The corridors out here were not only better lit and ventilated than those near the docks, they also had fabric deck covers (though in boring, ugly colors—dull blue and dull mustardy-yellow, in abstract patterns), and art that ran on dedicated wallboards. Now and then, the art turned off and a station-announcement played on the boards: informationals about when time-sheets were due, and where new postings were listed; warnings about lifts that would be closed for repair; a request to watch for a stray child, missing since thirteen o'clock from Level C.

Dwa's office was a few hundred meters spinward from the lift. Though it was twice the size of Elise Salo's entire workspace, Dwa was its sole occupant. She had a large L-shaped worktable and very nice wallcoverings with tiny animate comets soaring endlessly past. Real flowers—orange roses, purple irises, bright yellow daffodils—filled a real crystal vase on her table. Tiny and slender, with big brown eyes, she beamed at Tai as he entered. "I thought you had forgotten me!"

"Dwa! You missed me!" Tai came around her desk to hug her as she stood. "I brought you a present."

"So I see," Dwa said, nodding at Velocity.

"Puddlebug," Tai said, straightening the floppy bow she wore at her collar. "That's business. Here." He handed her a small dark bottle he took from his jacket pocket. "Some of Kas Salo's honey brandy. The new batch."

"Oh, how lovely!" Dwa held it to the light. "I can't wait to try it. How is Elise? And the new baby?"

"Already talking, if you can believe it."

"Tsk. They grow up so fast." Dwa took the scrap of paper Tai held out and went to work at her port. "Tell Elise she needs to keep 25:00 open, next tenth but one. Callie and I are having our Seeding."

"I'll remind her."

"06:00 the fifteenth good for you?" Dwa asked Velocity, and printed out a ticket, allocating space in one of the sections of the station's holds dedicated to Elise Salo, and issuing ten dockworkers to transport the cargo from Velocity's ship to this space, two station "days" from now. Sarat ran a 28 hour day, and it was nearly 26:00 by their clock now, so that meant...Velocity did the math in her head, and came up with Midwatch First, two spins off. She rubbed her eyes, and made a note through the uplink, reminding herself to check the time more carefully when she was back on the ship, and less exhausted.

After Tai chatted with Dwa a bit longer, he led Velocity out of the office again. His flirtatious mask fell away as soon as the office hatch shut behind them, leaving weariness behind it. "The labor agent on your dock will take that," he said, handing her the ticket. "Do you know where to find the kiosk?"

"I can hunt it up," Velocity started to say, but just then they came around a curve in the corridor, straight into a squad of Labor Security blockading their path. The Security were hauling three contract laborers from a service lift and shoving them up against the corridor wall. Tai stopped where he was, his breath drawing inward in one quick jerk.

A Labor Security wheeled. "You!" he snapped, pointing his stick at Tai. "Over here!"

Velocity glanced at Tai. His muscles were rigid. He went to join the contracts lined up against the wall. The Security who had shouted at him shoved him, knocking him into the wall. "Hey," Velocity objected.

One of the Labor Security, the Lieutenant, pulled out a handheld and began running data—on their chips, Velocity assumed. Most contract labor in the Republic had tracking chips implanted into their right shoulder blades. These chips could also be used to link to their labor files. "Your contract holder is Jeannot Azim," he informed Tai.

"Yes, kas."

Absently, the Lieutenant tapped the stick, hard, against Tai's collarbone. Tai flinched, but made no sound. "Sir," the Lieutenant said.

"Yes, sir," Tai corrected.

"Jeannot Azim of Azim Mines. In Skudai. On Sarat."

"Yes, sir."

"Why are you on-station, jess? Why aren't you in the mines where you belong?"

Tai swallowed. "I'm rented, sir. To ka—to Elise Salo. It should be in the file, sir."

"Elise Salo."

"Logistics, sir. Industrial docks. I can give you her com if—"

The Lieutenant hit harder with the stick this time. "You're a long way from the industrial docks, jess. Slip the fence, did you?"

"He is with me." Velocity spoke in her best and most icy Combine tone. She moved into the Lieutenant's space, her eyes narrowed. "Who are you, please."

The Lieutenant, who had stepped back by instinct, squinted at her, confused and annoyed. "I'm Lieutenant Calvo. Who are you?"

"Captain Velocity Kadir Wrachant," Velocity said, stressing *Kadir* slightly, "of the ship presently in your dock, the *Susan Calvin*. This man has been assigned to me by Elise Salo. He is here on my business. We'd like to be on our way, Lieutenant Calvo." She stressed *Lieutenant* also.

The Lieutenant stared at her. He knew he shouldn't let some stranger in a corridor push him around. On the other hand, she had a Combine accent, and a Combine name—Kadir—and she spoke like a Combine seat holder, and she was *acting* like she had the right to give him orders. He was Labor Security—recruited from the lowest levels of Republic society, trained from the cradle to do what anyone with the right accent and attitude ordered him to do. It was a hard habit to break, just because sense told him to break it.

"Do we need to consult your commanding officer, Lieutenant?" Velocity said, putting an even icier edge to her accent. The Lieutenant glanced down at his handheld. "One way or the other," Velocity said. "Make a decision. I do have business to attend to."

"You're free to go," the Lieutenant said, and turned away from Tai.

Riding the lift in toward the hub—she paid the premium for an express, mainly so that they could be sure of having the cabin to themselves—Velocity kept quiet, leaving Tai alone. When his breathing had slowed, and he was not trembling quite so openly, she said, "Sorry. I probably should have stayed out of it. I hope I didn't make things worse."

Tai hitched in a breath. "Ha. No." Then he said, "Probably not, anyway."

Velocity grimaced. "Sorry," she said again.

The lift stopped at the civilian docks. Velocity put her boot in the way of the hatch, to keep it open longer. "Why don't you come show me where that kiosk is?" she invited. "And I'll give you dinner after?"

Tai had been gazing at nothing. Now he focused on her, abruptly. After a sharp second, he grinned. "Dinner."

Half against her will, Velocity grinned back. "A very...hot dinner," she said, and licked her lips at him. Tai laughed and getting out of the lift came down the concourse with her.

Later that watch—well, halfway into the next watch, in fact—he pushed up on his elbow next to her in her bunk and observed that she had yet to produce that dinner. "I have something to confess," Velocity said lazily, half asleep, lax with the bone-deep ease she always felt after good sex. "I lured you here under false pretenses."

Tai grinned and ran a finger down her spine. "No. Really?"

"I can't actually cook, is what I mean."

He collapsed in the bunk, burying his face in the pillow. "No. Please. Anything but that."

She turned onto her side, petting the soft burr of hair on his scalp, just growing out from being shaved, petting down his back, which was marked with old white scars from long-ago whippings. "The mines," she said. His muscles flinched under her hand. "Your contract is to Azim mines?" she clarified.

He hitched up onto his elbows, though he didn't look at her. "Since I was nine," he said. "I came out when I was twelve, though. This boss...anyway, last summer, Elise Salo needed a runner. Someone smart. Someone who wouldn't cause trouble." Tai smiled, sort of. It was more like another flinch. "Salo's related to Azim somehow. Brother's kid, or kid's wife. Some way like that." Velocity said nothing. He lay down on his side, reaching to take her hand. "It's fine, Captain Whatever Your Actual Name Is. Here on the station, at least I get fed. And Kas Salo hardly ever hits me."

She could count every articulated rib under his fine brown skin. If Salo was feeding him, she wasn't feeding him much. She wondered what would happen to him when Salo got rich enough to quit her work and buy an estate downhill. Back to the mines, probably.

Out loud, she said, "Velocity."

"What?"

"Velocity Wrachant. That's my name." She sat up, reaching for her trousers. "Any chance you can cook?"

"Cook?"

"Want to hire on as my cook?" she asked. He squinted, all his muscles going still. "I need a cook," she said, "obviously. If you can't cook, other work is open."

He kept watching her. "Like bunk boy?"

Velocity pulled on her shirt. "Do you mean was this an audition? No. The work won't require anything like that."

Tai slid from the bed. She handed him the ratty coverall he had been wearing, and he pulled it on. When the front was sealed, he said, "I absolutely would have done bunk duty as part of the job. Just so you know."

Velocity's spine straightened. She started to answer forcefully, and then saw his slight smirk. "Did your boss ship you uphill to get rid of your troublemaking ass?"

Tai grinned. "How much pay did you say you were offering? And you do know this means you're making yourself a felon? Aiding someone to ditch their work contract is a fast ride into the system yourself. I'm just pointing that out."

"Bah," Velocity said. "Let's go see if you can cook."

On the *Susan Calvin*, all these years later, Velocity looked at the yams she had chopped and steamed, wondering what to do with them. Even she knew you couldn't just feed people steamed yams in a bowl. Tai came in through the hatch from the trail. "Are you cooking?"

"If you'll tell me how. Rida was supposed to teach me," she added gloomily.

"Here." He came over and took down the basket of vegetables Rida kept stocked from the Exchange. "Add in some peppers and celery, a bit of lemon. Grilled shrimp on the side..." He hunted in the keeper for shrimp, and set about cleaning them.

Velocity took a handful and helped. "Listen. I always meant to ask."

"Uh-oh. This sounds scary."

She elbowed him. He rocked with the impact, but—used to microgravity—caught himself on the anchor bar at their feet and hauled himself back into place. "You remember when we met, there on Sarat," she said. The laughter on his face sliding away, Tai gave her a sidelong glance. "Did you..." Velocity kept her attention on the shrimp, "...when you had sex with me that first time, was that because you'd been ordered to do it?"

"Captain."

She looked into his eyes. "I didn't even think about it, then. I thought, of course you'd want sex, who wouldn't want sex, of course you'd say no if you didn't, what would stop you?" She made a face. "I was so young then. Not even five years out of my father's habitat. I thought I knew everything."

"Captain."

"It didn't occur to me. When you said you were full-service. It didn't occur to me that might not be a joke."

Tai, moving with care, wiped his hands on a galley scrub, and dumped the scrub in the laundry. Then he cupped his hands around her face. "Captain," he said. "It was a long time ago." Velocity felt heat under her skin, and behind her eyes. "And of everything that happened to me on that filthy planet," he said, "you were the best." He kissed her above the eye. She shook her head. "We do what we can do," he told her, "and when we can do better, we do better."

She laughed, maybe a little raggedly. "You've been talking to the dagan." He laughed too, and kissed her again.

Nothing," Tai said.

"Nothing," Rida agreed.

"They've got impressive discipline," Velocity said, "for pirates." She pointed at the chili sauce in the rack by Tai's elbow, and he tossed the bulb her way. She caught it from the air and squirted some through the port on the cover on her bowl. Eating was the only unpleasant part of microgravity. Even when you took care to cook foods that stuck together—as her crew always did—you still had to use bowls with covers and drink from fiches. However, the shrimp and yams had turned out well enough. "Brontë is the key," she said, maneuvering a slice of radish through the small hatch in the lid of the bowl.

"She's a child," Rida objected, and then added, with a tone of concession, "A Combine child. One who didn't grow up in the line, if what they said is true."

"Why lie about that?" Tai asked. "We won't be more likely to take the job because she wasn't expecting to inherit this seat and now she is."

"They're lying about that because they're lying about everything. They're Combine. Lying is what they do."

Velocity slid her fiche of wine from its rack and rolled the fiche through a small arc, to encourage capillary action. Though theoretically wine, like the shrimp and yams, could be consumed from bowls in microgravity, liquids did better in these open-mouthed containers, named for the data tag covers they resembled. "She outranks Sabra," Velocity explained, "at least as they see it. That Security won't move without her whistle. Which means she's our key. That's if we want to continue with this job. Because we don't have to continue. I'll point that out. We have another option. We did get the up front payment. It's not much, but it's not nothing. We can head back to the Drift, ditch these pirates on some Free Trade Station, move on."

Rida flinched. Tai didn't, but he didn't look happy, either. Velocity said, "They lied to us. They pirated the ship. They assaulted you," she pointed her chin at Rida, "and they tried to play you against us," she moved her chin at Tai.

"Dump them with the freets," Rida said.

"It's not like ditching *you* there," Velocity argued. "They're not helpless. They're Combine. Brontë has plenty on that tag in her pocket. They'll be fine."

Tai shut the hatch on his bowl and sat back, folding his arms across his chest. "So why not take that path? Why are we even thinking anything else?"

"It leaves us right where we were," Rida said. "Liens on the ship, not much in the hold, out in the Drift with our tanks dry, and no job worth taking in sight."

"Whereas this is a job worth taking?" Tai said.

"Maybe." Velocity ate a shrimp. "That's why we need to get this pup to stop lying. She tells us where they were really going, and what they were really after—maybe that's a job we want." She finished the last bite of yam. "Maybe not. We won't know until she stops lying to us."

"You don't think it was really Woodlands they were aiming for. Or this aunt."

"I think they've lied to us from the start. I think this aunt is just another lie. Peel this back, probably we've got another lie under it." Velocity flicked her chin at Rida. "I had been thinking the dagan could get her to talk. But it's probably going to have to be you."

"Captain," he said, without any special force.

"She's been asleep for," Velocity checked her uplink, "twenty minutes and change. Give her another hour, then go wake her up."

Chapter 10

The *Fido*, in Transit to Gagarin, the Core
(Seven Months Earlier)

Brontë had booked Rec Cabin 5B, a double, for Shtai, and a private booth at Mori's Tea Shop for after. She and the Ikans meant to discuss their research on the hostile takeover at length over tea and satay, though she wasn't certain they'd be able to do this: Sabra had insisted on coming with them, and bringing Tully along as well, ostensibly so they could participate in the Shtai session. Brontë thought it more likely it was Sabra being fretful and overcautious.

When they arrived at 5B, Theo, who had the block before them for his dance lesson, was still there. Everyone in the House took dance, just like everyone took Shtai. But Theo took dance seriously. Leaning in the hatchway to 5B, Brontë watched the end of the lesson. Theo's dance tutor—apparently brought along on the ship just for these lessons—watched as well. Theo spun and floated through the chamber, light as air. The lower gravity of the *Fido* underway benefited his dance in interesting ways.

Watching, brooding, Brontë considered telling Theo about the coup. *Possible coup*, she reminded herself. ***Rumored*** coup. *Coup you're not even supposed to know about.* She understood, theoretically, the reasons Ikeda House Security wanted the suspected hostile takeover kept confidential. But Theo had passed his prelims. He was, at least nominally, an adult of the House. Also, though he got on her nerves, he wasn't an idiot.

His Security team wasn't with him, she noticed. As heir presumptive to the Primary Seat, he had a dedicated half squad— twelve full-time Security officers—just as she had a dedicated quarter. At least two or three of them should have been here. She glanced at Sabra, wondering if her Security or his had the better intelligence. She thought of the bonded workers they had overhead in the corridor, thinking through what they had said once more. Really, it could have meant anything. And if a coup was looming, would her mother have sent her off on this ship alone, with only half her usual Security to watch over her?

Nevertheless, as Theo gathered his kit to leave, she asked him to meet her at Mori's after her own session. Theo frowned. "I've got a full schedule. If you have something you want from me, ask me now."

"That's not it." Brontë glanced past him at his dance instructor. "It's more…something I want to discuss."

Theo grimaced again. "Look," he started, and just then the bone-jarring siren for Combat Stations blared through the ship.

Brontë jumped; all of her Security, including the two Ikans, spun toward the hatch in perfect fighting stance. Theo gave the overhead speaker an annoyed glance. The siren wailed, increasing in volume and tempo. A crew member ran past the hatch, and then another. "Captain Anador," Tully said to Sabra tensely.

"We move to aft," Sabra said. "Adder, you have Brontë."

"Yes, Captain."

"What?" Theo stepped forward, starting to reach for Sabra, and stopping. He knew better than to take hold of a combat-trained Security officer. "What do you mean? It's just a drill. Isn't it?"

Sabra pointed at Wolf. "You have Theo."

Theo's eyes widened. "It's a drill!" he insisted.

In the hatch, Sabra glanced both ways along the corridor. Then she stepped out and across the corridor, motioning to the Ikans. Adder crowded Brontë into motion. They followed Sabra down the corridor at a trot. Behind her, Brontë heard Theo objecting, and Wolf murmuring something in reply. Adder, beside Brontë, ran faster, so Brontë did too. Theo came with them, his expression apprehensive and grim. Sabra was heading for the aft lift, Brontë thought. But at the first service hatch, Sabra followed a crew member into that, and slid swiftly down the ladder. Brontë followed, her grip clumsy on the railing. She realized suddenly how hard her heart was beating.

On Deck B, Sabra led them aft again. The alarm was really loud now. Catching hold of Adder at a junction, Brontë said in her ear: "It's too early! We're not through the jump yet!"

Adder shoved her between the shoulder blades. "Move."

"But what if it *is* just a drill?"

"*Move!*"

Just behind them, Wolf had a grip on Theo, hauling him along. The dance instructor was rushing along in their wake, his mouth a huge gape. Adder shoved Brontë again. The alarm siren blared deafeningly. She whirled and ran. The corridors had emptied of crew: they had reached their stations. Just as Sabra got them to the escape pods, tucked aft up against the hull, the alarm siren cut off. The silence it left behind felt soft in Brontë's ears.

Six crew were stationed by the escape pod hatchways. The lieutenant among them frowned at Sabra. "Ma'am...Captain. You need to be in your quarters. Go there now, please, and secure your hatch. Take these children with you."

"Step aside," Sabra said.

"Captain—"

Somewhere on the ship a plasma weapon fired. The crew lined up along the hatchway twitched; one of them swore. "Lieutenant!" he said, as if in protest.

"Hold your station. Captain, take these children to their quarters, now."

More plasma fire, distant in the ship: two shots, three. Sabra pulled her short rifle. It was a Lopaka TAC-20, which she carried, as Brontë had once heard her tell Tully, because pulling it was usually enough to end any argument. Certainly it startled this commercial ship's officer into silence. He swallowed, though, and rallied. "Captain, regulations require all passengers to be in their quarters during Combat Stations."

More plasma fire, multiple shots, getting closer now. Someone screamed. Sabra stepped close to the Lieutenant. She didn't point the TAC-20 at him; she just held it. "I am taking a lifepod. These children are coming with me. Step aside." He stared at her, and Sabra added, "This is Elena Ikeda Verde. That is Hiro Ikeda Hayek. They are getting on a lifepod. I will shoot you, and all of your crew, if necessary." The Lieutenant started to speak. Then he looked at Brontë and Theo, and moved aside. Sabra hammered open the hatchway into the lifepod bay. "Adder. Now."

Adder shoved Brontë through the hatchway. Sabra started powering up one of the pods, using the exterior port. She pointed at Wolf, who started powering up a second. Bracing herself in the hatchway, Tully said something to one of the ship's Security, who nodded, her face pale. Sabra punched a final sequence of tabs on her port, and the first pod hummed into life. Its small hatch slid open. Down the line, at his own port, Wolf was struggling to power up the second pod; Theo moved him aside and started feeding in data himself. The plasma shooting down the corridor grew abruptly louder. Tully, still braced in the open hatchway, muttered a curse under her breath. "Captain Anador!"

"Get in the pod," Sabra ordered Brontë, and returned to the hatchway. Shouldering the civilian Lieutenant aside, she aimed her TAC-20 up the corridor and fired. The plasma blast was violently loud in the enclosed space. Adder, who was shoving Brontë at the pod, wheeled; and just then the dance instructor punched her—punched Adder—from behind with the stock of a rifle he had taken off one of the ship's crew. Brontë fell down, and skittered backwards out of his range. The instructor drove the rifle's butt down into Adder's spine and pivoted toward Brontë. Astonished, she dodged further backwards; Wolf yanked her to her feet and behind him.

Just beyond the dance instructor, Brontë saw Tully tumble into the pod bay, yelling, a great scorched plasma burn covering most of her belly and chest. She yelled too, in horror and panic, and scrambled backwards even faster. More plasma blasts came through the hatch. Theo swore and flung himself to the deck just before a plasma bolt hit the port he'd been struggling with. It exploded into blue arcs and broken plastic, and Theo, flat on the deck, snarled, and then flung himself to his feet, grabbing the instructor from behind. He twisted the rifle from his hands, knocked him to the deck, and spat an order at Brontë: "Get in the pod."

Stunned, Brontë just stared, and Theo pivoted, bringing the rifle up, aiming it at the instructor. "You, stay back! As presumptive heir to the Primary Seat, I order you back!"

"No! You can't leave me here!"

Sabra fired down the corridor again. "Adder!" she snapped.

"Wolf," Adder said, *"get her in the lifepod."*

Catching Brontë by the collar and upper arm, Wolf spun her and shoved her through the open hatch of the life pod. He secured her in the seat furthest from the hatch.

"Captain!" Adder shouted.

"Go!" Sabra shouted, still firing.

Adder climbed into the pod, her teeth bared. Theo scrambled after her, the rifle tucked under his arm, and when the instructor tried to follow kicked him in the chest, knocking him out again. Adder yelled again, *"Captain!"*

Sabra rapid-fired six or eight plasma bolts up the corridor, and dove into the lifepod. "Close the hatch," Sabra ordered. Adder did as she was told. The last thing Brontë saw before the hatch sealed was the dance instructor scrambling over Tully's body, wailing, as a skinny dark-haired kid with a biomask over her face pitched a plasma stick in through the bay door.

Chapter 11

The *Susan Calvin*, Chernyi Hub, The Drift

The pit was crepuscular, silent but for the rush of air from the vents. Rida hung in the hatch, one fist gripping its cleat, the other around the gear bag. Across the pit, the dagan sat braced in its open locker, Brontë Ikeda asleep in a knot in its arms.

Tai said to do this. Though only if he wanted to. But Tai thought the Captain was right, that this was their best chance of learning what was true. "Why me?" Rida demanded, sounding whiny even to himself.

"Everyone likes you, Ridashi," Tai said. "Must be those big dark eyes." Rida scowled at him, and Tai grinned, that slow sweet grin which Rida, as always, found irresistible.

Pheromones, Rida thought now, watching the child sleeping in the dusky pit. *You fat addled egg.* He released the cleat and launched himself, sailing through the air to land neatly next to the dagan, who hissed to say that Rida should stay quiet. "She's finally asleep."

Rida anchored himself on the locker door. "She's been asleep since Midwatch first."

"After being in a fret for the previous nine hours. Without food, or water."

Rida pulled a bento box from the gear bag and waved it at the dagan. "Water, too," he added, hauling out a flask.

"Are the restraints necessary?" the dagan asked.

Rida had been younger than this child when he'd been indentured into Guo House. No one had chained him up, but on the other hand he'd had to survive the House dorms. *Forgive me if I don't bleed for this delicate blossom.*

"The child thinks the Captain is withholding food as a form of torture," the dagan said.

From the gear bag, Rida took out a second bento box and two more flasks. These all had stick patches on their undersides. He stuck them to the pit wall, made certain the last item in the gear bag—a medkit—was secure, and rolling up the gear bag, stuck it to the wall as well. Then he nudged Brontë, still wrapped snug in the dagan's arms. The child twisted, muttering in her sleep. He nudged again, and she woke. Shoving herself away from the dagan, she rubbed her eyes and then glared at Rida. "Why are you here?"

"I brought you breakfast, mzala." Rida offered the first bento box. "Here's tea also."

She caught the flask and broke it open, her eyes squinted with temper. "I'm not telling you anything. No matter what you do to me."

"I'm feeding you breakfast." Rida cracked his meal open. "Mine is yam fritters, grilled shrimp, and sauce. Fresh berries for dessert. What's yours?" She glowered, and he shrugged and started eating. "Just we could swap if you liked."

"I'm not stupid! I know you know what's in mine! You made it!"

"The Captain," he said, eating his berries. He always ate fast, and ate the best part of the meal first. Even now, after all these years out of Guo House, after all this time living on the *Susan Calvin* where he knew no one would steal his food, he ate like this.

"What?" Brontë demanded.

"Captain made the meal. Can't you tell? The fritters are terrible. Captain Wrachant's got her fine qualities, but she's no cook." He ate another bite, and drank some tea to get it down. Too many peppers, and way too much salt. Still scowling, Brontë turned away, eating rapidly and savagely. Rida pretended not to notice her hunger. Or her thirst—though when her flask was empty, he did pull down the second and hand it over. "The Captain doesn't want to know anything awful," he said, when she had most of the meal inside her.

"Shut up," she said. "I'm not talking to you."

"Only information that you'd want us to have. Only information that can help the Captain decide whether to help you—whether she ought to do your job." Rida paused. "If we're going to finish your job. That's what we have to decide." Brontë stuffed a fritter into her mouth, still glaring. "We can't decide that without information." Rida had hypnotic patches in the medkit—they wouldn't make her answer his questions, but they'd make her more willing to. He didn't want to use these. No part of him wanted to. Even as a last resort. "You said you were going to Hokkaido Station, that your aunt was there, that you wanted us to negotiate with her for these contract labor that got left behind when you ran. Now you tell us that it's not Hokkaido, it's Woodlands, and they aren't just any contract labor, but special contract labor. But that the rest is all still true." Brontë kept glowering. "You can see why the Captain is reluctant to believe you."

"No. I can't."

Rida shook his head. "If that's all it was," he told her, "why not give us that story up front? Nothing in that story is scary, or threatening. You wouldn't have needed to try this idiot plan to pirate our ship if that was the real story. You're not very good at telling lies," he added gently.

"It's not a lie," Brontë spat. "You just don't know the truth when you hear it!"

"We can return to Hujan Point. The Captain's mostly inclined to do that, at this point. With what fuel you've left us, there's a mining station we can reach from there. Yoder Mining. It's unaffiliated, but mostly Free Trade. We can leave you there, take our cargo back into the Drift. All in all, that's the safest choice for us."

"Good," Brontë said. "Do that."

Rida nodded. "We can't get you back to the Bucket."

"No one's asking you to."

Rida nodded again. The dagan looked from Rida to the Combine child, and huffed through its nose—a purely cosmetic act, since mechanicals didn't need to breathe. "This is a child," it reminded Rida. "You need to explain to her what that means."

"I'm not a child!"

"Not all space stations are equal," the dagan said. "The Bucket has flaws, clearly. But its stockholders are mostly honest, and mostly do their best to keep their administration honest. Many of the smaller stations—especially mining stations—are very badly run."

"I said I'm not a child," Brontë snapped. "I'm not an idiot, either."

"We don't usually put in at Yoder Mining," Rida said. "Not usually." His stomach hurt; he shut his bento box. "Murder's not a crime there. It's a civil offense, like littering. Unless you kill a jess," he added. "A contract worker. That, they take seriously. That's capital theft. They'll impound you for that, put you in the system. That, and a hundred other offenses, including not paying your air tariff on time."

Brontë frowned.

"We'll leave you there," Rida said, though in truth the thought of making dock at Yoder, even long enough to ditch these two and negotiate for refueling, terrified him sick. "Or you can tell us where you really want to go, and what you really want the Captain to do for you once we get there. And if you're lucky, the Captain may even now agree to do your job. Despite your recent behavior." Brontë whipped up her head to fix her glare on him, and Rida repeated firmly, "Despite your recent behavior."

"Recent illegal behavior," the dagan added drily.

"Pirates don't care about laws," Rida said, ostensibly to the dagan. "Laws exist to keep the rabble in line. To come onto our ship," he told Brontë, "to eat at our food, to sleep in our bunks, and then betray us, was worse than illegal. It was rude."

Brontë flushed, color showing dark on her neck and ears.

"The Captain may still decide to work with you," Rida said, "if you explain what you have in mind." He took his flask of tea down from the wall and had a drink. "It's up to you."

Chapter 12

L ifepods had limited fuel, most of which was dedicated to climate control. Designed to locate the nearest station or sizable inhabited object not its own ship and aim itself at that target on the best-possible course trajectory (the one that would keep most of its passengers alive), the pod would also activate its distress beacon, sending out a continuous Mayday. Sabra's first move after launching them from the *Fido* was to disable this beacon. Her second was to override the pod's search engine, taking manual control of its drive.

At this point, Brontë yanked loose her safety restraints—something you were never supposed to do in a pod while it was under way—and shoved herself forward against the thrust of the engines. She grabbed the back of Adder's seat, next to the pilot's chair. "Get back to your couch," Sabra ordered, not looking up from her display screens.

"I'm a qualified navigator," Brontë reminded her. "Third class, provisional. Let me help."

Sabra growled and pulled down the seat on her other side. "Strap in."

"Hey!" Theo objected from abaft. "Third class, *provisional?*"

Brontë brought up the navigation screen, expanding and expanding again once it was loaded, to see what their options might be, as far as ports. Their original intention had been to make for the trade station at Kaguya Hub—but that had been when they had been predicting the hostile takeover to occur after the *Fido* had gone through its first jump, at Pickering Point. A coup after the first jump had seemed the most rational move, since it would have left the usurpers out of direct reach of Ikeda Security, and yet within one jump point of Ikeda House. Post-jump, and within a few hours of the first jump out of Waikato— that was the obvious best place to strike. Running the coup this side of the jump made no sense, and Brontë couldn't think why anyone would have done it.

Also, and worse from their perspective, the lifepod had few options when it came to seeking a safe port on this side of the jump. Brontë chewed her lip. The nearest port was KRC Mining, a mining platform held by Kumo-Rinehart Combine. This platform, based in the local asteroid field, was so small it couldn't really be called a station. The best route she could find to the mining platform put it seven hours away.

Keeping that option in reserve, she plotted several routes to their best option, Hayek Station, messing hopelessly with fuel use and a few other variables. Then she turned her attention back to the mining platform. Kumo-Rinehart was a small and not very powerful Combine, which held no voting stock in either branch of the Ikeda-Verde Combine. Also, since no one from either Kumo or Rinehart House had married into Ikeda House in almost a century, it was likely that their Combine would have no cock in this fight. Somewhat dispirited, she presented the best route to the mining platform to Sabra. "The other option," she said, "is we try to take the pod through the jump point."

Sabra gave her a dark look. Lifepods weren't intended to make jumps—neither their fuel capacity nor their processing power was built for it. "Making the jump puts us within reach of Chiba Station," Brontë argued. Chiba was the main commercial station on the other side of Pickering Point. "Five hours and a bit."

Theo, who had unstrapped from his seat, now took the bench beside her. "Have you ever plotted a jump?" he demanded.

"The system has the program."

"That would be no," Theo said. "Also, lifepods aren't designed for jumps."

"If it wasn't meant to make jumps, it wouldn't have the program in its bank."

Theo snorted and opened the port under his hands. "What are our other options?"

"Aside from the jump?" Brontë said impatiently. "KRC Mining. As I said."

"What about Hayek Station?" Theo asked, plotting a course to Hayek as he spoke. Brontë knew for a fact Theo hadn't done more than the basic navigational math everyone took. He certainly hadn't sat for any qualifiers. She also knew why he wanted to try for Hayek Station. It was the same reason she did. Hayek would give them the most choices for further transport and for finding allies. But it was twenty-one hours away by the best route. Twenty-one hours with five passengers was not survivable. While she watched, Theo changed a variable, asking the port whether they could make it to Hayek if they had only three passengers. "Who do you plan to jettison?" Brontë demanded. "Me and Sabra, or the Security cadets?"

"I'm just looking at data," Theo said.

Sabra reached over and shut down his port. "Set the course for KRC Mining," she ordered Brontë. "Best possible speed, please."

Speed was important. First, other lifepods, carrying other Ikeda heirs and their Security, might well have made it off the *Fido*. Beyond that, whoever was behind the coup—Brontë's two current leading suspects were David Ikeda Ito and Iriaka Ikeda Weber—if the attack on the ship had succeeded, the usurper might well now have possession of the *Fido*. That meant four of the top ten heirs in the line for the Ikeda Primary Seat could now be dead. It also meant the usurper had almost certainly determined, by now, any heirs that had slipped through their net, including her and Theo.

David, Brontë thought, was the more probable suspect. She didn't think Iriaka had enough support in the House. In any case, David had been seventeenth in line, Iriaka ninth. No matter which of them was behind the takeover, both Theo and Brontë stood in their path.

With far more resources to hand than Brontë, the usurper would send out Security teams (*kill squads*, Brontë thought) to Hayek Station, to KRC Mining, across the jump to Chiba Station—to every possible port within reach of a lifepod. They would take no chances on any heir reaching Ikeda House before they did. Once an heir reached the House, that heir could claim the right to inherit the Seat, and the usurper would go from victor and inheritor of the Seat to mass murderer, condemned to death the moment they crossed into Ikeda-controlled space. On the other hand, if they succeeded in killing off all the heirs who preceded them in the line, and returned to claim the Seat, then *they* were the heir, and all of this would be an unfortunate incident in space, which they could write off in any manner they chose—a hull breach, maybe. Or a vicious attack by exceptionally bold Pirian pirates.

They'd find some excuse, Brontë knew, which no one would really believe, which people would whisper about at parties for years to come; but which everyone would accept. Most people would even approve, more or less. Because this was how the system was designed to work. *Survival of the fittest! Competition! Natural selection! How else do you expect to breed the best leaders for our civilization, and our Combine?*

The plasma blasts and the choked little gasp Tully had made as she died, back on the *Fido*, echoed in Brontë's memory. She rubbed the bad ache in her forehead, and linked the route she had plotted to Sabra. Theo leaned to read the screen as well. Brontë bit down on her scowl. "Right," Sabra said. "Everyone's secure? We're at launch in three...two...one...*go.*"

The pod's engines, which had been moving them steadily away from the *Fido*, shifted position and kicked in hard. Brontë watched the screen, making certain they followed the trajectory she had programmed, though why wouldn't they, one, and two, what she would do about it at this point, she had no idea. The burn went perfectly, though, and when it cut off they were in the groove, their trajectory propelling them neatly toward KRC Mining: ETA seven hours, seventeen minutes, eleven seconds. Brontë heard Sabra let out her breath, a tiny huff of relief. This reaction didn't bother her, really. She felt the same way.

Having checked a few more readings on her display, Sabra sat back. "We will reach port in just over seven hours," she said, speaking to them all. "I suggest trying to relax as much as possible. There should be handhelds in your seat pockets, with limited banks—a few games and animates, some art and music programs. Find something to occupy yourself. I can also dispense anti-anxiety medication, if necessary. Also," Sabra said, meeting Theo's eyes, "we should all return to our seats and replace our safety gear."

Brontë had already been moving back to her seat. She froze in the act of locking shut her safety restraints, glancing from Sabra to Theo, and then past Theo to Adder, just behind him, slouched in her seat and to all appearances entirely relaxed. Theo swung one leg sidelong over the bench, keeping himself in place in the low gee with a grip on the desk, and then crossed both legs under it, so that he faced Sabra squarely. His expression was sardonic, faintly amused. "Tell me what we have planned," he ordered.

"This is a hostile takeover," Sabra said. "We must assume you are a target."

"Correct."

"Our charge," Sabra said, "however, is to protect the life of Elena Ikeda. We'll do that."

Theo studied her, his eyes narrowed. "Above my life."

"We are Security of Ikeda House," Sabra said. "Your life is also in our charge."

Theo started to speak, and then pressed his lips together. His eyes slid toward Brontë. "When we arrive at this mining platform," he said, slowly, "what is our plan at that point?"

"We'll secure alliances," Sabra said. "As heir presumptive, you will be useful there."

Theo made a noise in his chest. "At this point, I hold the Primary Seat. Unless these are extremely incompetent usurpers."

He meant that anyone running a coup would have taken out Dhia, the Primary Seat Holder and Theo's older half-brother, before they made any other move. That didn't mean Theo now held the Seat, though. He had to get back to Waikato and be confirmed first. Brontë decided not to mention this. Glancing at Sabra, she could see her Security Captain deciding not to bring it up either.

"You didn't bring me along just for this, did you?" Theo asked. "As a bargaining tool?"

Sabra's expression changed: surprise, and just an edge of respect. Then she smiled. "No, Mr. Ikeda. I did not."

Theo scowled, and looked down at the port. "Not that you would admit it if you had," he muttered.

"Not that I would," Sabra agreed cheerfully. "The offer for anti-anxiety patches stands, should anyone need them. Now. Please. Strap in."

Chapter 13

KRC Mining at Hayek Point, Republic Space
(Seven Months Earlier)

KRC Security met them at the dock with medical tuk-tuks that transported them directly to the station infirmary where medics waited, at high alert. "No injuries," the medic working on Brontë said, looking at his doctor and not at her. "You came into dock via a lifepod?"

"Right," Brontë said. "But our ship—it wasn't that sort of emergency."

"I see. Well, your stress level is high. Would you like something for that?"

"No, thank you." Everyone wanted to slap anxiety patches on her. "May I get up?" They had taken her clothing, so she lay naked on an elevated padded bench. Not only was it uncomfortable, she also felt exposed: the infirmary was one big open room. Not much medical equipment, and most of what she saw was rebuilt cobbled-together hobgoblins, machines patched together out of tape and spare gear. Beds and support couches stretched down the room, filled with patients, young men and women, as well as some children. They all seemed badly injured. Almost all were unconscious. Some recent accident, Brontë supposed.

The medic looked up. His face was round and puffy, and his head shaved. When Brontë pointed at her clothing, he startled, and handed it to her. Over on the next bench, Adder was submitting patiently to an examination. Beyond her, Theo scowled at the very young medic running his doctor. Brontë sealed her suit and went across the infirmary to where Sabra and Wolf sat on adjacent benches. "How are my Security?" Brontë asked the medic there, who had finished with Sabra and was now working on Wolf.

"Ah…" This medic, skinny and barely taller than Brontë, glanced around as if for help.

"Are they injured?" Brontë said.

"No. I mean, they, I mean, no, miss."

"Excellent. Captain Anador, collect your team, please."

"Yes, Miss Ikeda." Sabra sealed her uniform tunic and went off towards Adder.

Theo came up behind Brontë, fussing with his sleeves. "Who's in command here?" he asked the skinny medic.

"What? Of the infirmary, do you mean? Um, Vida…but—"

"What seems to be the problem?" A Combine Security officer appeared—Captain Hana Nyman, according to her name tag. Nyman wore a blue uniform, with red and orange piping on her collar to mark her as being bound to Kumo-Rinehart Combine.

"Captain Nyman," Theo said. "Excellent. I'll speak to your Executive Manager now."

"Fortunately," Nyman said dryly, "she'd like a word with you as well. This way."

"Our Security will attend us." Theo gestured to get Sabra's attention; but the Security officer shook her head.

"Just you two," she said, reaching for Brontë's arm.

Brontë moved closer to Theo, straightening her spine. She tipped back her head, trying to make her expression into a copy of her mother's at her most affronted. Immediately, Sabra and Wolf were flanking her. "The Ikedas," Sabra said, "go nowhere without their Security."

The two Security officers stared one another down—Brontë felt the air crackling between them—and then Nyman stepped back, her chin jerking sideways. "As you say," she growled.

Sabra spoke to Wolf without taking her gaze from Nyman. "Cadet."

"Captain." Wolf strode without hurrying over to Adder; they returned together. Jerking her chin once more, Nyman led them all out through the infirmary hatch.

With Wolf and Adder flanking her, Brontë could relax a bit, and give some attention to the station itself. When they had come off the lifepod, they had been bundled into the tuk-tuks so swiftly that she hadn't had a chance to see more than a blur. Now, once they were through the infirmary hatch, she found the dock level concourse basic and very grimy, with a low overhead. It was painted with green and orange sealant paint. Here and there, yellow stripes of warning tape were peeling away from the deck. No shops; not even a tea cart. Only two of its ten docking slips were currently occupied. Maybe KRC Mining didn't get commercial trade, so far out from the jump point as it was.

Brontë realized suddenly that, even though they were walking at a normal pace, she was finding it hard to keep up. Her heart pounded; she was gulping for air. She stopped, dizzy. Captain Nyman went on for several steps before she wheeled, scowling. "Are you ill?"

Brontë shook her head, fighting to get her breath. She was never ill, not with her rebuilt immune system. She had never felt like this in her life. Had the medic poisoned her? Had someone else, maybe back on the ship? Was this part of the coup?

Sabra stepped back and took hold of her arm, holding her up; she gave Nyman a narrow look. "You keep your air pressure low. Is that just in the common areas of the station?"

Nyman's mouth twisted. "Most people," she said, "aren't bothered." She looked along the corridor, pointed at a loitering tuk-tuk driver, and snapped her fingers. The kid scrambled into the driver's seat and pedaled toward them. *Low pressure?* Brontë was thinking. *Is this from low air pressure?* "Climb in," Nyman said.

"Four seats," Sabra noted. The driver was a spindly boy, maybe ten years old; like Brontë's medic, his face and hands were puffy, and his head shaved. His lips were blue, as was the skin under his eyes.

"Oh, get in," Nyman said. "Your Security team can follow on foot."

In the end, Nyan gave in and summoned another vehicle, this one hauled by a slightly older child. The tuk-tuk boys towed them all spinward to a block of lifts. As they climbed out, Nyman tossed the older child what looked like a toy, a ring of brassy metal—something Brontë might have found in a Spring Cake, as a child.

In the lift, Nyman ran a slim tag across a scanner plate and said, "Level A."

The lift surged into movement. The blood surged out of Brontë's head; her vision went dark. Sabra kept her on her feet. Brontë heard Sabra demand, her voice like an echo down a distant tunnel, "What *is* your air pressure here?"

"There must be something wrong with her," Nyman said coolly. "No one is troubled by the pressure, except contract labor."

Brontë closed her fist around Sabra's collar. Fighting for breath to speak, she gasped out, "Poison? Is this poison? Did someone—"

"It's the pressure," Sabra said. "Breathe deeply."

The lift slowed and stopped; its hatch opened. Theo got out first, looking both ways; Sabra half-carried Brontë to a bench and sat with her. "Breathe," she said again. "The pressure's better here," she added, with dark emphasis toward Nyman.

The corridor was brighter than the dock concourse, and had brilliant carpets on its floor; but the big difference was Brontë had no trouble getting her breath. In only a moment, her pulse slowed and the cold sweat dried from her skin. Her vision cleared.

"Better?" Sabra asked. Brontë nodded. Sabra helped her to her feet. Nyman led them down the corridor, past a variety of shut hatches, all round and faced with wooden trim. Almost all had a faux window at their top, with captures showing wilderness scenes—as if they opened on some planet-side lake or mountain pasture, rather than a station compartment.

The hatch Nyman took them through was wooden-faced like the others, but painted red, and with no fake window. It opened on a room which was immense for a station stateroom—at least fifty meters square. Nor was this the main room, apparently: a steward of some sort appeared from a connecting corridor, spoke to Nyman in a language Brontë didn't recognize, and led them through that corridor into an even larger room.

This one, decorated with wall-hangings and flowering plants and trees in wooden tubs, had low tables and couches. It also had a young woman in close-fitting white linen trousers and a knee-length blue qipao, who stood feeding slices of yellow pepper to a rainbow macaw hanging upside down from a pear tree. She turned as they entered, pushing her dark braid over her shoulder. "Monsieur, Madame Ikeda," she said, speaking to Theo and Brontë as though only they were present. "Please. Sit. You are quite well?"

Brontë sat down before she fell down—she felt better than she had on the concourse, but her muscles were still spongy. Theo ignored the sofa. "Madame Kumo?" he demanded.

"Oh! Oh!" Laughing, the young woman covered her mouth with her long fingers. Behind her, the macaw flapped its wings violently, echoing her laugh precisely. "I'm so sorry! I always forget that part! No! I am Fiona Rinehart! But please. You must call me Fiona."

The steward brought in tea and tiny teacakes. Fiona folded gracefully down to sit on the carpet, and held one of the cakes up to the macaw, who came swooping down to take it from her. "More," it demanded.

"Later, Toto," Fiona said. "Go eat your vegetables. Go on. Now," she said, turning back. "My Security has been through your lifepod, and they've spoken to you and your Security, and they tell me they haven't been able to form a clear understanding of just what happened on your ship. Perhaps you can help?"

"Hostile takeover," Theo said briefly. "I am the presumptive heir to the Primary Seat on the Ikeda House Board, as I am sure you're aware." Her expression bright with interest, Fiona waited. "We need a ship, and a crew. As fast a ship as you have available. Once I reach Ikeda House, and take the Primary Seat, I will be in your debt. Meanwhile, I will leave my heir," Theo nodded at Brontë, "in your hands."

Fiona's eyebrows twitched upwards. Behind them, Sabra shifted her weight. "That's…an interesting proposition," Fiona said. "However, I must ask—how certain are you that those running this takeover will fail in their attempt?"

"Not certain at all," Theo said evenly.

Fiona laughed. "That's such an attractive bargain. Very hard to resist."

Theo shrugged. "If the ship you supply is sufficient, the question should not arise."

"Hmm." Fiona sipped her bowl of tea. "Hana. Take our guests to the Liberty Suite, please. Be sure they have everything they need."

$$\text{ʔ ✝ Ƕ ʂ}$$

The Liberty Suite, on the same level as Fiona Rinehart's quarters, had a wide central cabin off the entry hatch, with staterooms to each side. Directly to the rear of the central cabin was a garden. "If you would like servants assigned," Captain Nyman said to Theo. "A cook, perhaps?"

"We'll manage," Sabra said.

Nyman gave Sabra a frosty look. Still speaking to Theo, she said, "My call-sign is my surname. You need only ask." She gave a small bow, and left the suite.

Brontë had gone to stand in the hatchway to the garden. Like every other hatchway on this level, this one was round. Out in the garden, water tumbled from a fountain, bright green bamboo palms grew thick, and giant purple wood poppies bloomed riotously. She glanced over her shoulder at Theo who was prowling through the suite, his elegant brows drawn low. Pulling her handheld from her jacket pocket, Brontë cupped it in both hands. The round blue light in the upper left corner shone clear, meaning that no one had infiltrated her system, or was trying to infiltrate it—at least so far as her wardens had detected.

As a data rat herself, Brontë knew how much credence to give to wardens. She opened the sentry file anyway, and launched a scan. As she'd expect, not just one but several feeds were operational in the suite. Sabra came to look over her shoulder. Brontë showed her the results of the scan. Sabra twitched one corner of her mouth down, letting out a slight huff. Then, pulling out her own handheld, she set out to locate the feeds—not to disable them. Just to know where they all were, so that they could work around them.

"What have you found?" Theo demanded.

Brontë jumped, because he was much closer to her than she had thought he was. She minimized the file on her screen, reflexively, and slid her handheld into her pocket. "What was that with the Rinehart? I am not staying here as your hostage, Theo."

He blinked, surprised. "It's the safest place for you."

Brontë scoffed. "Miss Fiona will sell me the minute your ship leaves dock."

Theo studied her. Brontë knew he'd never really thought about her until, well, ever, probably. She was a younger cousin, far enough down the line as to be essentially irrelevant. "You do realize," he said, "that I wasn't attempting to swindle Rinehart? That you may well now be the presumptive heir to the Primary Seat?"

Brontë's heart thumped, mainly at hearing this said out loud. It wasn't a revelation. Somewhere within her, she had already thought about the line of succession, and her new place in it. "That's an excellent reason not to leave me here to be sold."

"It's an excellent reason not to take you with me. The Primary Seat Holder and his heir don't travel on the same ship."

"You don't hold the Seat yet," Brontë argued, but he waved this off. "Besides, others might have survived. I might not be next in the line."

"There are ports in the study," Theo said. "I'll see what's on the feeds."

Brontë started to object, since any port in these quarters would certainly be jacked, but then kept silent. Theo knew enough to be aware of that. Both she and Sabra watched him go through the hatch into one of the staterooms. "I still feel queasy," Brontë told Sabra. "How can you be sure whoever is running the coup didn't get to me?"

"The medic ran a full scan, yes?" Sabra lifted her brows. Brontë bit her lip and nodded. "The doctor would have picked up on any toxin, including any toxin deliberately introduced to your system. Your symptoms are typical of low-pressure sickness. And they went away when we reached this level, where the pressure is higher."

Brontë couldn't argue with any of that, so she argued with something else: "None of the rest of you were affected. If the pressure was too low, why didn't it make all of us sick?"

Sabra looked away. "Not everyone reacts the same way to every stimulus," she said. "I need to check these rooms." She walked away without giving Brontë a chance to object, or ask further questions.

Somewhat annoyed, Brontë went into the garden. The garden benches, made of rock and iron, were entirely unpadded, but this level had such low gravity that even without a cushion these were comfortable. She chose one which would put her at a bad angle to the garden feeds and, pulling out her handheld, slipped into the system. Though designed and built in the Republic, and thus not unlike those used on Waikato, still it was not her home system. She moved with care, and a great deal of focus. It was some time before she noticed Adder watching past her shoulder. "Station Security won't even bother arresting you," Adder said. "Just chuck you in the nearest recycle."

"Here."

"What?" Adder asked. Brontë tapped the screen, showing she was into Fiona Rinehart's private bank. Adder swore under her breath and climbed over the bench to sit next to her. "They'll chuck you in *alive*."

Brontë flicked rapidly through Fiona's filing system, such as it was. The Station XO had folders and files grouped haphazardly, as well as duplicate and triplicate files and folders, and untagged files floating loose—some files, Brontë couldn't see any way of deciding what they contained without outright opening them. All had date-stamps at least, which made her task easier. Almost certainly nothing any older than thirty hours could be what she was looking for. Unless Kumo-Rinehart Combine had been part of the usurper's plot from the start.

Unlikely, she decided. The usurper would have to know that an Ikeda heir, or heirs, would escape the ship, *and* that they'd take refuge here, on this mining platform. That was…not impossible, Brontë admitted, especially if the usurper had planned to initiate the coup on this side of the jump from the beginning. While that had seemed unlikely to her back on the *Fido*, as well as in the lifepod, she admitted now that maybe the usurper knew things she did not.

Capturing the data into her X-box, Brontë isolated the files, then started sorting by date. She started with those less than 90 hours old, in order to have a manageable set, and ran a keyword search. A hit came up immediately: a priority post, eleven hours old, text-only, from Captain Esme Matsumoto, Chief of Security on the *We Are Faithful Unto Death*, to the XO of KRC Mining Platform. The post contained a request to detain any fugitives from the ships *We Are Faithful Unto Death*, *Tonbo*, *Azov*, or *Mirfak*, these fugitives being wanted for questioning in connection with the felony murder of forty-eight Republic Citizens and Combine Seat heirs (list of names appended).

Brontë read through the list of dead, her stomach filling with icy dismay. Everyone. They had gotten everyone in the House, including her two main suspects, Iriaka Ikeda Weber and David Ikeda Ito—all the heirs to the line out to the thirty-sixth heir, except for her and

Theo. Reading through the list a second time, she realized suddenly that Anja Ikeda Nowak was not on the list. Neither was Torres. She remembered, clear as a flashback, Anja stalking from her mother's office, her eyes narrowed with temper, and her heart thumped hard.

Anja had been fifteenth in the line, Torres thirty-first. Now Anja was third in line to inherit the Primary Seat, and Torres fourth. Adder, still reading over her shoulder, said, "Maybe they're working together. Maybe they have a deal between them to share the Primary Seat?"

Brontë shook her head. "They don't have anywhere near the support they would need in the House." She checked the rest of the hits among the files, looking for further information, widened the search to a 120 hours, and then to a 150, scanning the new hits that came up while she tried to think this through. She wondered if that was what the meeting between her mother and Anja had been about—Anja trying to gain her mother's support for a coup. *Impossible.* Never mind how that would mean killing off Brontë; Isra had never kept her contempt for Anja secret.

And even if her mother would consider Anja for the Primary Seat (impossible!), Isra would never support Anja on the Primary Seat with Torres at her back. Brontë knew what her mother would say. She would say that if Torres had the ambition to run a takeover, she was not going to be content to play second to Anja's Primary. Isra would say that they'd be doing this all over again in another six months, when Torres cut Anja's throat some night in her sleep.

She pictured herself making the argument to her mother that it was different with Torres and Anja, that they were partners, that everyone knew how much they loved one another. She heard her mother shoot air through her teeth, in the way she did whenever someone said something especially stupid. *Love is for the ballroom or the bedroom,* her mother had said, more than once, *not the boardroom.*

Adder shifted her weight, nudging her elbow into Brontë's ribs. Theo had entered the garden. Brontë minimized the file she was reading, and opened the one from Captain Matsumoto. When Theo drew near, she tipped the screen toward him. Frowning, he bent his head toward it, and then sat down and took the handheld. Brontë watched him read. Tall and lean like most Ikedas, Theo had the light Ikeda skin, their dark hair and eyes, their narrow nose and high blunt cheekbones. Growing up among the Ikedas, with her heavy bones, round face, and bright blue eyes, Brontë had always stood out, even before all the upgrades. Moodily, she watched him read through the file, thinking of how resistant Ikeda House was to any sort of genetic variation and wondering what would happen if she did end up in the Primary Seat—how the House would take that turn of events.

"Anja," Theo muttered. Brontë made a small sound, not quite a cough. "You were seventh in line," he said, quietly. "Yes?"

"Right."

Theo thought this over. Then he shut the file and gave the handheld back. He glanced up at Sabra, who had followed him into the garden and now stood a few steps away. "You'll accompany me to Waikato, Captain," he said. "You and one of the cadets."

"No, sir," Sabra said. "My charge is to protect Elena Ikeda. I stay with her."

Theo's jaw muscles bunched, but when he spoke his voice was calm. "You are bound to the House. Your contract is to me, and you will follow my orders."

"No, sir. My contract is held by Isra Ikeda Lopaka, who charged me with the protection of her child." She and Theo stared at each other, and Sabra added, "If you and Elena stay together, I'll attempt to protect you as well as her."

After a moment, Theo laughed abruptly. "Is that *blackmail*, Captain?"

"It is a counteroffer, Mr. Ikeda."

"Fine." He got to his feet. "You'll come with me," he told Brontë. "Assuming we go anywhere. Assuming this Rinehart viper doesn't sell us all on the open market."

"Yes, well," Brontë said. "Speaking of that. I have a suggestion."

Chapter 14

The *Susan Calvin*, Chernyi Hub, The Drift

The sauna on the *Susan Calvin* worked more or less like the laundry did, except that it had no microwave cycle. A half-size cabin at the aft-end of lower deck, the sauna had wooden benches that could be pulled out if the ship had weight enough to merit it. At microgravity, they left the benches stowed and drifted through the hot steam the sauna shot out from its hundreds of miniscule ports. The walls radiated warmth, heating the air as well as the free-floating water (which at microgravity tended to collect in floaty globs, rather remaining in a nice steam form).

Meanwhile, Velocity, Tai, and Rida scrubbed themselves and one another with rough bamboo scrub cloths and Pirian bath oil. The heated air made sweat flow. In micro, sweat didn't run; it just clung thickly to the skin. As the bath oil was made of olive oil, honey, and beeswax, among other elements, the entire experience could be interesting, richly scented, and gooey—not to mention, if you were in the right mood, erotic.

Velocity wasn't, at the moment. Once they scrubbed down, she switched the sauna to recycle—it started pulling out the soapy water, preliminary to the second blast of steam. She and Tai finished listening to Rida's recounting of what Brontë had told him. It was a complicated, convoluted story, filled with Combine intrigue and betrayal, but what it came down to was one member of the Ikeda family, Anja Ikeda Nowak, formerly fifteenth in line for the Ikeda seat, might have joined forces with another, Torres Ikeda Alonzo, to run the hostile takeover. Brontë said that Anja might be planning to make Torres her heir, if their coup succeeded.

This coup obviously required the removal of the heirs in the line before Anja, as well as those heirs between Anja and Torres. To be properly executed, the removal of these heirs should have been accomplished very soon after or even before Anja Ikeda went forward with the removal of Dhia Ikeda Hayek, the Primary Seat holder whose assassination had triggered the hostile takeover. Simultaneous assassinations, the Combine child had explained, would have been ideal. Otherwise, the line of inheritance could get muddied.

"They got rushed, Brontë thinks," Rida explained. "Brontë says something must have gone wrong. Maybe one of their allies let their plans leak. She says Ikeda House Security—Sabra and others—they knew a coup might be coming."

Velocity scrubbed a bit of oil through her hair, remembering the intelligence officer at her father's habitat, who issued an alert level every morning. *Someone is always trying to kill us,* her father had told her and Alice. *That's part of holding power.* Her father told them to take reasonable precautions, but not to let fear run their lives. As if anything about being in line for a Primary Seat at one of the top twenty Combines in the Republic was reasonable.

Brontë thought that those running the takeover moved earlier than they meant to. This let Brontë and one of her cousins escape. "They made it to a mining platform," Rida said. "That's where Brontë left her cousin. This is Hiro Sayid Liao Ikeda Hayek, the heir to the Primary Seat. That's the same cousin she told us she sold on Bastiat, the one she calls Theo. Theo's his milk name, apparently. Now she says she didn't really sell him. She hid him. He's the heir, he's valuable. She stashed him at this mining platform, and then she and her Security booked passage for the Drift, using his credit line as funding."

"Or that's her current story," Velocity said.

Rida dumped the towel in the laundry chute. "She and her Security kited out to the Drift. Found a message waiting when they arrived. Fetch this Hiro home, or Torres will gut every Ikan cadet Brontë left behind her."

Velocity finished scrubbing down. "Torres. Not Anja?"

"I asked that. Brontë says the message came from Torres, but she thinks Anja is still in charge. She doesn't think Torres would kill Anja." Rida emitted a huff of disdain. "They *love* each other."

Since Velocity shared his opinion concerning the possibility that any Combine citizen would let love stand in the way of their chance at a Primary Board Seat, she didn't argue. "Home," she said instead. "Where's home?"

"Waikato."

Velocity stared at him. Rida spread his hands. "First of all," Velocity said, "no. Second of all, are you kidding me? Third, no. Fourth, absolutely not. Fifth—"

"That's not even the worst part," Tai interrupted.

"What?" Velocity demanded. "What could be worse than this Combine puppy expecting us to take our ship into the heart of the Republic?"

"Tell her the worst part, Rida."

Rida punched up the next cycle on the sauna, mostly so he wouldn't have to meet her eyes, she suspected. "Hiro Ikeda Hayek is already dead."

Warm clear water began fizzing in high-pressure streams into the sauna. Absently, instinctively, Velocity put her palm over the jets near her face, blocking them so she could keep watching Rida. He grimaced, lowering his eyes. "Someone got to him. Anja or Torres—who knows which? Not that it matters. And not that Brontë's reliable on the point. But Hiro is dead, she says. She says she got the post while she was still out on the Bucket. She says that this means *she's* heir presumptive. If she can get back to the House, she'll hold the Primary Seat."

"If she reaches the House," Tai said. "Which explains the hostages. Bait."

Velocity nodded, still absently. Lure Brontë in and remove her. With her gone—along with every other possible heir right down to the third and fourth cousins, and no one in Ikeda House eager for succession battles at that level—Anja might well gain support from the remaining Ikedas in the House. "Where?" she asked.

"What?"

"Where is Anja holding the bait?"

Rida stared at her, and then looked at Tai. After a second, Tai reached over and shut down the sauna. "Captain," he said. "Are you...you're not still thinking of taking this job?"

Velocity focused on him, and grinned abruptly. "Still?" she said.

"When it was a job out here near the Drift, a quick drop and scoop, with a nice payoff, that was one thing. But this," Tai shook his head.

"When it was a *risky* job out here at the edge of the Drift," Velocity said, "for what looked like a minimal payoff, it wasn't worth maybe getting shot over."

"And now it is?" Tai said, his voice scaling high.

"Now this kid is heir presumptive to the Ikeda Board Seat. Do you know the kind of wealth she commands, if we help her clear Anja and Torres?"

Tai and Rida stared at her. Rida wet his lips. "That's not the job we're being hired to do."

Velocity showed her teeth. "Maybe not yet it isn't."

Chapter 15

KRC Mining at Hayek Point, Republic Space
(Seven Months Earlier)

Stepping to one side of the lift hatch, Adder stood breathing deeply, steadying herself. Captain Anador took position against the bulkhead on the other side. Adder's heart thumped adrenaline through her blood. She felt as short of breath as if she, and not Brontë, suffered from low-pressure syndrome. More now than at any moment since leaving Ikeda House, she missed the solid warmth of her brothers and sisters around her. She breathed. She breathed. She looked around her, scanning the concourse for threats.

Like many stations, KRC Mining didn't keep to the planet-side schedule of day and night, with some arbitrary number of those hours being called day and some others being called night. Rather, they kept three shifts per cycle, each nine hours long. Combine Labor Agents considered which shift a worker was assigned unimportant. This was held to be especially true for station workers, because external circadian signals could be manipulated on stations, and workers (in theory) adjusted to whatever schedule was needed. On most Combine-held stations, contract labor worked two shifts, back-to-back. For the most part, free labor did too, since wages were sufficiently depressed that making box rent and air fees was always chancy.

Right now, in the middle of Bantam Shift, with almost everyone at work, traffic on the concourse was scarce. Over by the service lifts, the handful of kids working tuk-tuks hunkered near them. Another kid ran a deck scrubber far down the way, its racket muted by distance. Up in the overhead, contract laborers were braced among the girders, changing out lights, and over by the bank of vending machines, which was what this station seemed to have instead of teashops, an old man scrubbed down tables in a desultory fashion. No Station Security anywhere, or at least none that Adder saw. She drew a long breath, wanting her absent siblings badly.

"Wolf," Captain Anador said, not looking away from the concourse. From inside the lift, Adder heard Wolf's low, polite murmur. The two Ikeda heirs emerged, with Wolf behind them. Brontë was looking around her, but Theo's attention was straight ahead, fixed on the immense hatch that led to the docking slips. "Stay behind us," the Captain instructed, and set out across the concourse. Adder fell in with her, with the heirs beside and just behind them, and Wolf at the rear. So much area to cover, and only the three of them. Once again she missed her siblings with a fierce ache.

From her earliest memory—memories so early they were really just bright scraps of image and sound—they had been there: Maggie, Nora, Ian, Ruçar, and Wolf. Her other selves. Her brothers and sisters who always knew what she was thinking, who felt what she felt, who trusted her as she trusted them, absolutely and without reservation. When they'd been little, in the dorms, where bigger children beat up the smaller ones, stealing the best gear, the better bedding, stealing food at meals, everyone knew not to try that on Ikan16. They stood together. Even when, once or twice, bigger hatchlings ganged up on them, well, they learned. You didn't cross the Ikans. Ikans didn't cry, or sulk, or tattle. Ikans just waited, and made you pay.

Later, older, they'd had their own room, with a facility they didn't have to share. Sometimes, for a few hours, or even a few days, they'd spent time apart for training modules. But other than that…Adder shook her head, a quick hard shake, and kept walking.

The night before they left Ikeda House, they'd sat in a circle on the floor of the sitting room of their quarters—their much bigger quarters, now that Brontë held their bonds. None of them had been happy. "It's not safe," Maggie said. "We're Ikan16. We trained together. Everything we learned, it's how to fight and work together. Now we're being broken apart?"

"Only for a while," Ian said.

"How do you know that?" Maggie said. "Anything could happen."

"It probably won't," Adder said. Everyone had looked at her, quiet, their mouths and eyes troubled. They'd all gotten the same intelligence briefing from Captain Anador, about the possible hostile takeover and the consequent increased level of threat. "It's a family vacation. They do this every year. Two months, and we'll be back."

"Two months," Maggie echoed.

"Most things never happen," Adder said, which was something Coach Jasper said—*Most things never happen, so don't put your energy into fretting, put it into training.* Coach had also warned them that they might, from time to time, find themselves assigned apart from one another. Adder reminded them of this too. "It's only a little while," Adder repeated. "In two months, we'll be back here, and finding something new to fret about."

That night in their bunk—they shared a bunk, she and Maggie, as they had done since they were six minutes old—Maggie hugged her close and whispered fiercely, "Two months. You better not be late."

Now, on the mining platform concourse, she and Wolf glanced across the Ikeda heirs, meeting one another's eyes as they reached the hatch leading into the docking bay. Brontë edged up to point past the Captain at a docking slip at the far end of the bay. "That one," she whispered. "Sabra, listen. Let me go first. You wait here with—"

"No. We stay together." Captain Anador, after a swift reconnaissance of the docking bay, headed toward the slip. As Brontë had learned, that slip was registered to a short-haul cargo ship, the *Hegre*. While the *Hegre* was independently owned, Verde House held liens against its title. According to Brontë's admittedly swift analysis, the Captain of the *Hegre* was most likely, of all those in dock, to be pliable to their specific combination of bribes and threats.

"Listen," Brontë said, catching up to Captain Anador. "When we get there, Sabra, let me talk."

Theo snorted. "Yes, because threats coming from a little girl will work so well."

Brontë straightened her spine and opened her mouth to reply, except just then an alarm began sounding, a deafening mechanical blare, two seconds long, and a pause, and then another two seconds, over and over. Adder wheeled, her hand going to where her Lopaka SC should have been—their weapons had been confiscated as they'd come off the lifepod.

The tuk-tuk kids had scrambled into the seats of their vehicles, and were peddling top speed down the concourse, vanishing like mice into various alleys and dark corners. The alleys and corners vanished as well, as blast doors thudded down across every hatchway, shutting off access points. The noise echoed through the concourse. Then the concourse blast doors themselves came booming down, immense sectional slabs isolating every 300 or 400 meter chunk of the concourse.

Adder stood, breathing deeply, filled with calm. She recognized this feeling—it was how she always felt in real danger. All her senses were clear, her muscles easy and loose. Time felt endless. She took inventory of their section of the concourse, which was empty of any immediate threat, with access to the ships on the docks still available, and turned to Captain Anador. Brontë had her handheld out and open. "Incoming ships," she said. "Two. No, wait, a third. Three incoming ships confirmed. Refusing station's request to stand off. Ah!" Brontë yelped, shock and surprise; the station had shuddered under their feet.

"They fired, the station fired on the ships," Brontë said, just as the station shook really hard, nearly knocking them down. A ship firing back, Adder guessed. Captain Anador pointed two fingers at

Wolf and Adder, and then the same fingers at Theo. The alarms were blaring so loudly now—several of them, not just the first one—that speaking was impossible. But Adder understood what the Captain meant. They were on Theo; the Captain had Brontë.

They all ran spinward, toward the far end of the docking slips, toward the *Hegre*. Before they had made more than a few steps, an immense clang shook the station. With a great *whump!* of an explosion, a dock hatch to Adder's left blew out.

Theo had fallen to his knees. Cold all through, clear and calm, Adder hauled him back into the shadow of one of the immense curved aluminum beams that ran like ribs up the bulkhead of the docking slip. Wolf, scooting in the rear, flattened out with them into this shadow. Wishing fiercely for her Lopaka, Adder watched a squad of Combine Security deploying through the blown hatch. They fanned out into a defensive perimeter, all around the slip apron. A second squad deployed on their heels, and formed an interior perimeter. "Those are Ikeda House Security," Theo hissed.

"Hush," Adder hissed back. She scanned up and down the slip, looking for Captain Anador. She glanced at Wolf, who pointed with his chin. The Captain and Brontë had taken cover inside the hold of a cargobot. The bot was only half-filled, but even so there wasn't much cover. "Do you have a weapon?" Adder whispered in Theo's ear. He shook his head, watching the Ikeda House Security intently.

A third squad emerged. At its center of this squad—even small with the distance, even half-hidden by the blast helmet—was a face Adder recognized. Isra Ikeda Lopaka. Theo made a sound, half cough, half stifled cry of pain. Adder found she was trying to flatten herself into the bulkhead. The third squad formed up around Dr. Ikeda. Even from this distance, Adder could see the Combine citizen was giving out orders.

Wolf hissed, and Adder looked back. Captain Anador was pointing at her and Wolf. Adder nodded, watching as the Captain pointed down the hold, toward the *Hegre*. Adder felt her heart thump hard. The Captain was staring straight at her. Adder drew a breath, and nodded again.

"Adder," Wolf muttered. It wasn't a real objection. He knew as well as she did what Dr. Ikeda being here meant—being here like this, in charge of three squads of Ikeda Security that had fired on this station. He knew what it meant for them if they stood against her as well. But the Captain had given an order. Baring his teeth slightly, he got a grip on Theo's arm. "Sir," he said. "Fast, now, and quiet, or we'll have no chance at all."

Adder knew they had almost no chance at all anyway, but she followed Wolf and Theo down the dockyard, keeping low, moving quickly, and staying in the deepest part of the shadows. Theo moved ahead, swiftly, reaching the *Hegre* some distance ahead of Wolf. Adder kept watch on their rear.

When the alarms finally cut off, Adder flinched at the silence, and crouched lower behind the shipping crate she was using for cover. Down the dock, IVC Security were working their steady way along the slips, toward the *Hegre*. Behind her, she could hear Theo arguing in whispers with a *Hegre* officer, trying to talk them onto the ship. Adder's most pressing wish in that moment, and Wolf's too, she knew, was that they would hurry. She didn't want them to have to tangle with IVC Security. Even if they won, which they wouldn't, they'd be killing her own.

"No," the *Hegre* office said, her voice rising. "What bribe you think you can pay out, that butters no tea. We're not taking sides in any Combine coup. Get off our gate."

Theo's voice rose too. "If you deny us this retreat, Lieutenant, you take sides. And we will not forget. *I* will not forget."

The *Hegre* Lieutenant spoke even louder. "Get off my gate, you Combine crumb."

The nearest IVC Security officer was only thirty or so meters away, poking through the shipping crates on the next slip over. He turned at the raised voice, his head lifting. Adder grimaced and scooted backwards. Rolling to her feet she scrambled over to where Theo faced off the *Hegre* Lieutenant with her fist on the Sima short rifle in her belt. "Uncle's here," Adder said.

A muscle by Theo's eye twitched. He didn't react otherwise, just kept staring at the Lieutenant, who stared straight back at him, her bony face grim and fixed. Just as Adder, all her nerves alive, was about to speak again, Theo spoke: "I might do the same, if I stood where you are." The Lieutenant raised her chin slightly. "You're still a coward," Theo told her. "And if I live, you'll learn the price a coward pays." He turned, meeting Adder's gaze. "Options?" When Adder pointed toward the far end of the docks, he scowled. "Hide?"

"Now, sir."

Theo shook his head, but started in the direction Adder had indicated. Behind them, the *Hegre* Lieutenant drew in a quick breath and bellowed, "Here they are! They're right here!"

Adder spun. Wolf flung himself at the Lieutenant, except her crew surged out to grapple with him—not effectively, given that Wolf was combat-trained, but they delayed him, and meanwhile the Lieutenant was still yelling. Adder knocked down one of the crew, stripped his Sima from his belt and crowded Theo back against the gate fence, raising the short rifle.

But Theo reached past her to put his hand on her wrist. "No point in that now," he said, and stood beside her, watching the IVC Security converged on them.

Chapter 16

Franklin Station, Freiheit, Republic Space

Velocity hadn't been this deep since she was nine years old.

On that occasion, her father, having a case before the High Court at Acre, had brought her and her sister along. Their part in the journey had been part pleasure, part education. Her father had mostly left them to the charge of their tutors while he attended to the Court. The tutors had made certain they'd toured both the Court and The Parliament of the Republic, which was also housed on Acre, and that they'd seen all the important museums and interactives. But what Velocity remembered best from her four months at the Core had come during their six weeks on Earth, which they had spent mostly on a tour of the Devastations in Europe.

She didn't remember that much about the Devastation Zones themselves, except that after nearly two thousand years, they had been more like parks than devastations. What she remembered best was eating candy floss in the teashop at the main overlook of the Travada Memorial. (Her father, in the normal course of events, never allowed them sweets.) The adult members of the tour had been clustered around the broad windows, as their guide explained the environmental and political causes that led to the short, vicious war that had devastated half the planet. She and Alice, the only children on the tour, sat on the banquette against the far wall, swinging their heels and crunching bright green spun sugar blissfully between their teeth. The heat, humidity, and gravity of Earth had been horrible: this tea shop had wonderful climate control, and just sitting down was bliss in itself. But candy floss, besides?

This station, the Rosalind Franklin, orbited Freiheit, which was fifteen jumps from Earth. It was two jumps from Dresden Station, where the Taveri-Bowers Combine main House was located, as well as the habitat in which young Tallis Taveri and her sister Alice had been raised. Neither Franklin Station nor Dresden were precisely the Core, but they were close enough for most customs to be similar. Elaborate and complex docking rituals; docking slips so stuffed with ships they bristled; two Security for every six citizens; ten rules for any action anyone might think of taking; and every nexus channel restricted or privatized or otherwise inaccessible to common use. It was this last that shocked Rida the most. "How do people access?"

"People?" Velocity smirked at him. "Do you mean people like Brontë or do you mean people like you?" Rida frowned. "If you mean people like Brontë," Velocity said, nodding at the child, "Combine seat holders and their heirs, well, they have open access to multiple venues, obviously."

"We do not," Brontë said. "That's not true at all."

"If you mean people like *you*, you filthy scrod, you don't get access, because Brontë's people know exactly what you would do with it."

"That's not *even*—"

"If there's something you have a legitimate need to know, you can submit a request to your bond holder. Then, if your holder agrees you need to know that specific thing, you'll be given access to that data file, and that file alone."

"Freedom of access," Rida protested. "What about Freedom of Access? Isn't it right here at these Core planets where they *made* the Compact?"

The Fifteen Freedoms were the foundation of the Republic— the first part of the Compact that had been written and agreed on when the six Sovereignties and twelve Combines began building the Republic of Sovereign Nations (now the Republic of Sovereign Worlds) after the Devastations. The First Freedom, and in theory the most important of all the Fifteen Freedoms, was that every citizen of the Republic had the Right to Access any and all information created with or stored by means of government funding, as well as the Right to Means of Access to that information. But other questions arose in later years, such as:

- Were bonded workers citizens?
- Were Combines part of the government?
- Did information created by the Combines fall under this law?
- Did the Emergency Embargo of Access to Information, enacted in 3215 during the height of the Pirian Conflict, still hold, even now, in 3365?
- And dozens of other interesting points of law the courts of the Republic were wrangling over even yet.

Velocity settled for saying, "Here at the Core, the Combines decide what the law is."

"That's not even *close* to true," Brontë said. "Not *remotely* true."

"But if people can't post," Rida said, and his frown deepened. "If people can't access…"

"The other part isn't entirely correct, either," Velocity said. She stood behind Rida, watching past his shoulder as he negotiated their docking procedure with Station Control. "Contract labor, bonded workers, and those living outside Combine Houses don't have *official* access. *That's* true."

Brontë gave her a look, and then shot a second, furtive look at Sabra.

Velocity grinned. "Not new information, is it, Rida? Where there's autocracy, there's an underground. And someone who knows how to use it," she added, looping an arm around Brontë's neck. The child moved away, affronted at this liberty.

Eventually the docking procedure concluded, and they were cleared to dock—an anticlimax, since in fact the ship had been docked for the past ninety minutes. But now they were officially listed as docked, and could, at least theoretically, board the station. In actual fact, Velocity still had to meet with several station officials, including someone from Combine Security, a Medical Officer, and a team from Customs.

The Medical Officer would want to inspect health certificates for both her and her crew, making certain they weren't bringing any plagues or vermin onto the station. And Customs would at minimum examine the *Susan Calvin's* manifest, and almost certainly come aboard as well, to inspect the cargo they were planning to offload, and possibly search for contraband. The Fifth Freedom of the Compact of the Republic was the Freedom to Trade without Intrusion or Restriction, but—once again—all sorts of interesting questions had arisen about who this Freedom applied to, not to mention when and how it could be abridged.

But it was the Combine Security that worried Velocity the most. Though Combine Security took an oath to uphold the Compact and protect the Republic, their first loyalty was and always had been to their Combines—it was right there in the name of their service, not to mention their funding. And until Brontë made it back to Ikeda House, and had her succession to the Ikeda Seat confirmed, her status was uncertain, at best. Maybe she was a Combine heir; maybe she was a potential assassin. Maybe Combine Security would put her in detention and let their bosses sort it out. Brontë in a box at Combine Security was a situation Velocity wished to avoid. The mission wasn't doomed at that point; but hunting frogs in a bucket would be putting it mildly.

Six weeks earlier, they had put in at Kingsbury Station, in orbit around Oz, a sensibly larcenous settlement planet one jump past the Drift. There, Velocity had offloaded much of the cargo in her hold, including everything that was proscribed in the Republic, and taken on cargo likely to be in demand at the Core—local spices, hardwood, wines, art. She had made a decent though not spectacular profit, especially since she had used Brontë's credit to buy the trade license and to top up her fuel reserves. Meanwhile, Sabra and Rida had made connections on the station, under the deck, organizing better tags for Brontë and Sabra—ones Rida believed would pass inspection, even at the Core. Velocity, who had procured her own forged data tags at Kingsbury Station more than a decade earlier, and a few years after that tags for Tai and Rida as well, hoped he was right.

"Medic at the gate," Rida said now.

"About time." Velocity swept her gaze over their passengers. "Remember the instructions. Not a word unless you're asked a direct question. Then answer exactly what you're asked and only that. Volunteer nothing." She looked from one of them to the other. "Clear?"

"Clear," said Brontë.

Velocity grunted. "Go let him in, Sabra."

$$ \text{𝍞 ✝ 𝍦 𝍥} $$

The Medical Officer ran their tags, considered the dates on their last immunizations, gave each of them a cursory examination, and then approved them for station access. Planetary access would be another, much more complex issue. Once the Medical officer had been served tea and little cakes (part of the process, like making offerings to a local deity) and had taken her leave, Velocity sent Rida and Sabra off-ship on their job. Tai and Brontë's job required them to stay on the *Susan Calvin*. "If anyone comes to the gate," Velocity instructed, as she got ready to go out herself, "don't let them in. Say I'm out, and let them record a message."

"Yes, Captain," Tai said.

"You," she said to Brontë. "Do what Tai tells you." Brontë, affronted at all these infringements on her dignity, frowned. She was an Ikeda heir, which—in her opinion—meant she was not a child, to be ordered around and confined to the ship. "And stay by the com."

Velocity pulled on the keffiyeh required on Core stations, even for those who wore their hair as short as she did. It was more about propriety than sanitation at this point, and had been for centuries. She wound the white and blue scarf deftly into place, her hands remembering the motions though it had, impossibly, been twenty years now at least since she'd worn one. "I'll ping you directly."

"We *know* all this." Temper gave Brontë's voice an edge.

Velocity tucked the keffiyeh around her mouth and nose. "Shouldn't be more than half an hour." She ducked through the umbilical hatch and waited on the other side until she heard Tai both seal and lock it behind her.

She had forgotten how ugly the public areas of Combine-built stations were—ugly, barren, badly constructed and badly maintained. This was the main civilian station for Freiheit, which was arguably the sixth most important planet in the Core after Earth, Acre, Hayek, Waikato, and Gagarin; and this was its second most important concourse, the one most merchants and tourists would initially encounter. This concourse was, for many of them, their first impression of the Core itself. And yet, looking downspin, Velocity saw a long curve of dull grey deck paint, dull grey railings and girders, dull beige bulkheads. The overhead huddled low, with minimal lighting, and that lighting bare and glaring. No attempt had been made to relieve the utilitarian architecture with any sort of variety of form or ornamentation—every surface was flat, every line straight. Every hatch to every cabin or lift or corridor was set flush with the bulkheads.

The shop hatches were currently open, however, and within many of these, Velocity could see the color and life that was missing from the public spaces—as she passed a shop selling crockery, for instance, the brilliant display of teapots (a tiny jewel-bright pot shaped like a ladybird; a larger pot, purple as an amethyst, made of shining glass) made her pause, and nearly drew her in, though what did she need with a teapot? She didn't even like tea. Velocity shook her head and hurried on. The medical inspection had taken somewhat longer than she had hoped, with the result that she was running late for her appointment.

Rather than leasing a habitat or a block of suites, Ikeda-Verde Combine had purchased an entire level of Franklin Station. Velocity had been out in the Drift so long that this had the ability to shock her. Her Combine, Taveri-Bowers, had been wealthy enough—on Dresden-3, the station where they had their House, they'd held what had seemed to her then an immense habitat. It had occupied fully a tenth of one of the midlevels: service quarters, more or less, for these Ikeda-Verdes. And that had been the main Taveri House, where almost every Taveri lived most of their lives. This habitat here on Franklin Station was just a guesthouse—a place Ikedas might stay occasionally, and short-term.

The Taveri House habitat had also been very well defended, as Velocity remembered. So was this habitat. The lift would not stop at the habitat level without the special code, which had been sent to her; and once she emerged from the lift, Velocity emerged not into a foyer, but into a koban, a guard station. A half-squad of Ikeda-Verde Security met her here, all armed not just with charged sticks, but with Lopaka HJ19 short rifles, plasma weapons. The Security put her through a thorough search and interrogation. During this search, Velocity toggled her uplink, sending a ping to Tai back at the ship, making sure that the dagan's worm through the Ikeda House shieldwall was functioning. *You there?*

Yes, Captain, Tai sent back.

I'm inside. Stand by.

Try not to get killed.

The Security officer finished running her tag. "Captain Wrachant. You'll surrender any weapons here."

Given his fellow officers had just run a search on her, as thorough a search as she had ever experienced without being made to strip down, this struck her as an odd comment. Velocity squinted at his lapel badge. "Officer Moral, is it?"

"Morel," he said, correcting her pronunciation.

"Morel. Why would I bring weapons to a civil negotiation?"

"You'll surrender your weapons before we admit you."

Velocity sighed. "I am not carrying weapons, Officer."

Officer Morel paused, his eyes remote. Velocity felt her eyebrows twitch—he was listening to an earring link. This was a smart room: he was checking her biolevels. That explained the useless question. They were establishing a baseline. *Interesting.*

After a moment, he nodded, and led her down a wide corridor. Here, in contrast to the public spaces, the deck plates were covered with deep golden wooden planks, polished and gleaming; the overhead was three meters high at least, with muted indirect lighting. On the walls, gold and green striped silken cloth. All very pretty. Officer Morel took her through a double hatch into a wide cabin with a terrace that opened out onto a garden. The light out over the garden was as bright as actual sunshine. Velocity stood squinting, and a honeybee came buzzing through the room, zipping past her to circle and burrow into a vase filled with purple carnations and lemon-scented verbena.

Without actually meaning to, Velocity moved out onto the terrace. Out in the garden, the overhead stretched perhaps five meters, and in that height, brilliant lights simulated sunlight; below, a quarter of a hectare of cultivated space bloomed and shone. Much of it was flowers; but there were dwarf pines and fruit trees, a tiny meadow, a pretty little stream. Velocity saw a kitchen garden at one end, and two shirtless boys at work in it. White wooden beehives lined up along the wall behind them. Closer, on the stone steps leading into the garden, a small child in a loose jacket and short trousers sat with her heels tucked under her. Bonded labor, she wore no keffiyeh; her silky dark hair was clipped close to her skull.

"Lovely, isn't it?" A Combine woman came up beside Velocity, hands behind her back, nodding out at the garden. Velocity stepped back, turning to face a tall woman with a close-fitting cap of short feathery curls. Her nose was prominent, her eyes dark, and she was not

Torres Ikeda Alonzo. This was Dr. Isra Ikeda Lopaka. Brontë's mother.

Velocity thought of the messages sent back and forth from the *Susan Calvin* to the station over the past twenty watches, as they had come into dock—hers addressed to Torres Ikeda, the replies which had allowed her to believe, by omission, that it was Torres writing them. Studying Isra now, she wondered if this woman expected her to be green enough not to have run image searches. Did she really think Velocity would be fooled? Or was this some sort of test?

Isra lifted elegant eyebrows at her silence. "You don't like gardens, Captain Wrachant?"

"I don't like slaves," Velocity said, "nor that which is built on the blood of slaves."

Isra's face froze. Then she smiled wider, sincerely amused. "That's adorable," she said. "Why don't we have some tea? You drink tea? Even tea grown by slaves?"

"I'd prefer moving straight to the negotiation."

Isra snapped her fingers. "Nina."

The child on the steps scrambled up and trotted into the relative dimness of the cabin. Taking a hold on her patience, Velocity unwound her keffiyeh, letting it settle around her shoulder and lowering the front enough to show her face. This was manners, if they were going to negotiate. Isra's own keffiyeh, a dark garnet silk scarf, was already settled in a loose puddle around her neck.

Nina reappeared, bearing a tea tray. She settled it on a table near Isra and began pouring out tea into tiny, intricately painted bowls. "The contract labor boy on your crew," Isra said. "What was his name? Nahas? The one who is delinquent on his contract?"

From just beside the cabin's hatches, Captain Morel said, "Tai Nahas, sir. From Sarat. He currently owes thirty years, plus twenty-six penalty years."

"Nahas." Isra held a teacup out to Velocity, who did not take it. With a twitch of her lip, Isra put the cup on the table next to Velocity. "He's an attractive child. I can see the temptation."

"Man," Velocity corrected levelly.

"Attractive young man, then," Isra said indulgently.

"Attractive. Erotic. Luscious. An excellent First Officer." Velocity shifted her weight, settling her feet further apart, the left just behind the right: the first attack stance in Indaiyi, though she didn't consciously think of it in that way. "And not the point. I thought we were here to negotiate, not discuss my ethics."

Isra laughed and strolled back into the shadow of the cabin. "Indeed. Well, let us negotiate. You claim to have a child I'd be interested in ransoming. One of our heirs, I understand, ranked highly in the line to inherit our Primary Seat."

"Elena Kora Hodaya Ikeda Verde." This was Brontë's register name, which Velocity had used in the messages. "Ranked very highly at this point. She inherits the Primary Seat, if she makes it back to Isra House. From what we understand."

Isra Ikeda settled into an armchair by the tea table. "You must know we have been getting hundreds of such claims a day, ever since the takeover."

"And yet you let me through your door."

"Your preliminary evidence was persuasive. Persuade me further."

The preliminary evidence had included a code phrase which every child in Ikeda House had been taught. They were to use it to communicate to the House that rescue attempts and ransom demands were coming from legitimate sources. Brontë had warned the phrase wouldn't be enough, though, since it could obviously have been tortured out of her before she was killed, or extracted while she was under medication, or achieved by some other equally appalling method. "A capture will not suffice, I assume," Velocity said, to which Isra snorted. Spreading her hands, Velocity shrugged. "Propose evidence you will accept."

"I will see her in person."

"I think not," Velocity said pleasantly.

"I will not trade for a phantom."

"And I will not surrender my only leverage before we have completed negotiations." It occurred to Velocity that she had slipped into the cadence and vocabulary of the Combine House where she had spent her childhood. Picking up the tea bowl, she tossed its contents into the garden and deliberately shifted her dialect to that used on the decks of the Drift stations. "I'm no fool, Kas...Ikeda. Stop thinking you can juke me."

Isra's pupils widened. She smiled. "Propose a different solution."

Velocity smiled as well. "I link my ship. You speak to your pup via the link."

"And this will not be your contract boy, the attractive Tai, aboard your ship using an image synthesizer to simulate my relative."

"If you don't know your pup well enough to read a synth, why are we here?" Velocity came to the edge of the interior cabin and glanced about. "Wallboard?"

"Nina," Isra said to the child. "A port, please."

The child trotted from the room. Velocity went back out onto the balcony. The two garden boys were hunkered by the bee hives, eating their dinner from a tray while a kitchen girl leaned in a hatchway talking to them. Through the uplink, she reached out to Tai: *Here we go.*

Ready on this end.

Velocity kept her expression schooled to blankness as the child, Nina, lugged in a port nearly as large as she was. Captain Morel took it from her and proffered it to Isra. "Doctor?"

"Come inside, Captain Wrachant," Isra said. "My yard boy gets testy when I dim the garden lights."

Velocity followed her off the terrace into the cabin, dusky after the bright lights of the garden, and over to a worktable of fine polished wood. Morel set up the port there, unrolled its keymat, and stepped aside. "The guest password is *deathtrap*," Isra said.

"Charming." Velocity coded in the password, simultaneously toggling her uplink and entering the password there. Her uplink accessed the Ikeda House system—or as much of it as the guest password would allow her. This was not much, but both Rida and the dagan thought it would be enough. She made what she hoped was not a too obvious show of entering the ship's access code into the Ikeda House port. Tai, piggybacking through her uplink, was already infiltrating the Ikeda House System using the pirate code that Rida and the dagan had built.

The dagan had been able to worm its way inside the Ikeda House shieldwalls, but not into its data bank. Both Rida and the dagan were sure that with a password they could get into the banks. When Velocity asked if they were sure they could do this without raising alarms, Rida had given her an exasperated look. Every wizard out in the Drift knew how pathetic the Republic was at packing code, and Rida was not only a Drift wizard, he'd worked with the dagan, who *was* Pirian code. "But right," Rida added. "I can't promise anything. Maybe Ikeda House is the one house at the Core that has wardens who know code. Or maybe we missed something. Nothing's a hundred percent, Captain."

Velocity thought how much better she would have felt if anyone out at the Drift knew anything at all about what the Combines were actually like. Still, a moment later, through her uplink, Tai said, *We're in*, and then, a brief moment later, *Implementing*.

Velocity felt, or imagined she felt, the faint, surreal whisper of the data streaming through her uplink. On the keymat, she finished feeding in instructions. The house system buzzed the com of the *Susan Calvin*. After another buzz, the channel opened. The dagan appeared on the screen. As Core custom dictated, it wore a crisp, high-collared shirt with long sleeves and a keffiyeh, this one white and black with a fine blue line running through the pattern. It covered the dagan's mouth only loosely, enough to seem polite. Velocity was interested to see that the dagan had made itself darker-skinned than usual, with broad, blunt bones. Very Pirian, in other words.

"Captain," it said, its diction crisp, its vowels pure. In contrast to its appearance, this was perfect Core dialect.

"Lieutenant," Velocity said. "Our passenger, please."

"Yes, Captain." The dagan put the screen-holder up a moment. When it re-opened the channel again, its fist gripped Brontë's collar. She had been also carefully prepped—her bright orange hair smeared with grease so that it lay matted on one side of her skull, and her skinsuit changed for a stained, worn, and oversized undershirt. Tai had also used considerable ingenuity and some of his eyeliner to construct bruises around one temple and on her chin.

Isra made a sound under her breath. Velocity shot a sidelong glance at her—had that been a grunt of empathy? But the Combine woman's face was expressionless. Velocity looked back at the wallboard. "Greet your aunt, Elena."

She was careful to put a delicate emphasis on the penultimate word. Brontë lowered her head further, her face set in a mute glower. "I told you this was a terrible idea. Ikeda House doesn't want me ransomed. They want me dead."

The dagan shook her roughly. "Stop lying, najis."

Isra folded her arms. "You found her traveling alone, you said."

"Out on Hell in a Bucket." Velocity smirked at Brontë on the screen. "All I ask is a reasonable finder's fee, plus a ten-year trade license, good at any Republic port."

Isra tipped her eyebrows up. "Not three wishes and a magic carpet as well?"

"I know what I have here, kas." Velocity tapped the port screen.

"Perhaps not as much as you think." Isra moved her chin at Brontë on the screen. "Even if that is who you claim she is, there is some dispute as to her place in the line. She's a proscribed g-set. Did she mention that to you?" Brontë reacted to this as well: a bare shift of her eyes toward the screen.

"Talk that eugenics smut with someone who cares," Velocity said. "The funds and the trade license. Give it up, or I sell this scrawny little twitch to some other Ikeda seat holder. Sell them your name and location, too, while I'm at it, will I?"

Isra smiled. "Not a solution I'd advise, Captain."

Velocity smiled back. "Are we making this deal or having tea? I'm getting bored here."

The lights out over the garden flickered—just for a micro-second, so brief a time it was barely noticeable except to someone who had been expecting it. Isra snapped her fingers at Nina. "Show our guest out. I'll speak to you in time," she added to Velocity and, picking up her bowl of tea, strolled toward the balcony.

Nina skipped forward, beaming. "This way, Captain."

Morel dogged them through the corridors and down the lift to the koban. Velocity ignored him, keeping well ahead, with the little bonded child at her side. As they rode the lift, she said, her tone friendly and idle, "Your name is Nina, yes? You seem like a clever child." Velocity looked straight down. Nina looked back, and Velocity held her gaze. Morel stepped forward to punch open the lift. "Thanks for your help," Velocity told him. "I look forward to seeing you again soon."

Morel scowled, already turning away, not noticing how, on this last sentence, she dropped her eyes, so briefly, down to meet Nina's gaze once again.

$$\text{𝕂 𝕥 𝕏 𝕊}$$

Momo Makan, Concourse D, the sort of eatery frequented by dockworkers, clerks and construction techs, was packed at this hour, Afterwatch First. Its chef and two sous-chefs were working at top speed in the galley. Maja Gupta, owner of Momo's, stood scowling at Sabra and Rida in the service corridor. "You're not affiliated."

Rida had no idea what this meant, except it couldn't mean what it would have meant in the Drift, where this Gupta would have been asking about a station or a ship's political affiliation—if they had sworn loyalty to the Republic, or to the Pirians, or to some Free Trade Merchant leader. Out in the Drift, this was a question usually raised just before weapons came out. However, given that he was supposed to be bonded labor, he knew what that called for in these circumstances: eyes down, mouth shut, look stupid.

"We are not," Sabra answered Maja Gupta. "At the price you're offering, though, I can't imagine our lack of affiliation is going to be an objection."

Gupta's scowl deepened. Skinny, with the reedy bones of someone who had grown up in low-gee without the Pirian fix, she had a small jaw and narrow dark eyes. Her dark skin shone with the sweat of her kitchen work. Her glower fixed on Rida, she said, "I give you the work, he don't fix it. He makes it worse even. Then what?"

"If he can't fix it, he'll tell me," Sabra said. "He knows better than to mess about. If he can't fix it, all you're out is the front money—what it costs for the diagnosis."

Gupta kept scowling. But this was fair, and she knew it. Hiring a real environmental tech to diagnose and repair the glitch in her filtration system would cost more than her eatery would earn this quarter—maybe put her at risk of losing Momo's. And losing her business might well put her and her family into a debt spiral from which they would not recover. Unreasonable Debt was a criminal offense in the Republic, with only one penalty: bonded labor, until you and your family had paid out the debt, and the court costs, and any debts incurred while you and they were serving out the bond. Since "any debts" included food, clothing, and medical expenses, that meant, essentially, eternal bondage, for you and your heirs.

Maja Gupta's shop already had readings edging into the red. If she didn't repair her environmentals—the system regulating the air coming into, and sterilizing the water and waste coming out of, her physical plant, she would soon draw the attention of Station Environmental Authority. If that happened, she would incur hefty fines *and* mandatory repairs, by station repair crews at station prices.

"Fine," Gupta said. "Send him down. You," she said, thrusting her small bony face at Rida. "You don't touch one thing down there besides what you're meant to. Ha? You don't put your filthy fingers into anything."

"Yes, miss," Rida said, keeping his head down.

"He's a good boy," Sabra said. "He does what he's told."

Gupta grunted. Then she led them through the kitchen into a dank service corridor, barely wide enough for one person to pass through at a time, and only then if that person had skinny shoulders. The deck plates underfoot were of salvaged cargo pods, cut into squares and bolted down. These had warped with time and damp. Most of the lights set in the overhead were no longer functioning, and damp streaked the metal walls—there was definitely something off in the local climate control. Gupta stopped and hauled up a hatch. Darkness below. Rida hesitated. "Go on," Gupta ordered. "I got work to do if you ain't."

Taking a breath, Rida braced his hands on the sides of the hatch and lowered himself into the dark. Gupta shut the hatch above him.

It was not as dark here in the underdeck as it had seemed from the service corridor. Still, it was dim. Rida stood a moment, letting his eyes adjust, before taking his handheld from his cargo pocket. The light of its screen was as bright as a torch in this dusk. He tried to raise Tai, back on the ship, but as they'd expected, he was denied access. Grimacing, he fetched up the schematic he and the dagan had cobbled together, working from various banks they'd wormed into, and turned this way and that in the cramped crawl space until he oriented himself. According to the schematic, the intersection they needed was 25.5 meters that way. And then he should go right another six meters. All of it in a space where—while crawling was an exaggeration—he couldn't stand straight, either.

Moving in a bent scramble, he headed toward the intersection. Gupta would assume bonded labor was lazy, stupid, and slow, which gave him a little leeway; but he didn't have infinite time. Fortunately, the vent was exactly where the station schematic had said it would be—one bit of luck, since stored data, in his experience, was often not just wrong, but wildly wrong.

Unshipping his satchel, Rida pulled out the toolkit, and located the box of bugs at its very bottom. Twenty-five of them, of Pirian manufacture, they came in a variety of forms—earwigs, flour beetles, woodbugs, ladybirds, several sorts of ants, discreet grey spiders. They had all been built for both storage and short-range transmission. On the ship, they used these bots to run checks in places too tiny or too uncomfortable for human oversight—plumbing lines, for instance. But in this case, since retrieval was not certain, Rida had set them to self-destruct in twenty-eight hours. At that point, the bots would turn to literal dust inside, leaving their very real insect exoskeletons as their only remains. If they were found before then, he was fairly certain no one would be able to crack their code, or at least not within 28 hours. Pirian wizards were famously good at this sort of thing.

Activating each insect one at a time, he released it within the grid. This particular air duct led up into the private level held by Ikeda House. Though that level was an enormous space, nearly six hectares total according to the station schematic, 28 hours ought to be enough time for the insect drones to infiltrate, investigate, and transmit a good deal of what went on within that level. He set the last one free, and then checked their feeds on the chart on his screen, making sure each was transmitting. They would not be able to pick up these transmissions on the ship—the bots' transmission range was less than 3000 meters— but the receiver which Rida now locked into place behind a water pipe would store everything they sent back in its data bank. If everything went well. If nothing glitched. If the insect drones didn't get seen, stepped on, or go wrong in six or eight other ways.

Rida started to kiss the knuckle of his thumb for luck, grimaced at how filthy it was from crawling around down here in this pit, and then kissed it anyway. He retraced his path, back to Momo Makan's bank of systems, where he pried off the tin cover—both damp and corroding, not a good sign—and shone the light from the screen of his handheld inside. What he saw made him wince. Not just damp but mold, and slimy mold at that. He cast the light of the screen around, muttering under his breath. The filtration tanks had corroded through. The sediment meant to filter toxic particles and CO_2 from the air of Momo's was leaking through the corroded gaps, spilling into mucky puddles on the station's hull. These puddles meant more trouble, something else leaking, probably either the cooling system or the water filtration. Maybe both. He'd have to pull up this whole section of deck and run checks on everything. He made captures and then shifted the handheld so that the screen tilted toward him, to start the list of components he would need, beginning with a dedicated dehumidifier.

⅞ ⊹ ⅄ ⅀

When Rida emerged back into the kitchen, Sabra was leaning up against the storeroom wall, drinking tea and chatting with Gupta, who was cleaning a giant perch at the nearby sink. They'd been laughing, but Gupta's humor dropped away when she saw Rida. "Well?"

He gave Sabra his handheld. She swiped through the captures, ending on the requisition list, which she read with some care before passing the handheld to Gupta. Gupta had washed and dried her hands; taking the handheld, she repeated Sabra's actions, her bad humor deepening. "Is this a joke?" she demanded, when she read the list. Rida said nothing. "I'm not some benny you can kip, deck-licker." Gupta flung the handheld at him; he caught it deftly.

Sabra took it from him. "If you think we're thieves, bring in another tech." Gupta growled, and Sabra added, "Or bring in Station Repair. Could be they'll have a better diagnosis."

"Your filters clogged," Rida said, "months back, from what I can tell. The coils on the environmental clogged after that. Then your dehumidifier went. Once you lost that—"

"Did someone ask you to talk, jess?" Gupta demanded. She braced her fists on the sink edge, her mouth a compressed line. Rida glanced at Sabra, and then lowered his head again. If they couldn't get back down into the underdeck, they couldn't retrieve the data. Which Sabra knew, same as he did.

Sabra waited, her broad-boned face—to all appearances—bored and unconcerned. "Right, fine, right." Gupta wheeled, slashing the blade of her hand at the corridor. "Get it done," she said, and stomped off to curse at the kitchen boy.

Chapter 17

Franklin Station, Freiheit, Republic Space

Most stations kept gravity, but Franklin Station kept full gravity, at least on the levels where most of its residents lived. Velocity couldn't think who had imagined this was a good idea. Here on the commercial dock level, where the *Susan Calvin* had her slip, the gravity was a mere bone-grinding 0.7 standard. Locking the umbilical behind her, Velocity exhaled gustily and collapsed on the bench, reaching to haul off her boots in the same motion. Her feet felt raw and broken, like the rest of her.

Tai spoke through the feed: "Captain?"

"I'm here," Velocity said, collapsed against the bulkhead, her eyes shut. "Everyone in?"

"You're the last. Wait till you see what Rida brought us for dinner."

Velocity was too exhausted for hunger. "Bath first," she said. "And maybe someone could bring me brandy and Opix in the bath."

"Absolutely."

"And a précis of what we've learned so far." With another gusty exhalation, Velocity forced herself back to her feet. By the time Rida arrived in the sauna, she was stretched out on the long bench, her feet up on the shorter one, and both the walls and the steam on high.

"Gah," he said, squinting. "Are you trying to cook yourself?"

Velocity sat up, reaching for the bowl of brandy. He gave it over, and then peeled the backing from the Opix patch and stuck it on her neck. Velocity lay back down on the bench, exhaling, the brandy resting on her belly. Rida unbuttoned his trousers and slid them off. She watched him moodily. Most sex on the ship was between her and Tai, or Tai and Rida. Rida didn't really like sex with women. Also, she didn't feel like sex right now. More like punching someone. Sitting up again, she swallowed the brandy and put the bowl aside. "How'd the job go?"

He snagged a scrub cloth from the bin. "The bug drones are launched. And Sabra talked the bistro chaff into paying for the repairs."

"I like a job that pays its way," Velocity commented, taking up her own cloth. The pain patch was taking effect, as was the brandy, and her mood was improving steadily. "You brought something nice home for dinner, I hear."

"The markets here are ugly. And overpriced. But well-stocked." Rida used the sluice, and then lay down on the bench across from hers. "I got chocolates."

Velocity glanced up, interested. "Real chocolates?"

"And that coffee you like. Also goat."

"*Goat?*"

"I know a recipe. You'll like it." He yawned and shut his eyes. "I ran the search when I got back, looking for Isra and Torres. It was a bit tricky. All the data here is behind shieldwalls. But Isra arrived just over a month ago. She brought five full squads of dedicated Security with her, and forty-six staff members."

A hundred and twenty Security officers. Velocity pulled the sluice hose from the wall and rinsed her hair, tipping back her head and scrubbing through the short soapy strands with her free hand to aid the rinsing process. She wondered idly how many of the hundred-twenty were combat-trained, and dismissed the question. It wasn't as if an assault on the habitat was anywhere on the list of likely contingencies.

"It looks like Torres only just arrived, maybe three or four watch before we did. Station Security has a hold on the crew and most of the passengers."

"Huh. Most?"

"Torres Ikeda Alonzo was given an exit permit. Also a half squad of Security with her, and two other staff members."

Velocity lowered the sluice and sat studying Rida, thinking this through. "Just Torres. No other Ikeda House member."

He shrugged. "Might be someone still on the ship. Might be one disguised as Security."

Half a squad was only twelve Security officers. That wasn't much, for someone who was now within spitting distance of the Primary Seat on the Ikeda House Board. "What's the Security hold about?"

"That, I don't know yet. The report's sealed, maybe just because it's an on-going investigation, or maybe because it's something sweet."

"Sealed, as in you can't access it?"

"Pssh." Rida hadn't met the wall he couldn't worm through, and when he did, it wouldn't be one built by some Republic tech. "Torres has rented a block of dorms and cabins out in the cheap seats. Level Fourteen. It wouldn't be hard to infiltrate out there, especially if she's only got a half-squad minding her gates."

"Let me think it over," Velocity said, and set the steam cycle going.

$$ \text{🝰 🝙 🝲 🝮} $$

Dinner was tasty. The goat had been cooked into a spicy stew, with fresh vegetables. The only flavor she recognized was the ginger, but it was good. And Rida had found an excellent local wine, which went well with the stew. Also, the chocolates were a big hit. Velocity hadn't had chocolate in years, and Tai had never had any. "Is it supposed to taste like this?" he said, after his first bite.

Rida laughed at him, and taking away his piece—a dark chocolate-covered bit of salted mushroom—hunted through the fancy gold-lined box for something more pedestrian.

"Give me the name of the shop where you got these," Velocity said to Rida, tapping the lid of the box. Out in the Drift, chocolate would sell even better than Pirian medicinals. "Also the wine merchant." She refilled her wine bowl, and added, "Everyone take the next watch off. Get some rest. No one leaves the ship without letting me know. Brontë, you don't leave the ship at all. That order stands. Tai, you're onboard as well. That bit from Ikeda about you, that was a threat."

Mouthing a new piece of chocolate Rida had fed him, Tai grimaced. Being restricted to the ship was never pleasant; when they were in dock, it was a kind of torture. "It's not like our gate will stop Ikeda House from coming for me if they want me bad enough," he argued.

"Keep working on the communications problem, too. We need to be able to talk to each other."

"Ah. About that." Rida ate his last bite of chocolate and wiped his fingers on his shorts. Then he dug a little rice paper packet from the pocket of his undershirt. "We had these in storage. The dagan reminded me."

He shook them out on the table: eight little brown gadgets, dark and shiny as ticks. When Velocity nudged one over with the tip of her forefinger, she saw it had miniscule cilia on its convex side, too many to count. "Bots?"

"Netbots. Pirian design. They create a closed network, using nanotropes. Short-term, about a hundred-twenty hours. You put them in your ear," Rida explained, "and they rebuild about one percent of the, uh, I forget what it's called. It's part of your bones."

Periosteum, the dagan said through Velocity's uplink.

"Basically, they turn your body into a link," Rida explained. "The netbot in your ear is the receiver. But it's a closed network. We'll only transmit and receive to one another."

That's best case, the dagan said. *There may be leakage.*

Leakage.

Any transmission can be detected. Once detected, any transmission can be decoded.

Rida was still talking. "...six to nine hours to fully implement. They're fully active for 20 watches—Pirian watches, which is about

124 hours, universal time. Five days UT, more or less. It should be plenty of time." He hesitated, watching Velocity. "Captain?"

She picked up one of the ticks. "In my ear?"

"Nodes side down."

The nodes were the cilia, she assumed. She studied the netbot and then inserted it in her ear. "Push down," Rida advised, and she did. With a little crunch, the tiny instrument deployed. Velocity suppressed a shudder. One by one, everyone else, including Sabra and Brontë, picked up a netbot and tucked it, with more or less squeamishness, into their ears.

"The main engine is a virus," Rida said, "as with most nanotropes. So we might see some side effects. Fever, nausea. Nothing severe, the dagan says."

"Fine." Velocity got to her feet. "Brontë. I'll see you in my cabin."

The Combine child glanced up, startled. "What? Why?"

"Now, please." Velocity took along what was left of the last liter of wine. Moving with obvious reluctance, the child followed her through the hatch and down the trail to Velocity's cabin. Though Velocity had the largest cabin on the ship, still when she and Brontë were inside with the hatch shut, space was tight. Velocity hauled down the bench from the bulkhead, nodding at the bunk. "Sit."

Since they'd left Kingsbury Station, Brontë had spent much of her time sulking in her cabin, or in the pit with the dagan. This latter was fine with Velocity. The more time Brontë spent with the dagan, the more time the dagan had to subvert her. Rida had also set the pit feeds to capture every interaction between the dagan and Brontë. Every few watches, Velocity spent some time, out of all the copious time she had to spare, reviewing these captures. A number of these had been interesting, with Brontë giving the dagan details about her life back on Waikato which she hadn't put into the versions she'd given Rida; and *much* more detail about what exactly had happened on that KRC Mining platform. But what had happened during the previous Midwatch had been the bogey Velocity had set her watch for.

Midwatch was when Brontë usually slept. Reviewing the ship's records, Velocity saw that the child hadn't slept more than five hours at a stretch since they'd left Oz. This past Midwatch third, Brontë had slipped into the pit and fed in the manual code that woke the dagan. Emerging, it had been even more round-faced and plump of arm and body than usual. Smiling, it had knelt on the deck. "Back for another session already, mzala?"

"Would it be all right if I slept here?" Brontë asked, her head lowered.

"Of course." The dagan reached to cup a gentle hand around the child's face. "You seem unhappy. Is there anything I can do?"

At which point Brontë had begun to cry. Not noisily, like a child, but in steely silence, her arms hugging her chest. The dagan, reaching out, pulled her into a gentle embrace, which Brontë did not resist, though she didn't relax into it, either. Somewhat to Velocity's surprise, the dagan began singing, some Pirian song Velocity didn't recognize. The only Pirian Velocity knew was the simple version used for talking to Free Trade merchants and other barbarians. This was real Pirian, and probably in some ship's dialect as well. She understood only one word in five or six, enough to know it was probably a lullaby.

Eventually Brontë stopped crying. The dagan stopping singing, but kept humming. And after some time, Brontë began a long and incoherent story about some intra-Combine society. The Atlas Society. Velocity ran an Orly, but her banks didn't have much on it. Another of the many societies with which Combine citizens, too wealthy to actually work, occupied their idle hours. The Atlas Society, according to the squib which was in her bank, dedicated itself to the intersecting areas of history, economics, and science. All the rambling Brontë fed to the dagan didn't add much detail, except for one key point: that her mother was a member of the Atlas Society, and for some reason this was a terrible thing.

Now, huddled in the small space of the cabin, knee to knee with her, Brontë looked even more exhausted and miserable than she had in the capture with the dagan. Velocity studied the child for a long moment. Then she reached to tug open her locker, hunted out a bowl that was mostly clean, and poured some wine. She handed it to Brontë, who took it dully.

"So," Velocity said. "Jobs went well today. I didn't see any of your Ikans at Ikeda House, but I've got a possible hook. And Rida launched the bug drones. We also inserted the ferret he and the dagan wrote into the Ikeda House system." No reaction, unless the faintly green color of her skin was a reaction.

"Meanwhile." Velocity settled back against the bulkhead. "That must have been a shock. Seeing your mother instead of Torres at Ikeda House." Brontë twitched, her pale face wrenching into a grimace for just one second. She shot Velocity a swift frightened look, color coming up bright across her cheekbones. Velocity saw her consider denying it, and then rejecting the tactic. She bent her head over the wine again. "Well? Do you want to pretend you didn't know your mother was sending those messages?"

"I wasn't sure," Brontë said faintly. She was gripping the bowl so tightly her fingertips were white. "Adder…when we got to Bastiat, we found a message waiting, from Adder. Or…the message said it was from Adder." Brontë bent her head further. Velocity wondered if she was crying again. "Sabra said we couldn't be sure it was from her. Because of the coup. Because maybe whoever was really behind the coup had sent it, to lure me back."

"Sabra said." Velocity meant to say this evenly, but a certain amount of sarcasm flavored her words. The child flushed again, and looked up. No tears. It was dark anger in those eyes, and an even darker torment. Velocity grimaced, and drank wine from the carafe. Bright and stinging, it was as excellent alone as it had been with the stew. "What did this message from Adder say, exactly?"

"It wasn't just Sabra," Brontë said. "I didn't want to believe it either." She hitched in a breath and looked for a place to put her bowl. Velocity took it from her, putting it on top of the locker. "Adder's message." Brontë took another rough breath. "The message said my mother was behind the coup. It said my mother had killed Theo, and killed Wolf," Brontë's voice broke, just a fraction, when she said Wolf's name. She paused, getting it under control. "That she killed Wolf when he tried to protect Theo. That I should run away. Run out to Pirian space and keep running."

"Hmn. Sounds like a fake message to me, certainly."

Brontë gripped a fistful of her short hair—fresh-scrubbed and shiny after their charade earlier—and twisted it fiercely. "If my mother had, had done that, she would never let Adder have access. So how had Adder sent the message? If it wasn't my mother, if it was… someone else, why would Adder send that message?"

"Someone else."

Brontë twisted her hair harder. "My mother running the coup makes no sense. Why would she? To put me in the Primary Seat? I haven't qualified, and I'm not old enough. Not nearly old enough."

"So you decided it was Torres."

"No." Releasing her hair, Brontë rubbed at her eyes viciously. "David was my first hypothesis. David Ikeda Ito. He had enough support in the House, he was ambitious, his daughter, Talia, had already qualified, and—" The Combine child shut up, abruptly.

"And then they were both killed in the coup," Velocity said. "David and his kid."

Brontë lifted her head. Her eyes looked bruised and swollen. Fixing her gaze on one corner of the cabin, she said, "But Anja wasn't. Neither was Torres. Given how deep into the line the assassinations went, the two of them running the takeover made sense."

"But you didn't believe it."

The hectic color on Brontë's cheekbones burned bright again. "They don't have enough support in the House. Neither of them has ever been active, politically. They don't sit on committees, they don't come to parties. They don't make allies. They don't even belong to any societies."

"Like the Atlas Society."

Brontë shot Velocity an indecipherable look. Anger? Fear? "If my mother had Theo, she'd have Adder and Wolf. And in that case, Adder sending that message made no sense. But if Anja and Torres took Theo, they would have to go through Adder first."

"And maybe that's how they knew to use Adder to lure you in?"

Brontë exhaled wearily. "Or Theo told them. But if they're running the coup, they need Theo dead. They'd have no reason to keep him alive."

"Why can't it be your mother using Adder to lure you in? Here she is, after all," Velocity pointed out, "running the coup."

"She's here. That doesn't mean she's behind the takeover. And she wouldn't have sent that message. She'd already sent me off to hide. Why send a message telling me to run and hide, when I was already hiding? Especially *that* message?"

Velocity admitted this line of reasoning seemed sound. She thought what Rida had said, how Torres had brought only twelve Security officers and two staff members off the ship. Could one of those be Theo? Much more likely Theo was among the 150-plus people Isra had arranged exit permits for. And…if Isra had Theo, did she also have Anja? Was that why Torres had lured Brontë here, to swap her for Anja?

If Torres had lured Brontë here at all. Velocity shook her head. She needed more data. "Go get some sleep," she ordered Brontë. "We'll talk more when you're rested."

Brontë left at a speed that revealed how much she still had to hide. Velocity finished the last of the wine and then sent a post to Rida, instructing him to run further research on Theo, Anja, Torres, and Isra Ikeda Lopaka. After a second, she added both David Ikeda Ito and the Atlas Society to that list. Then she went down ship to wake the dagan.

Chapter 18

KRC Mining at Hayek Point, Republic Space
(Seven Months Earlier)

She and Sabra were the diversion. Gripping her upper arm, Sabra marched her out of the shadows straight for the main body of IVC Security formed up in a thick square around Isra. Brontë wasn't entirely at ease with this plan, but she could follow Sabra's logic—that a main aim of this invasion was almost certainly to collect her, and that if she showed up, she'd capture everyone's attention. This ploy would give Adder and Wolf time to get Theo aboard the *Hegre*. Also, her mother was far less likely to shoot her than anyone else in their party. So she didn't object.

As a diversion, it worked well, though not precisely for the reason Sabra intended. As Sabra hauled her forward, the alarms cut off abruptly. In the immense silence afterwards, her boots and Sabra's boots clattered loud on the metal deck. The Security swung toward them, their eyes and the heavy muzzles of the Lopaka HJ19 plasma rifles dark in the dark light. Between the speed at which Sabra moved, the panic swamping her, and the thin air on this level, Brontë grew shorter of breath at every step. Her muscles went boggy; her head filled with a buzzing mist. Someone shouted, but the rush of blood in her ears was so loud she couldn't focus on their words. The shouting increased; people rushed at them. Sabra jerked her to a stop and just like that she was falling. She tumbled toward the deck, pain knife-sharp her throat and chest, waiting for plasma fire, waiting to die.

Instead, when her vision cleared, IVC Security officers in their deep black suits jostled around them, the masks of their armored helmets lowered, the HJ19s no longer pointed at her at least, but still ready in their fists. Sabra, kneeling, had pulled Brontë up into her arms, and had curved herself forward, making her body a shield as best she could. Someone was snapping orders. After a fraction of a second, Brontë recognized the voice. Her mother emerged from the ranks of the Security. She stared down at Sabra and Brontë, shut her eyes briefly, and then went to her knees beside them.

"Little Mach," she said, cupping Brontë's cheek. "Are you injured? Is she hurt?"

Sabra, not relaxing, shook her head. "It's the environmentals. KRC has their pressure and mix set too low."

Isra muttered under her breath, and shouted, "Medic!"

IVC Security medics swarmed up, driving the crowd around her back, dragging her from Sabra's arms. They strapped her into a combat doctor, closed its environmental hood, and slapped patches on her. New patches were added as the doctor returned data. While the medics talked about her instead of to her, the patches fed their medication into her blood, loosening both her lungs and her mind. The world went lucid and surreal. Time turned eternal; she lost any concern about anything. Past the polarized hood of the doctor, Isra's face loomed among the medics. Brontë watched with no interest at all as her mother turned aside to ask something of the medic in charge. "Better," the medics said, her voice muffled. Plump and light-skinned, she had a bright red caduceus tattooed on her temple, just by her right ear. "O2 sat is up to 94."

Her mother put her hand on the hood, as if she wanted to touch Brontë's face again, and this was as close as she could get to that. "Think you can join us, Mach?" she asked, speaking loudly to reach through the doctor.

Brontë thought through this sentence, one word at a time. Each word made sense, each word was lovely. One corner of her mouth turned down, her mother straightened, said something to the medic, and went off somewhere. Sabra appeared beside the medic. The muscles were tight around her eyes and mouth. Brontë tried to ask why Sabra was worried. But the medication from the patches infused her, warm and heavy, and she slid down sweetly into sleep.

⅞ ⼗ ⅔ ⅖

When she woke again, she wore a portable doctor with a mini environmental mask strapped over her mouth and nose. She was lying on her back on a padded bench in a ship's stateroom. No ship she recognized. A short distance away at a polished cherrywood conference table, Sabra and her mother sat talking. "—property there," her mother was saying. "You'll be safer there than anywhere."

Brontë pulled off the mask. "Mama?"

Her mother's eyes tightened. Getting up, she came to the bench. "Little Mach. How's your breathing? Better?"

"Where is this?" Brontë looked around. "What ship is this?"

Her mother helped her sit up. "Everything's going to be fine."

Pulling away, Brontë got to her feet. She was still wobbly from the drugs, and moved slowly to hide that. Her heart beating hard, she turned to stare at Isra.

Later, on the ship traveling out to Branden Hub, she would think that it was at this moment, facing her mother in the conference room, that she drew the line between them—this was the moment she classed Isra as her adversary. "This is an armed cruiser," Brontë said. "Is it yours?"

Eyes narrowed, Isra was watching her speculatively. "It's a courier. Registered with one of our subsidiaries. It's been loaned to us. Its captain and crew are charged with getting you to safety."

"An armed courier. Are you running the coup?"

"Captain Anador will escort you out to Durbin. We have an estate there, and an agency with a regiment of Security at its disposal."

"Are you running this coup?"

"It's not a coup," Isra said. Brontë, unable to help herself, made a rude noise. "We are not the government, or the state. Taking over our mechanism of leadership is not a coup. Imprecise language leads to imprecise thinking."

"You're here with an armed cruiser." Brontë was not able to keep her voice steady. "An armed cruiser and four squads of Combat Security, less than ten hours after, after—" She shut her eyes. Behind them, Tully slammed to the deck, eyes wide with shock, the plasma burn boiling up out of her belly. "Where's Theo?"

Isra turned to open the locker above the bench. Taking out a bottle of soju, she moved to a different locker, one filled with stacks of boneware and crystal. Isra selected a crystal bowl. "I've made funds available for you to draw on while you're on Durbin. They're linked to your tag. Keep your head down. Captain Anador will keep you safe until I can get this sorted."

Brontë opened her eyes. She still felt dizzy. The medication, she tried to tell herself. But she was finding it hard to focus on her mother. "You didn't answer me."

"As to who is running this hostile takeover," Isra said, spacing the final two words evenly, "my Security is still in the process of investigating that."

Brontë stared at her.

"As to why I am here..." Isra handed Sabra the bottle and the bowl. Unsealing the cork, Sabra poured the bowl half full. Isra took it and swirled the soju ritually. "I am here because those of us in the Atlas Society put together data that led us to believe this takeover was coming sooner than we expected."

Brontë folded her arms across her chest. She couldn't remember exactly which the Atlas Society was, an association or an advisory group. There were so many societies, and her mother was a member of so many of them. "What does the Atlas Society have to do with this?"

"At the Atlas Society," Isra said, sitting down at the table, "we consider long-term consequences of present-day actions."

"Whatever that means," Brontë muttered, though she understood what it meant exactly. Swiveling out the stool across from Isra, she sat down too. Her muscles were quivering. Sabra pushed a bowl her way—this one filled with tea. Cupping it with both hands, Brontë drank. Hot and sweet, the tea made her feel better, at least a little. "Why am I like this?" she demanded.

Isra blinked. "Ah—what?"

"You gave me all those upgrades, why do I get pressure sickness?"

"Oh. It was a trade-off." Her mother waved a hand, as if dismissing the point.

"*What* was?" Brontë demanded.

Isra twitched one corner of her mouth impatiently, and then said, "You understand how genetics works, yes? If we give you one trait, we might not be able to give you another. The ability to tolerate low pressure rests on only a few genes. Selecting for those is not a high priority in g-sets of your status. How often will you be in a low-pressure environment?"

Brontë rubbed the pain behind her eyes, too harried and distracted to ferret out the flaws in this argument. "What does the Atlas Society have to do with the coup?"

"Don't call it a coup," Isra said again, more sharply this time. She tapped the rim of her bowl, and Sabra got up to fetch the soju bottle. Isra watched, her eyes narrowed broodingly. "The Combines saved humanity. That's no hyperbole. After the Devastations, humanity wasn't just at risk of sinking into stone-age barbarity. We were at risk of extinction. The national governments—even those few still functioning—had no resources, no power. It was the Combines that created the early arcologies, the domed cities, the filter technologies needed for infected air and water."

"I've had Republic History," Brontë said.

"We created the Republic. Before us, humanity was ruled by literally tens of thousands of governments. Attempting to mediate between these governments, these tribal regimes, led to one war after another—led directly to the Devastations. The Compact we created, which created the Republic, has given us the peace and stability of the past fifteen centuries."

"This is peace?" Brontë said. "How many of my cousins died in this coup?"

"Do you remember one evening when you and I discussed the Pirians?" This was not a direction Brontë was expecting the conversation to take. She frowned at her mother. "The Pirians and their use of genetic engineering," Isra explained. "Specifically, why it might be necessary for the Pirians to employ genetic engineering to a greater extent than we have, traditionally, in the Republic."

"What does this have to do with the coup?"

"The Combine Houses are a relatively closed system. For the first millennium of their existence, they were essentially an entirely closed system. We intermarried within and between the Houses, but we never married outside the Houses. People sometimes left, but we almost never took new citizens—or new genetic material—into the Houses overall. You've had three years of genetics seminars, plus extra tutoring from Sabra. What would that do to a genetic bank?"

Brontë licked her lips. It wasn't a difficult question—she could have answered it halfway through her first seminar. "Our bank is too small. Just like the Pirians'."

"Worse than the Pirians'. They took nearly ten thousand people with them, and at least a third of those were from Africa, which had a very diverse genetic bank. Also, unlike the Combine Houses, the Pirians seem to practice habitual exogamy—it's easier to marry into one of their ships than to get a job scrubbing floors at Ikeda House. And as near as I can tell they also adopt every stray child they find running about on a dock. Meanwhile, the first citizens in the Combines came either from Japan, or from very specific, homogeneous populations in New Zealand and Australia. All these groups had relatively limited genetic diversity, and we had less than six thousand people in all eight of the first Combines. What happened next?"

"Genetic drift. Loss of genetic material. Insufficient diversity. Less genetic resilience."

Isra nodded. "About five hundred years ago, the Atlas Society—"

"*Five hundred years* ago?" Brontë couldn't help interrupting.

"—the Atlas Society became convinced the Houses would not solve this problem on their own initiative—by exogamy, for instance, or by adoption of promising new citizens, or in any other way. At that point, we began advising the Science Boards of our Houses to begin editing the germlines of select bonded labor candidates." She nodded at Sabra. "This was proposed as an experiment. If these bonded labor candidates proved successful, we argued, we could edit their genetic material into germlines of our own citizens—into citizens of our Houses. Not all the Houses agreed to follow our advice. Adding bonded labor genetic material to our own children, even material that had been engineered, was too much for many of us. Even those who agreed insisted on certain sureties, including that no House citizen with such genetic material would be kept in the line to inherit a Board Seat."

Brontë found she was gripping her empty tea bowl. Isra watched her steadily. Brontë drew a shaky breath, and then another. "Is that why you're not in the line?" she asked. "Are you, did your parents—you're gengineered?" She drew another breath and asked at once, "Am *I* genetically engineered? But I can't be. I'm in the line to inherit. If I'm in the line to inherit—and you can't have done it anyway. It's proscribed. You can't engineer the germline. Not on human gene sets. It's a capital offense."

"Those Houses that adopted our policy have seen some good effects," Isra said. "But keeping the new genetic material from the lines of inheritance has limited the extent to which we have been able to integrate that material into the Houses. It has also limited our influence."

Brontë watched her mother's dark unreadable eyes. Isra had not answered her earlier question about Theo. That could not be accidental. Brontë swallowed, and said, "If you're not behind this coup, who is?"

Isra got to her feet. "You break in half an hour," she told Sabra. "Have her secured."

Chapter 19

Franklin Station, Freiheit, Republic Space

T he entrance to Theo's suite had its own separate koban, staffed with Dr. Ikeda's own dedicated Security, a full squad, twenty-four of them, all from the same Ikhen set. They were at different stages of maturation, ranging from cadets to a brace of Captains in their thirties. Adder's attempts to cozy up to the cadets had come to nothing. They wouldn't even admit to individual names, all going by their set-name, Ikhen54.

This morning, Adder submitted to being searched by an Ikhen28, before being escorted into the suite by one of the cadets. Theo was in the study, seated at the worktable reading something on his port. "Thank you," he told the Ikhen54. "That will be all."

The Ikhen saluted and returned to her station. Theo kept Adder waiting while he finished reading whatever file was on his port. Then he pointed at the bench across from him. "Report."

Adder settled onto the bench. Ever since Torres Ikeda had arrived on the station, Dr. Ikeda had kept Theo restricted to the habitat, and mostly to this suite. Though Adder was still, technically, under contract to Brontë—or at least she assumed she was, since no one had told her differently—Theo had corralled her into working for him until Brontë returned. Right now he had her running intelligence. The rumor was that Torres Ikeda Alonzo had come off-ship alone—Anja

Ikeda Nowak had not been with her. Theo wanted to know if Anja was dead. If she was dead, he wanted her death confirmed. If she was still on the ship, he wanted to know who was with her.

Adder knew Dr. Ikeda had her own intelligence working those questions. She almost mentioned that to Theo, before realizing he obviously knew it, and then further realizing, with a jolt, that she was Theo's check on Dr. Ikeda. This was so alarming—that an unsupported cadet could be the only resource available to the heir to the Primary Seat—that she said nothing.

That morning, she had little to report. She had spent most of the previous day wandering the market on Level Twelve, which was the closest market to the block Torres had rented on Level Fourteen. On the concourse, Adder had bought a bowl of pork rib tea at a stall and sat on a bench against the market wall to eat it.She wore her off-duty gear, grey canvas trousers, slippers, and a much-mended dull-green kurta. She knew from experience that a kid her age was invisible, dressed like this.

After not too long, she spotted the cook from Torres's kitchen, accompanied by her usual kitchen girl, and followed them for a while, keeping close enough to eavesdrop, but far enough away not to draw attention. She hadn't learned anything new—they had mentioned Torres, but not Anja; they had mentioned one new name, which Adder didn't recognize, but which when she ran a search came up as a probable Nowak House Security officer.

Theo listened to her report, but she could tell his attention was elsewhere. He was simmering with edgy energy, and as soon as she finished, he told her he wanted her in-House today. Dr. Ikeda was meeting with someone. "They claim they're holding a hostage," Theo said. "They claim it's an heir to the Primary Seat, high in the line. Find out who they are, and who the heir is."

"Do you think it's Brontë?" Adder couldn't help asking. She hadn't heard from Captain Anador or Brontë since the mining station. She hadn't seen Wolf since then either. One reason she had agreed to work for Theo was he said he would try to find out where the Captain and Wolf were.

"That's what you'll find out." He dismissed her with his customary wave.

Later, dawdling over the tea and cake she had wheedled out of the cook while eavesdropping on House gossip—kitchens were always the best place to tap into the banks of House gossip—it occurred to her that Theo's information almost certainly hadn't come from Dr. Ikeda. And clearly it had not come from her. This was good news, she realized. This meant he had other people working for him. That meant his base of operations was broader than he'd revealed to her. The situation might not be as hopeless as she had estimated.

After the cook chased her out, she went back out to Level Twelve for a while, then returned to the House to loiter in the barracks common room. Near tea time, she returned to Theo's quarters. For once, he did not keep her waiting. Impatient to hear what she had learned, he shut down his port at once. "Well?"

"Dr. Ikeda met with a ship's captain, Velocity Wrachant. Mid-thirties, with a Combine accent. Her ship is the *Susan Calvin*. It came into dock just over twelve hours ago. Nina, she works in the kitchen, says this Wrachant is tall, with dark hair, a big nose, and big ears. Says she claims to have Elena. Brontë," she added, as if Theo wouldn't know who Elena was.

Theo's eyes tightened. He said nothing, clearly thinking hard.

Adder continued: "Nina says Dr. Ikeda spoke to the hostage via a sync to the ship. The hostage has the wrong color hair—Nina says it's red—but otherwise the description fits Brontë."

Theo grunted. "Hair is easy to change. Did Isra seem convinced?"

"Nina wasn't sure." Adder shifted on the bench, sitting straighter. "I went out to Level Twelve again. I didn't hear anything about Torres and Wrachant. But I'm only one set of ears."

"Nina," Theo said. "This kitchen girl. Worth recruiting?"

"She's sharp," Adder conceded. "I don't know about her loyalty.

She's a little too free with her tongue and her favors."

Theo sat back, his eyes focusing into the distance. "Recruit her. See if she can get closer to Torres than you have. You look to this Captain Wrachant. Find out what you can about her. Confirm that she has Brontë."

"Yes, sir." Adder got to her feet. "Sir. About Wolf. And Captain Anador. Did you..."

Theo didn't look up from his port. "Get it done, cadet."

ᛉ ᛏᚱ ᛪ ᛦ

Velocity made her way through the market on Concourse D, her scarf tucked loose around her face, watching the sparse crowd. All the years out in the Drift, she had forgotten what life was like in the Core—how everyone moved with leisure, and spoke so quietly; how no one met anyone's eyes. Even here in the market, when people bought fruit or fish from a shop, they only looked at what they bought; they didn't look at the merchant. And no shouting, no beggars, no thieves. Or, well, no poor thieves, hungry enough to steal from market stalls.

She strolled the concourse, pretending to browse this wealth her ship's Exchange could not produce—bananas, pineapple, luscious ripe cherries, potatoes, fresh cream, bins of cane sugar, bakeries fragrant with racks of tender bean cakes, shimmering tarts, great puffy loaves and crusty baguettes. She bought a box of bagels, mainly as camouflage. Though her crew would love them, she wasn't here to shop. Concourse D, and especially this end of Concourse D, was the prime location for the job she needed to do.

And here, past the fruit sellers, scattered among the bakeries, were several tea stalls, one with tiny round tables set out in the plaza before it. Velocity settled her purchases on a chair at one of these tables and herself into another chair. Almost at once a bonded labor child showed up to offer a handheld menu. Velocity waved the menu away, ordering a pot of white tea and salt biscuits.

All around her, besides bakeries and tea shops, were spice shops and wine shops. This end of the market smelled wonderful. But nowhere were any of the musicians that would have filled the concourse on any Drift station; no children dancing or juggling colored cubes or hawking handmade flowers; no artists offering instant tattoos or to draw your icon, two different poses, one low price, you keep the file! When she had first arrived out in the Drift, on the Free Trade stations, Velocity had been rattled by the racket and clatter of the buskers who made such a snarl of every marketplace. Now she couldn't help thinking how dull this market seemed without them.

The tea shop child showed up with the pot of tea and plate of biscuits. Velocity paid him, and settled in, to all appearances enjoying the tea while she watched the market. But in fact, she had toggled open her inskull uplink. According to station schematics, this tea shop was located directly under the level held by Ikeda House: almost precisely under the garden where she had met with Isra Ikeda. Now, merging this ferret to the ferret Tai had set loose in the Ikeda House system, she ghosted into Isra Ikeda's data bank and began a download of all files stored or updated in the past ten months. She also ran a search of the Ikeda House security feeds, using the image capture she had made of the bonded labor child, Nina. Besides this, she made an attempt to capture data from the insect drones. As she had expected, she was too far away to access most of the drones, which only had a range of a few thousand meters. She collected data from those she could reach, meanwhile continuing the hunt via the House feeds for Nina, whom she found, finally, in the Ikeda House kitchens, cleaning some sort of bulky brown root vegetable and chattering to the cook.

Keeping the data from the feeds open in one window, and the data from the insect drones open in another, she chose a wood tick which her schematics showed her was near the kitchens, and began guiding the beetle to the child. Since this was a skill common to the games she and her crew played during long voyages, Velocity had some practice in the tactic. Nevertheless, managing multiple windows and keeping the necessary situational awareness of her surroundings, here in the market, left her somewhat queasy.

Though that might have been side effects from the Pirian netbot. Inserting her forefinger into her left ear, Velocity rubbed the itchy bump which was all that was left of the nanobot.

In time, she had the beetle latched on the bonded child's trousers. Its chameleon circuit immediately began turning it the same red as the silk cloth. Slicing out the string of numbers which was the NPM for that beetle, Velocity set up an alarm which would tell her when Nina crossed the Ikeda House shieldwalls. Then she shut that window, saved all the data she had collected to her temp bank, and set it streaming back to the *Susan Calvin*.

That done, she finished her tea and started back to the ship, detouring to visit the costermongers down the concourse. Their bins were heaped with multicolored fruits and vegetables, some of them grown on Freiheit, some here in the station Exchange. Circling among the ripe figs and oranges, the carnelian pomegranates and golden papayas, Velocity selected and bought ten small bright oranges and was negotiating over a pound of dark cherries when a spear of pain drove through her temple. Unable to keep from it, she hissed in pain, almost dropping the oranges. Someone had sent her a high alert post, triggering the physiological reaction. She shut her eyes: two posts flashed scarlet at the edge of her eye. She flicked open the one from Rida first, then caught her breath and opened the one from Tai.

$$\text{\textreferencemark} \; \text{\textdagger} \; \text{\textnumero} \; \text{\textsection}$$

Back at the *Calvin*, she hauled the umbilical hatch shut behind her and scrambled up the ladder two rungs at time, though moving at that rate in this gravity hurt her hands and her knee joints, and made her heart pound hard. She hurled herself through the hatch into Command. "Report. What do we know?"

"Shit. Shit and shitsticks." Tai had Rida's post, the same one she had received, up on the board: *Captain, they're coming, I—* "I've posted him, six times, he doesn't answer."

"Nothing from Sabra?"

He shook his head. His eyes were wide, his skin flushed dark. "I pinged Gupta. She doesn't answer either."

Closing her fists on the back of his saddle, Velocity breathed deeply, centering herself.

"My mother took them." Brontë stood on the ladder, framed in the hatch, her expression miserable. "Hostages, probably. Maybe to interrogate."

"*Is* this Isra Ikeda?" Velocity asked Tai.

"Who else would it be?" Tai demanded. Then he shook his head. "We don't have evidence, if that's what you're asking. It could be Station Security. Or Torres, for that matter."

"It's my mother," Brontë said. "You should trade me to her. I'm what she wants."

"What about the Pirian netbots?" Through her uplink, Velocity sent an order to the dagan, *Wake up. Raise Rida through the netbots.*

"I tried that. They're not active yet." Tai tapped up another feed— the data on the Pirian bot network, which showed an activation bar, currently at 68%.

Even once the bot network is active, the dagan said through her uplink, *there remains the problem of getting through the shieldwall. I've got a tunnel into Ikeda House at the moment, but it's only a matter of time before their wardens detect my invasion and shift protocols.*

Velocity knew he was right. Rida had programs that did nothing but hunt for tunnels in their shieldwalls; it was an elementary precaution. Anyone who had a data bank of any size or value had such programs. *But you can be ready to worm through again*, she argued.

I can. I will. It may be more difficult the second time. Our focus now is Rida and Sabra. And I don't believe Isra Ikeda has taken them. Attend.

The wallboard to Tai's port came to life. A capture from a surveillance feed popped up and began running, and then next to it another, and then a third and a fourth. These all showed a corridor from different angles. *This is the service corridor behind the dining establishment leased to Maja Gupta,* the dagan informed her.

In one capture after the next, a half squad of Combine Security officers surged through, six from each direction, converging onto and then vanishing through a pair of access hatches set in about ten meters apart in the corridor's deck. Nothing for several minutes, and then the Security emerged, dragging with them first an unconscious Sabra and then Rida, his eyes and mouth open wide, and his hands restrained behind him. Tai cursed softly.

The Security rushed the pair of them down the service corridor. The dagan brought up another feed, this one by a cargo lift. This showed both Rida and Sabra being loaded into the lift, with six of the Security crowding after them. The dagan froze the capture at this point, centered it on the lieutenant in the squad.

"Lieutenant Zhang." Brontë said from the com hatch. Velocity wheeled. The child was pale, her jaw set with determination. "Ayu Zhang," Brontë said. "Torres has her contract. Zhang is Torres Ikeda's dedicated Security."

She is correct. The dagan brought up an image on the wallboard, of Torres Ikeda Alonzo surrounded by Combine Security officers in dark uniforms. The lieutenant from the capture stood just to the left of Torres. *Further, just after this point*—it started the capture running again, Rida and Sabra in the lift as the lift doors closed—*they pass into restricted space. That space is leased to Torres Ikeda Alonzo.*

"Torres' Security took them," Velocity confirmed. "And they took them into the block Torres rented."

"You should still trade me," Brontë said. "Torres will want me."

"Go to your cabin," Velocity ordered. "Stay there."

"They took them to get to me."

"That was an order. Move." Velocity studied the wallboard. What would Torres want with Rida? Or maybe she just wanted Sabra. Maybe Rida was collateral damage. If Ikeda House was anything like Taveri House, Torres and Anja might well have known the young heirs to the Primary Seat, and their Security teams as well. *What about their tags?* she asked the dagan. *Rida and Sabra's tags? Their handhelds? Can you access those?*

The dagan's reply was immediate—both handhelds were in the crawlspace under Gupta's service corridor. Both devices were still active, unlike the tags, which were showing as cleared, Rida's thirty-six minutes and twenty seconds ago, Sabra's forty-two seconds before that.

"Breach the Ikeda Alonzo shieldwall," Velocity told the dagan, speaking out loud for Tai's sake. "I want them located, and I want real-time captures."

Yes, Captain, the dagan said.

"Meanwhile, I'll brace Gupta. Someone told the Security Rida and Sabra would be there. And I'll download the data from the rest of the bug drones, while we still have access. You stay here," she ordered Tai. "Work with the dagan."

"Captain!" Tai spun on the saddle, distressed. "What makes you think they won't take you too?"

"I'll be back before end of watch."

𐰴   𐰦   𐰚   𐰺

Rida paced the room, trying not to panic. He couldn't stop shivering. The Captain wouldn't leave him here, he told himself. Tai wouldn't. Anyway, no one had hurt him. Much. Yet. He dug his finger in his ear, pressing down on the welt the netbot had left, and subvocced: *Tai? Captain?*

Nothing. He wrapped his arms around his ribs, shivering even harder. Sabra had fought them. That had been his first indication that something was wrong—Sabra making a sharp sound, deep in her chest, and moving so swiftly, moving like something made of liquid, launching herself straight at the Security coming through the crawlspace. So many Security—swarms of them. Too many to count, but for a minute it had seemed Sabra would defeat them, fighting so fluidly, so perfectly, one against their multitudes in that narrow space.

Rida had fallen back, further into the crawlspace, away from the condenser he'd been replacing. He had just pulled his handheld from his pocket to send a mayday to the Captain when, from behind, the second horde of Security surged up on him, knocking the handheld from his grip. When he shouted, trying to warn Sabra, they had punched him, in the chest and in the neck, putting him on his knees. That had been the only time they'd hit him. So far.

Sabra had been hurt worse. He'd seen her as the Security officers hauled them up ladders and through service corridors, to lock them up here, wherever this was. Sabra had been bruised and dazed, bleeding from the nose and mouth. In the lift, when Rida asked if she was all right, she didn't seem to hear him.

The Security had taken him and Sabra to Level Fourteen. That told him this was Torres, or Torres and Anja. Here, they had locked him in a bonded labor cabin: two bunks bolted to one wall, no wallboard or port, dull grey anti-rust/fungicide paint on the bare walls and deck plate. No ventilation except the tiny slit vents alongside the lights in the overhead. No sound except the pounding of his heart in his ears. Unable to keep from it, he pushed down on the swollen spot in his ear again, subvoccing: *Tai?* **Tai?**

But once again, nothing. *You'll be fine*, he promised himself. *The Captain won't let anything happen to you. Tai won't. You **know** they won't.*

It was hard to keep himself steady. Even though his memories of his early years had worn to bare wisps, fragments and echoes, he could not stop thinking of his indenture—how his parents had told him everything would be splendid at the school, how his mother had dressed him in a new suit, stiff new trousers, his first real shoes, and a deep red achkan with bright brass buttons. Though he could not remember her face now, or his father's face, he remembered still how she had fought not to cry as she buttoned him into that jacket.

Up on the station, Guo House had taken away his new clothing at once, and taken the data tag his father had given him, with its pitiful scraped-together bit of funds. They had dumped him in the barracks with forty other boys, some even younger than he was, but most much older, some so old they had seemed adults to him—sixteen and seventeen year olds.

While Guo House had given him, over the years he had lived there, the education they had promised his parents he would receive, teaching him Public French, deportment, mathematics and mechanics and how to pack code, the greater part of his education had taken place in that barrack. At first, he had sent post after post to his parents, telling them what was happening to him every night, begging them to come save him. He'd never gotten a reply. Eventually, he quit sending the posts. Eventually, he was big enough to fight back. Eventually, he met Tai, who took him to meet the Captain.

Folding his arms around his head now, he fought to breathe, to stop shivering. This wasn't Guo House. He wasn't five years old. The Captain would not leave him here. She would not abandon him. She would never do that.

When the hatch lock rasped and turned, every muscle in him jumped. Two Security officers stood in the corridor. The Lieutenant who had opened the hatch regarded him, her light eyes level and sober. "Will you give us trouble, jess?"

Rida hitched in his breath and shook his head. The lieutenant stepped back, indicating with her chin the direction he should move. Rida went that way, and they flanked him. His muscles felt light and uncertain. He concentrated on walking. They didn't go far—just through a connecting hatch into a corridor, and down that to a storage compartment, empty of anything except a small bench. Standing near this bench, reading something on a handheld, was Torres Ikeda Alonzo. From the captures he had watched, Rida recognized her square body and her choppy way of moving, even before she turned toward him and he saw her face. "Mr. Tdemir," she said. "Please. Sit."

Fighting to think, Rida did not move. Torres nodded at the Lieutenant, who pushed the bench into the center of the room. Rida sat down. It was a low bench, maybe twenty centimeters high. With all three of them standing around him, it felt even lower.

"Mr. Tdemir," Torres said. "Do you know what a smart room is?" Rida nodded, his head down. "Answer me verbally, please."

"I do. Yes."

"Excellent. Then you won't try to lie to us." She strolled over toward the far wall, which he now noticed held a slap-up wallboard. Torres pointed her handheld at it, tapping her thumb against the handheld's screen. A capture appeared: the commercial docking slips here on Franklin Station. A pan, and then a sharp focus. Gate 11. That was the gate to their slip, to the umbilical that led to the *Susan Calvin*. Rida knew what was coming, but Torres rocked on her heels, letting it play out. First the Captain emerged, then Sabra, and then he himself.

"We know your ship's provenance. We know that your allegiance is not to Isra Ikeda Lopaka." The capture switched feeds; he and Sabra were standing outside a lift, waiting to ride out to Gupta's level. Torres paused the capture, and zoomed in on Sabra's face. "Given that you are working with this Security officer, we know Elena Ikeda Verde is almost certainly on your ship."

She paused here, waiting for him to speak. But interrogations were part of the disciplinary program at Guo House, as well as a favorite form of breaking what little social cohesion formed in the dorms. He had learned very young not to fall for that one.

Torres switched feeds again, showing the Captain entering a lift. It was the small private lift, the one she needed the code from Ikeda House to use. "Your bond holder," she said. "Dealing with Isra Ikeda. Has she made you aware that Isra Ikeda does not hold any true power in Ikeda House?"

Rida watched the Captain enter the lift, which closed behind her. It occurred to him that Torres had not yet said Captain Wrachant's name, or Sabra's either. Was that a tactic? Or did she actually not know who they were?

"Has she told you that Isra Ikeda murdered children and innocent bystanders in her attempt to take the Primary Seat for her puppet— that little brat on your ship?" Torres clenched her fist around her handheld and came over to him. "She murdered my wife, on our own ship. In our bedroom. Has your bond holder told you that?"

"The Captain doesn't hold my bond," Rida said. "The crew on the *Susan Calvin* serve port-to-port. We're shareholders, and we can buy out whenever we want."

Torres looked down at him. Rida kept his head lowered. His heart was still thumping, but he couldn't deny it—the answer had made him feel better. *Careful*, he told himself. *You've got no power here.* After a long moment, she settled to her heels, forcing him to meet her eyes. "I was in the gym. Anja liked to get her exercise in the afternoon. I've always liked mornings. I took a little longer that morning because my coach wasn't happy with my wrist rotation." She shook her head, shaking this off. "The suite, when I entered the suite, I thought—the smell—I thought..." She shook her head again. Her eyes were open, but she wasn't seeing Rida. "Anja never was much of a cook. I thought, *whatever she's burned this time, that's a new low.*"

The compartment was silent around them. Behind him, neither of the Security officers seemed even to be breathing.

Torres swallowed audibly in this silence. Then she focused on Rida again. "In our bed. She didn't even have time to call for help. Do you want an alliance with someone who would do that?"

Rida drew a careful breath. "If you want an alliance with us, kas," he said, "this is a strange way to go about it."

A muscle flinched beside Torres' eye. She stood abruptly, turning her back. "I should walk up to your ship and knock on the door instead? Trust people who are dealing with the woman who murdered half my family?"

"No, you should assault me and...my friend and take us hostage.

That will get my Captain on your side."

Torres kept her back to him. "You are in violation of your indenture with Guo-Innis Combine, Mr. Tdemir. Guo-Innis has an agency right here on this station. They'd be happy to come collect you. Probably they'd even offer a small premium, as a reward for my trouble."

"Are you trying to make a deal with me or threaten me?" Rida said. "You're really bad at this, if you don't mind a little constructive criticism."

Torres wheeled. Her dark eyes flickered, and Rida realized abruptly that this was someone whose grip on sanity was not strong. *Oh*, he thought. *Oh, help.*

"Lieutenant," Torres said, through set teeth.

One of the Security officers behind Rida stepped forward. "We need the codes to access your ship's data banks," she said. "We need names for everyone on your ship, along with their personal access codes. We need you to agree to speak to your Captain, and persuade her to surrender Elena Ikeda Verde to us, in exchange for you." The Lieutenant paused, expectantly.

Rida stared at her. Then he shook his head. "I'll speak to my Captain, of course." He fought the impulse to look at Torres. "I won't do any of the rest of that."

The Lieutenant looked past him, at her fellow Security. Then she gave him a sad smile. "We're not just asking, sweetheart."

Rida felt his muscles ratchet tight. Almost involuntarily he tried to stand, and the Security behind him shoved him back down onto the bench. The Lieutenant took a medical kit from her pocket. Extracting a patch from it, she peeled it from its backing and stuck it to his neck. "You're a lucky boy," she said. "We're trying the nice way first."

𝌀 ✝ 𝍖 𝍦

Momo's, bright with music and light sculptures, was packed full.

Scowling at the crowds around its front bay, drinking and talking in shouts while they waited to be seated, Velocity started for the service corridor, meaning to take that around to the kitchen hatch. But while she was still working her way through the spindrift on the edge of the crowd, the alert she had set on Nina's drone chirped in her skull.

She paused, and then ducked into the service corridor, quieter and less crowded than the concourse. Getting her back to the wall, she enlarged her uplink screen and opened the file to the drone's feed. Nina had, indeed, crossed out of Ikeda House. The child was riding a lift somewhere. The drone feed only had a limited scope on its view feed, and with the beetle fixed to the child's trousers, that scope didn't include the lift controls. She also couldn't see what Nina was carrying. A box? A bundle? Baring her teeth in frustration, she attempted to find the child via the security feeds in the lifts available to Ikeda House. But Ikeda House boasted more than thirty lifts; with three feeds per lift, she was still running the search when the lift doors opened.

Swearing under her breath, Velocity shut down the search, and focused on the data from the drone: a bright plaza, a kiosk selling flowers, a shop selling fruit (Nina moved out of the lift at a brisk pace), another shop selling both flowers and vegetables, a tea shop—Velocity stood straight, adrenaline spiking hot through her blood. She knew that place: the tea shop where she'd had the salt biscuits. It was five minutes from here. Two if she ran.

She didn't run, having no wish to alarm Station Security, but she did move briskly. She kept the drone feed open in a small window at the edge of her right eye, but her attention was on the concourse, watching for the tea shop, and for Nina. She found the shop quickly, and stood by its apron, scanning the sparse crowds browsing through the bakeries, fruit, and wine shops, hunting the bonded labor child.

"Looking for something?" Nina said from beside her.

Velocity controlled herself admirably and did not jump. "I am indeed. Someone to have tea with me. Interested?"

Nina grinned up at her. "Rather hot chocolate."

"Hot chocolate," Velocity said, struck with memory. She hadn't had hot chocolate since that trip to Earth.

Nina's grin widened. "Klara makes the best on the station," she said, and headed for the interior of the tea shop. Inside, Nina greeted and chatted with the woman in the galley. "The Captain will pay," the child said, waving at Velocity, before going to clamber into a booth. The woman, Klara, brought them a pot of hot chocolate and a basket of cakes, along with three pots of different sorts of jam. Nina poured the chocolate into little white boneware bowls. "Try it," she said. "Go on."

Velocity did. It was wonderful, she admitted—rich with cream, heavy with chocolate. "Amazing," she said.

Nina beamed, drank more of her own, and reached for a tea cake. Loading it up with black currant jam, she said, "You want information? Because that I can do, and I'm not even going to make you sweat, much, on the pricing. You want more than information, though." She nodded and ate the entire cake at one bite.

"Information," Velocity said, "and infiltration."

Nina chewed industriously. "Infiltrate. Do you mean them out on Fourteen?"

"Does Dr. Ikeda know Torres is living on Level Fourteen?" Velocity asked idly. Not idly enough, though—Nina's dark gaze sharpened. "Is that why all of you came here? Because Dr. Ikeda knew Torres was headed here?"

"Ha." Nina scrubbed her mouth with the back of her wrist, though the tea shop had supplied a perfectly good napkin. "Trying for free information, are you?"

Velocity spread her hands. "I need to know your soup is worth the bucket, mzala."

Nina thought this over while she ate another cake, this one spread with cherry jam. Then she said, "Not Torres exactly. Dr. Ikeda knew someone had an Ikeda-held ship, and that it was headed here. But she thought it was someone else."

"Who?"

Nina licked jam from her fingers and smiled beatifically. "Let's talk payment."

𝒵 ✝ 𝕏 𝔖

Out in the corridor behind Gupta's, two scrub boys sat on their heels, passing a bowl of fried dumplings back and forth. Neither spared Velocity a glance. In the kitchen itself, the harried cooks and their assistants paid her even less attention. Gupta was nowhere in sight. Velocity was trying to decide if she might bluff her way into the crawlspace—she needed the downloads from the bug drones still in Ikeda House a great deal more than she needed to twist Gupta's arm—when the bistro owner came out of the galley to scold the scrub boys back to work. Spotting Velocity, her already angry scowl became darker. "You've some face showing that high-born ass around here," Gupta said.

Against her will, Velocity's eyebrows shot up. "My what?"

Gupta snorted. "Rivkah!" she shouted. "Watch the till!" Jerking her chin at Velocity, Gupta stomped down the corridor. Velocity followed her past a storeroom hatch to another hatch, which led to what turned out to be Gupta's own cabin, back of her eatery. The cramped cubicle had probably been meant as an office. Now it held a worktable and a sofa that clearly doubled as a bunk, with another hatch standing open to show a very small facility—just an oubliette and the spigot above it. Everything was scrubbed and tidy, but Gupta, still scowling, banged shut the panel that covered the facility hatch anyway. She jerked her chin at the sofa. "Sit."

Velocity did not. "Who told you I was highborn?"

Gupta dropped onto the banquette behind the worktable. "You're just passing through. The rest of us live here. We have loans we're paying, deeds we signed, family we care about. You kick over the hive, you can kite off in your ship. Not us."

"That's a sad story. Who told you I was highborn?"

"You used me. You put my shop, and my family, at risk. You get what you deserve."

Velocity studied her. "That answers that." Scowling even darker, Gupta folded her arms over her chest. "Here's my second question: who did you sell us to?"

"Do I look like an idiot?" Gupta snarled. "I'll be loyal to you over my own blood? Like shit."

"No, you'll roll over like the dog you are. Which is what the Combines count on." Velocity shook her head. "I want the rest of the payment."

Gupta had started to argue the first point; this second shut her up. "You what?"

"Rida fixed your filthy environmental filter. Pay me the rest of what you owe me."

Gupta flushed. "First, your jess didn't fix shit. Second, he wasn't down there to fix shit, and you know it."

"I don't know anything like that. If you sold him out like the lying dog you are and kept him from doing the job he was there to do, that's your doing. We had a contract. Pay me, or I go to Station Security." Gupta stood, her lips skinned back from her teeth, and Velocity added, "Now. Dedicated funds. I don't want you canceling the payment when I walk out of here."

"Combine *viper*," Gupta spat. She stalked out. Left alone in the cabin, Velocity drew a long breath. Shutting her eyes, she opened her uplink, and reached out for the drones. Here, in this cabin, she was nearly as close to Ikeda House as she would have been in the crawlspace. It would be close enough—she hoped it would be close enough—to access all of the drones. And with any luck at all, Gupta would take long enough with the hard payment that she'd have time to complete the downloads. Time and more than time for luck to run their way, Velocity thought, waiting for the drone feeds to appear in her link.

𝕀 ✝ 𝕏 𝕊

Adder brought the bonded labor child, Nina, in through the service hatch—both entrances to Theo's suite were guarded, but during dayshift, the service hatch had just one Security officer. And Nina, who knew everyone in the habitat, knew this Security (Lewis) by name. She knew what certification he was studying for, and about the fellow Security officer he was hot for. "Ask him to join your slam-ball team," Nina advised. "Then when he gets his head broken you can carry him off to medical and confess your love while he's high on pain patches."

"What a good plan," Lewis said dryly. "Why are you here?"

Nina jerked her chin at the hatchway. "Kas Heir isn't eating. Cook sent me up to ask if maybe there's something he'd like better." When the Security glanced at Adder, Nina added, "It's the cadet's idea."

"All right," Lewis said, and even opened the hatch for them.

Theo was in the study, in the armchair with his feet braced on a foot stool, his data port open on his knees. Dr. Ikeda was speaking to him via a sync; he did not look up as the two of them entered. "The risk can't be higher than the risk of staying here," Theo said. He wore an earbud, so Adder couldn't hear what Dr. Ikeda said in return, but Theo shook his head. "I can't run the Combine by remote. Furthermore, I shouldn't. Making decisions without the rest of the Board to advise me makes me a despot, not a leader."

Another pause, and Theo shook his head even more decisively. "Your advice has been helpful. And I'm aware of your experience. But you're not on the Board. We should return." He shut down the port and yanked the bud from his ear. "Well?"

"Nina thinks she can get into Torres' block," Adder said, without preliminary. She herself had not been able to get closer than Torres's kitchen boy, who would let her buy him breakfast, but hadn't told her anything worth knowing yet. "She's also been approached by the ship captain, by that Captain Wrachant who has Brontë hostage."

Theo focused past Adder on Nina. "Approached. Toward what end?"

"Information," Nina said. "That's what she says. She wants to know who's in the House, and who Dr. Ikeda talks to. Like that. She says that's all she wants."

"You suspect otherwise."

Nina shrugged. "People never start with what they really want."

"Huh." Theo's eyes narrowed, in amusement Adder suspected, though he was always hard to read. "And did you agree to sell her this information?"

"I did." Nina smiled winsomely. "But I came right here to tell I'm doing it,"

"Also, you'll bring me any information you sell her before you give it to her. And you won't sell her anything without my approval."

Nina locked her hands behind her back. "Exactly."

Adder eyed Theo speculatively. But Nina, focused on her own duplicitousness, didn't seem to notice what he had just slipped past her. Satisfied, Theo leaned back in his chair. "Tell me how you plan to get past Torres' security protocols," he ordered.

Chapter 20

The *Singing Turtle*, in Transit to Branden Hub, Republic Space (Six Months Earlier)

The *Singing Turtle* was a courier ship—small, fast, used for getting documents and diplomats from one end of the Republic to the other at priority speed. As such, it had little cargo space, and only six passenger cabins. However, what living space it did have was luxurious, as were the few common areas. Brontë's mother had secured two staterooms for her and Sabra. The larger of these, housing Brontë, had a study separate from its sleeping cabin. The ship had both a gym and a large galley which doubled as a game room, with scheduled entertainments each Topwatch, at least when the ship wasn't running up to jump. Jumps were frequent, every thirty to fifty hours, given the high-speed schedule the courier kept.

However, Brontë had no time for games. Her mother had entrusted certain files from the Atlas Society to Sabra. These contained documentation on the genetic changes that Atlas Society members had implemented first on the germlines of certain bonded labor zygotes, and then on specific children born to House citizens. The file also contained reports tracking the progress of those created by Atlas Society genetic engineering. These files were extensive, complex, and filled with data beyond Brontë's education level. Some of the files, the ones dealing with bonded labor germlines, were hundreds of years old, and referenced historical and political situations Brontë knew nothing about. She kept having to stop reading to access the ship's bank, to read (sometimes briefly but more often deeply) in some area of history or science or math, or all three, and then return to the files for another run at the patch that had jammed her up.

Sabra had at first been reluctant to turn over the files. "Dr. Ikeda was very clear in her instructions. She wants you to have these files when you come of age. Not before."

"*Instructions*. Not orders. Who holds your contract, Captain?" Brontë had meant to speak flatly, without affect, but she heard the anger sharpening her voice. Sabra's lips tightened. Looking away, Brontë rubbed her wrist over her eyes. "Theo still hasn't answered my post. Neither has Adder or Wolf."

"Nor mine," Sabra agreed. "But that could mean many things. We've made five jumps since leaving KRC Mining. The replies might be stalled at any one of those relays. Or the IVC Board might have quarantined your cousin, to protect him. He may not be receiving posts from unauthorized sources."

"And Adder and Wolf have been quarantined as well?" Brontë demanded, and then shook her head. She knew as well as Sabra that in a crisis like this two Security cadets were even more likely to have their access limited than the heir to the Primary Seat was. Switching tactics, she said, "My mother took the scholar's exemption. She voluntarily removed herself from the line of inheritance."

"I'm aware of that."

"The Primary Seat Holder holds all the contracts in the house," Brontë said, though of course Sabra knew this also. "The Primary only leases bonded workers to others in the house." When Sabra frowned, Brontë continued, not giving her time to consider that point: "Theo may well be dead. That may be why we're not getting replies from him. In which case, I now hold the Primary Seat. Your contract is with Ikeda House. That means I hold your contract, and that means you follow my orders. Not my mother's orders."

"That's a long string of ifs," Sabra observed.

"The point is, whether I hold the Primary Seat or not, you don't follow my mother's orders. Even if Theo is still alive," Brontë paused, getting control over her voice, and continued, "even then, I outrank Isra Ikeda, a scholar nowhere in the line to inherit."

Sabra kept frowning. Brontë shut her burning eyes and let her think. The courier ship stank of industrial cleaner and the spices the cook was grilling for ship's dinner. That mix didn't help the headache that had been nagging her all morning. She knew her argument was slippery. The biggest hole was that she herself wasn't—yet—technically in the line to inherit, having never gone up for, much less passed, her preliminaries. Sabra wasn't fool enough to forget that detail.

Slumped in the big over-stuffed chair in her stateroom's study, Brontë thought through everything she had learned over the past days, certain specific details hurting the inside of her stomach, sharp as ragged metal. Sabra shifted her weight. "Your mother believes these files contain information which might do you harm."

"Belief is nothing. We need data. And we won't have data until we know what the files contain." When Sabra shook her head, Brontë spoke again, adopting, though she didn't realize this until later, the forceful tone her mother used when she issued commands: "Anja Ikeda Nowak may still be alive. I'm between her and the Primary Seat. I need to understand the entire situation—including my mother's part in it—if I'm going to be effective against her. Right now, I'm operating blind."

Sabra started to shake her head again, and then did not. Brontë pushed her advantage: "My mother would not have given you that information if she didn't think I should have it. Give me the files, Captain Anador."

With obvious reluctance, Sabra had turned the files over to Brontë. That had been sixteen days ago, universal time, or just over sixty watches by the ship's log. Brontë thought maybe she'd slept fifty hours out of all that time. Sabra dragged her down to the gym every morning, and made her eat and bathe. Otherwise, Brontë was left alone to work non-stop through the files.

"Are you learning anything useful?" Sabra asked, showing up for dinner with two bins of the fried noodles the evening cook did so well. Brontë reached out and Sabra put a bowl of noodles in her hand, as well as a set of paper-wrapped chopsticks.

"Plenty I wish I didn't know." Brontë shoveled in a wad of noodles and shrimp, and used her free pinkie finger to poke up a file excerpt she had saved at a corner of the screen. "The Atlas Society had twenty-five different sets they were running, through twelve different Houses. Calypso sets. Your set is just one of those." Brontë glanced up at Sabra, ate more noodles, and then said, "I'm a variation of your set. Did you know that?"

Sabra's eyes tightened fractionally, but she said nothing.

"My m…Dr. Ikeda used your egg when she created my zygote," Brontë continued, making her point more clearly. "Or, well, she had the Ikeda House geneticists use it. They edited in selections from her g-set, along with selections from the Calypso set the Atlas Society is running in Ikeda House—one of the sets the society is running in Ikeda House. Ten different specific sequences were edited into the germline. Into my germline."

"My egg. But your mother's genetic material. Except for these sequences edited in. Yes?"

"No. Some of Isra Ikeda's genetic material was edited in, along with selections from the Calypso set. The rest is yours." Brontë waved a hand. "Yours and Leonard Verde Hayek's." The man she had always been told was her father. The one she had never actually met, because his work kept him far off in the settlement planets, at least according to the stories her mother had always told her. According to these files, although Leonard's sperm had been used to fertilize the donated egg, the resulting zygote had been heavily edited. So how much of his set had been left, afterwards, or whose child she could therefore call herself—no one seemed to have worried about any of that. "Theo is also edited," she added. "He's not your set, but they edited his germline just like they did mine."

Sabra stood with her own bowl of noodles in her hands, motionless, not eating.

"The Atlas Society have been doing this, edited select germlines in the line to inherit in every House, including Ikeda House, for the last twenty years," Brontë explained. "Before that, the society was only working with bonded labor—they've experimented on hundreds of bonded labor subjects over the past five centuries. More than a thousand, total. The complete list is in here. The Ikan16s, our Ikans, they're just the latest. Most of the bonded labor subjects are either Security cadets or professional level workers—physicians and tutors. About a hundred years ago, they began working on citizens in ancillary positions—engineers, advocates, administrators. Like my mother."

"Twenty years," Sabra said. "How many subjects? Do the files have names?"

"Only those in Ikeda House. The rest have lab numbers. There must be a master list somewhere, but my mother didn't include it. Theo and I are the only Calypso children in the line to inherit in Ikeda House," Brontë added, moodily. Over the past sixteen days, she had spent a certain amount of time trying to understand who had authorized her editing, and more importantly Theo's editing. If it had only been her, it would have been an easy question—as chair of the Ikeda House Genetics Advisory Board, Isra undoubtedly had a certain amount of influence. But why would she have authorized the editing of the zygote that became Theo?

"Calypso children?" Sabra asked.

"That's what the Atlas Society calls us. The project is the Calypso Project."

"Why Calypso? Isn't that a mining planet, somewhere off Sol?"

"It's the constellation of traits you should be asking about. Also, why the Atlas Society engineered not just new genetic combinations but defective zygotes."

"You're not defective," Sabra objected.

Brontë tabbed up another excerpted file. "Some of the traits, they're what you would expect—higher intelligence, better reflexes, greater endurance and physical strength. The usual. Others, though. Look at this list."

Sabra hesitated, and then took the handheld from her. She read out loud from the list: "Heightened aggression and reaction time. Heightened need for variation in the environment. Reduced risk of anxiety/distress. Reduced tendency for thalamic emotional reactions. Reduced risk of depression."

"These are the traits my—that Dr. Ikeda wanted me to have. That the Atlas Society wanted. This is why they couldn't give me tolerance to low pressure, or a decent metabolism. Because they wanted to select for *this* crap."

Sabra was paging through a file. "How many in Ikeda House knew about this project? Because if it's more than two, how did they keep it secret?"

"The Atlas Society has strict security protocols."

"Bonded labor know everything. You don't keep secrets from us." Sabra shook her head. "I'll be surprised if this project involves more than a few people." She emphasized the word *project* faintly, disparagingly. "At least not at the planning stage," she added, when Brontë started to object. "Execution, yes. That's a mass job. But you wouldn't have to tell those people what they were doing or why. Just their own bit of the plan. Also, are those even traits you can edit into a set? Genes that create a desire for variety? That's not how genetics works."

"The Atlas Society has supporting research." Brontë ran her hand through her hair, which Sabra had cropped short, both because short hair was easier at low gravity, and as a way to disguise her appearance. They were thinking about changing its color and her eye color, for the same reason. "I don't know how reliable it is. This research shows that these certain genetic clusters occur in people who test for this or that. For a love of variety, for instance. Or a family history of a low incidence of depression. Apparently their theory is that combining all these genetic constellations will create subjects with these traits too."

Sabra scrolled down the file, and then switched to another tab. Brontë ate another chunk of noodles and shrimp. Chewing industriously, she moved her chin at the handheld. "According to their files," she said, "at first, in the early days, their main purpose was an attempt to increase genetic diversity in the citizen lines of the Houses. The House geneticists were charged with finding new and potentially useful sequences and editing them into the germlines. That makes sense, if it's true. It's at least understandable."

"Say all this about this Calypso Project is correct," Sabra said. "Say this genetic editing does give you the traits these engineers claim they do. Why does the Atlas Society want heirs in the line—a Primary Seat heir, no less—with these specific traits? I don't even see why they would want to create *bonded labor* with those traits. Aggressive, easily bored, reduced ability to create emotional connections? That's a classic ASID diagnosis."

ASID, Anti-Social Identity Disorder, was one of the common ways to be convicted into bonded labor—as opposed to being born into it, or sold into it by impoverished parents. An ASID conviction happened when a non-citizen child under the age of six committed an arrestable offense. Such children were examined by a court physician, who usually diagnosed them as ASID. Adults and children over six given an ASID diagnosis were shipped out to the settlement planets, to be sold into contract labor there. But ASID children under six were usually bonded into one of the Houses, and put to some labor-intensive, strictly supervised task, such as laundry, or grounds maintenance, or wastewater crew.

Brontë gathered the last of her noodles onto her chopsticks. "You're assuming the Atlas Society thinks these are non-desirable traits."

Sabra glanced up, eyes narrowed. "I've worked with ASIDs. The lower floors are full of them. You can't trust them, you can't turn your back on them, they'll steal anything—even things they don't need, things no one would steal. I had one steal end caps from the chairs in the common room. She didn't want them—she flushed them down the facility. When I asked her why, she just gave me that empty stare they all have." Sabra scowled. "ASID is nothing to select for. Shipping ASIDs out to the mines, that's the best solution. You don't make more of them, not intentionally."

"The bonded labor you dealt with, they came from outside the House walls. From less than ideal environments, if what..." Brontë started to say *if what Tully tells me is so,* and bit her lip instead. Sabra glanced at her, and she said, firmly, "From less than ideal environments. That's not just them—those bonded, their phenotype—it's their parents, too, and their grandparents. It affects them on the epigenetic level."

"As it does you, if your engineers are using selections from these ASIDs. From bonded labor outside the House."

Brontë hesitated, trying to think what the files had said about that—which bonded labor the Atlas Society had selected from. "Maybe. It depends on when they edited that material in. From which generation of bonded labor, I mean. Also there are ways to suppress epigenetic activity. The point is, when we change the environment, we change how the phenotype is expressed."

Since Sabra had taught Brontë most of what she knew about genetics, she knew more about all of this than Brontë did. She gave an absent grimace, her mind clearly elsewhere. "What is undesirable in a gutter pup might be beneficial in bonded labor," Brontë elaborated. "And those same traits might be highly desirable in a leader."

"Gutter pup," Sabra said mildly, her gaze focusing suddenly. Brontë felt her skin heat. It was Tully's term, and one she had used to describe herself and her friends cheerfully. It had never occurred to Brontë that anything might be wrong with term. Sabra grimaced again, and looked away. "ASIDs are criminals," she said. "Literally so."

"My—Isra says that the ASID diagnosis gets over-used." This was something she had heard her mother say fifty times. Now, belatedly,

Brontë wondered why Isra had put such emphasis on the point. "She says it's an excuse to create convictions into forced labor. That even when physicians think they have cause, it's mostly diagnostic bias—that the children they're examining are fresh off the street, and have just been taken from their parents, that they're terrified, and the physicians are primed to see what they want to see."

Sabra folded her arms, scowling. "So are you saying that having these constellations of traits does make people criminals, or that it doesn't?"

"A key issue," Brontë agreed, "given I've got all of them, along with above-average height and wit."

Sabra raised an eyebrow. "Witlessness, you meant to say, I think."

Brontë grinned. Sabra almost never teased. "Fuckwit. *That's* what I meant." She put aside the handheld, getting up to stretch. She had been sitting reading for hours, and her muscles were stiff with lack of use. "Hey, you realize this makes your children my siblings."

Sabra snorted. "My ass it does."

"It does, though. Genetically, I'm more closely related to them than I am to my mother." She grinned. "In fact, I think it makes them my spares."

Sabra snorted again and gathered up the empty bowl to return them to the galley. "You should suggest that to Dr. Ikeda. Make sure I'm around, so I can see her face."

Chapter 21

Franklin Station, Freiheit, Republic Space

As it developed, Velocity had plenty of time. She completed the downloads, ran a backup for good measure, sent both of these data packets back to the ship, and was still waiting for Gupta. With nothing to do, she realized for the first time how tired she was. Sliding down a little in the chair, she shut her eyes. Tension buzzed along her nerves and muscles. Sounds echoed. Her bones ached. Bits of memory played and replayed: Tai's tense face as he watched her leave the ship. Rida, years ago, when he had been new to the ship, flinching whenever she moved too quickly.

She rubbed the broken bone in the back of her hand. The little bonded labor child, Nina, said they had all been aboard a Combine cruiser, headed for Waikato, when suddenly Isra ordered a course change. That they had come here, to Franklin Station. That everyone said it was because Dr. Ikeda had heard some heir to the Primary Seat was headed for Freiheit. *No one knew who the heir was*, Nina had said. *Most people thought it was David Ikeda Ito, but I think that's just because everyone likes him.*

When they had reached Franklin Station, the courier ship owned by Nowak House had still been three weeks from port. *Nowak*, Nina pointed out. *Not Ito*. So everyone knew it was almost certainly Anja Ikeda Nowak that was coming in. Though Isra still hadn't said anything to anyone. And then when the courier ship made port— here Nina had spread both her hands wide.

"What?" Velocity had demanded impatiently.

"No one comes off," Nina said. "For the longest time. Then Torres and her Security do. But the ship still has a Criminal Investigation seal on it."

"Criminal Investigation."

Nina nodded, reaching for the last tea cake. "Everyone says it's a murder. Anja Ikeda Nowak got murdered. Some people think Torres did it. But everyone else thinks it's more of the coup. Whoever's behind the coup. Probably David."

"I thought David was dead," Velocity had said, with only half her attention. She was thinking through the details of the Ikeda House inheritance line.

"That's what they want you to think," Nina had said darkly.

Gupta came back through the hatch—no longer alone. Captain Morel was with her. Velocity got to her feet, casting a swift glance behind Morel, a reconnaissance to see who he had brought along; or rather, how *many* Security he had brought along. She didn't see any, and when she used her uplink to access the single working feed in the corridor, no Security waited out there either. No one was in the corridor except another of Gupta's kitchen workers on break. Velocity scowled at Gupta. "Exactly how many parties have you sold my highborn ass to?"

"I've brought you an offer from Dr. Ikeda," Morel said.

"I've heard Dr. Ikeda's offer." Velocity put an ironic stress on the last word.

Morel took out his handheld and started a pre-loaded capture playing. It showed a split screen: Isra Ikeda speaking to someone Velocity felt certain she should recognize: a woman with short grey hair, wearing a conservative jacket and a dark green keffiyeh loose around her neck. "Adelina Bowers," Morel said, touching pause a moment. "Prime Counsel for your Combine."

"I don't have a Combine."

"Your former Combine, then, Miss Taveri," Morel said patiently.

"I am Captain Velocity Wrachant, of the merchant ship *Susan Calvin*, registered out of Lotus-5, in the Drift."

Morel started the capture playing again. Velocity watched while Isra explained to Adelina Bowers Taveri that she thought she might have located a Taveri heir long thought lost, and that she wondered what the procedure would be, should this heir wish to return and claim her Board Seat. Would it be possible, Isra wondered, that was her first question.

"Possible," Adelina Bowers said. "Yes. Probable? That depends very much on who the heir in question is, and which seat we are discussing."

"The Primary Seat," Isra said.

Adelina's face changed. "Ah."

"Possible?" Isra asked.

Adelina's eyes were distant with calculation. "I assume the missing heir is the young woman we had such hopes for."

"With our support," Isra said, "and given who holds the Seat now..."

"Our current seat holder," Adelina murmured. "Such a disappointment." She shook her head, and said briskly, "We would need to meet with this young woman. The planning committee will need to. But, yes. Possible. Even probable."

Isra started to speak further, but Morel stopped the capture again, giving Velocity a weighty look, his brows lifted. "Is that supposed to be a bribe?" Velocity asked. "I ran away from that when I was sixteen years old. Why would I go weak in the knees when you wave it at me now?"

"You're no longer sixteen years old. You're smarter, and tougher. And you'd have an alliance with Ikeda House."

"I've told Isra my terms. They haven't changed."

Morel tucked the handheld back into his jacket pocket. "We're also aware of your situation with Torres Ikeda Alonzo. Specifically, that she has taken your crew members hostage. She means to use these hostages to convince you to give her Elena Ikeda. You should understand that an alliance with Dr. Ikeda will benefit you much more than an alliance with this ineffectual traitor."

Velocity stared at him. He stared back. Licking her lips with a suddenly dry tongue, Velocity said, "My alliance is to my crew and my ship. No one else."

"That may not be effective at this point. Or even possible."

"Go tell your—" Velocity paused, fighting to steady herself. "Tell Dr. Ikeda that my terms have not changed."

Morel lifted his brows again. When Velocity said nothing more, he shrugged and left the cabin, going past Gupta as if she were a broom leaning in the corner. Velocity stared after him, and then switched that stare to Gupta. "Where's my payment?"

$$\text{ᛉ ᛏ ᛦ ᛧ}$$

Brontë couldn't sleep. She couldn't eat, either. Tension wound tight through her muscles and down her throat into her belly. Hard exercise helped some, so that was what she had been doing for the past four or five hours. Now, exhausted, she lay on her back on the pit floor, the cloth of her hakama damp with sweat, her hair soaked with it. The dagan sat nearby, the soles of his feet together, his knees flat against the deck, his back straight. "Guilt isn't useless, exactly," he said.

He: Captain Wrachant always called the dagan *it*. Because it was a mechanical, Brontë knew—as if a mechanically-created person was somehow not a person. As if the dagan were an object, no more aware or alive than any other tool on the ship. Brontë dug her fist across her eyes, wondering why things like this were bothering her so much lately. They never had before.

"As an alert signal, guilt can be helpful," the dagan said. "But letting that alarm overwhelm every other signal, that's adaiya."

Adaiya, daiya. The dagan's favorite words. Early on, Brontë had translated *daiya* as good, and *adaiya* as bad. But when she talked to Captain Wrachant about these terms, the Captain said no, that wasn't exactly right. Captain Wrachant said *dai* was a Pirian root word that meant center, or equal, or balance. The Captain said this word, *dai,* was the key value in Pirian culture. Everything had to be centered, she said. Everything had to be in balance. It was why the Pirians loved circles so much. They said circles were always in balance.

"Why don't you have a name?" Brontë demanded, still breathing hard from the hour she had done on the rowing machine. "That seems adaiya to me. That the Captain never even *named* you. And I *don't* feel guilty. Why would I feel guilty? I haven't done anything wrong."

The dagan surveyed her. "You failed to rescue Captain Anador. You allowed her—and the Ikans—to be captured. Also, according to the ethos of your culture, you are a proscribed creation. A monster."

Brontë sat up. Sweat thick on her skin, muscles trembling from exhaustion, she stared at the mechanical. Then she swiped sweat off her face with her sleeve. "So are you," she pointed out. "A proscribed creature. A monster."

The dagan smiled. "By the ethos of your culture. Not by mine."

"I don't feel guilt, anyway. That's the entire point, remember? They built me *not* to feel guilt. Nothing but intellectual curiosity, and boredom. The perfect monster."

The dagan shifted position, stretching the muscles of his legs. "Captain Wrachant knows what she's doing." Her temper blazing up like a lit spark, Brontë leapt to her feet and headed for the hatch. "You're not a monster," the dagan said, behind her.

Wheeling, Brontë snapped, "She *doesn't* know what she's doing! She doesn't have any *idea* what she's doing!"

"Mzala," he said gently, and before she could stop herself, everything poured out of her in a torrent, none of it in any order, none of it careful or guarded. She told him everything, which she knew was stupid. Not only was he was a robot, he was part of Captain Wrachant's crew. He was part of her *ship*. Anything she said to him, she might as well say to the Captain herself. And yet she told him everything.

"Captain Wrachant is out of her depth," she finished. "She doesn't understand my mother, or what she will do. I need off this ship." When the dagan kept silent, Brontë looked up, into his eyes. "I'm heir to the Primary Seat. I should be taking charge of this. I should to be on the station." She hesitated, and added, "I know she set you to watch me."

"That's not precisely the case."

"I know you're part of the ship, too. Perfused with the ship."

"Again, not precisely the case." The dagan shifted into a new position, one that let him stretch his back. "Are you asking a question, little bee?"

"I need to leave the ship. What will you do if I do that?"

The dagan tipped its head. "The umbilical is locked. How did you get the Captain's codes?"

Brontë hissed impatiently. Everyone on this ship thought it took an arcane level of genius to be able to hack into a system. Well, Rida. Maybe Rida knew better. "What will you do if I leave the ship?" she repeated.

The dagan studied her. "If you have the Captain's codes, you can just shut me down," he pointed out. "Then you wouldn't have to worry about what I might do."

"I know that."

The dagan seemed to think this over, though Brontë knew his mind, computer-based, worked so swiftly that this pause was for verisimilitude only. At length, he smiled. "Sit down, mzala. Perhaps we can work together."

𞤩 𐊕 𐌞 𐌙

Rida soon lost track of how long he had been under Lieutenant Zhang's boot. Long enough to realize she was a professional at interrogation, varying medication with force, force with kindness, and never letting him rest. The lights were kept on, for maximum disorientation, and he hadn't been given anything to eat or drink since the interrogation had started. The most recent tactic was psychological. McCann, the Security officer on duty now, had him standing on the bench in the middle of the cabin, knocking him off occasionally to keep him off balance. She had just knocked him off again when her com button chimed. "Get up," she ordered, and thumbed the button. "McCann here."

Rida climbed back on the bench, exhausted. Having said, *Yes, Lieutenant, Yes, Lieutenant*, about eleven times, the Security released the com button and pointed her stick at him. "Don't get down from there. That's an order."

"Sir," Rida said.

McCann left the cabin—left him alone, standing on the bench. Rida wobbled a moment, staring at the shut hatch. It was a trap, he knew. But he decided he didn't care. They would hit him no matter what he did, so he might as well do what he liked. He stepped off the bench and, going to the far corner, collapsed into it. Exhaustion pulled him toward sleep, but he rubbed his finger in his ear. The welt was entirely gone. He clenched his teeth in the way the dagan had shown them and subvocalized: *Tai?*

Nothing. Still nothing. The bot network wasn't working. They would never come for him. He heard himself whimpering, more misery than pain, and choked off the sound. Before he could try the netbot again, he fell into sleep. What felt like only a moment later, McCann was kicking him awake, swearing. "Now, now, Officer McCann," Lieutenant Zhang was saying. "I'm sure Mr. Tdemir is sorry he disobeyed. Aren't you, Mr. Tdemir?"

Rida slid as far out of range as he could. "I'm sorry you weren't gone longer."

McCann yanked her stick from its holster; Zhang put out a hand, palm raised, to stop her. "Bring us some tea, please, Officer."

McCann's skin went scarlet in patches. Shoving the stick back into its holster, she did as she was told. Lieutenant Zhang gripped Rida under the arm and hauled him to his feet. She led him, limping, over to the bench and sat him down. Then she took a handheld from her pocket. "Here now," she said. "Data. To help you make your decisions."

Rida didn't know what this meant, and didn't care. When she pushed the handheld at him insistently, he took it, though his damaged hands hurt so much he almost dropped it. A capture was playing: Dr. Isra Ikeda, speaking to some other Core citizen. Another Combine seat holder, probably, from the dialect she spoke and how she was dressed. Rida couldn't follow what they were saying. Even if he hadn't been stupid with hunger and exhaustion, he didn't think he would have understood them, between the dialect they were using and the fact that they were talking that way Core citizens did talking, saying everything without actually saying anything.

Zhang punched the screen with her forefinger, pausing the capture. "You understand?"

Rida grunted a laugh. "Shit. Might as well been speaking English all I got from that." He scrubbed blood from his chin with the back of his wrist. "*Was* it English?"

The Lieutenant jerked the handheld away. "Do you know who your Captain really is?"

Rida squinted at her. Zhang stared back, all her false good humor vanished, intent earnestness in its place. "What do you mean?" Rida asked. "She's the Captain."

"She's heir to Taveri House's Primary Seat." Zhang thumped the screen of the handheld. "That's what they're dancing around, here. Isra Ikeda Lopaka, she's not content to destroy our Combine. Now she's entered into negotiations with members of Taveri-Bowers Combine, to run a coup on them." When Rida did not react, Zhang added, "Ikeda Lopaka has been talking to your Captain. Promising to restore her to the Primary Seat on the Taveri House Board. Your Captain is listening."

Rida laughed again. "Pull the other one, najis."

As if in reply, Zhang ran back the feed on the capture, playing the last few moments again. If this was meant to be dramatic, it failed, since Rida still didn't understand a word either Isra Ikeda or the other women was saying. The Lieutenant, watching his expression, shook her head and shut the capture down. "You cattle should pull your heads out now and then. Do you know how much power we're discussing when we talk about a Primary Seat? Never mind the wealth."

Rida said nothing. He knew she was right, that he didn't know anything about either power or wealth, especially power and wealth on that scale. On the other hand, he knew the Captain, whereas this Lieutenant did not. The Captain wouldn't come back and be a dog for the Combines, not for any heap of power or wealth. Anyway, he hoped that was true about her.

Zhang tucked the handheld into her pocket. "Think it over," she said. "I promise you one thing, though. Your captain's not spending one minute worrying over what happens to you."

She walked to the hatch. It opened just as she reached it—McCann coming in, along with a kitchen girl bearing a tray of tea and cakes. "We won't need those after all," Lieutenant Zhang said, and ushered them all out, shutting the hatch behind them.

They didn't return. When Rida was sure they weren't coming back, or at least not soon, he retreated to his corner and tried to sleep again. The cabin felt colder, and he couldn't stop shivering. After a moment, he clenched his teeth and subvocced: *Tai? Are you there? Tai?*

No one answered, and he knew no one would. But for a long, long time he kept trying just the same.

Ꝛ ✝ Ꝕ Ꝥ

When Velocity got back to the ship, Tai was up in the com, staring at images of Rida up on the boards. Shirtless and barefoot, Rida knelt in an empty compartment. An Ikeda Security officer stood behind him. His face and ribs were marked with livid bruises. Long raw welts crossed his back. "Torres Ikeda Alonzo sent them over," Tai said. "She wonders if you would like to talk."

Velocity slid into the nav saddle. "What about the link with the netbots? Surely it's up by now."

It is up, the dagan said through her link. *But as I feared, I have lost my tunnel into the Ikeda House bank, as well as the one through the Torres shieldwall.*

At almost the same moment, Tai said, "We've got the com link. What we don't have is a tunnel through their shieldwalls. Not anymore."

Get the breach back, Velocity ordered the dagan. To Tai she said, "We'll get him back."

"Tell me why we're not trading that brat for him," Tai said. "What do we care who holds this mafi board seat? Not like they'll survive six months in the seat anyway."

Velocity bit back her first hard words. "What about the downloads I sent from the bug drones? Did we get anything off those?"

Tai said nothing. Then, moving slowly, he tapped up four captures, one after the next. One showed a child with short dark hair; the others were various captures of a very young man. "This is one of the Ikan16s, I think," Tai said, nodding at the first. "Her image is a 98% match with those Sabra gave us. Also, I'm pretty sure she gets called Adder at one point."

The bug drones didn't have the capacity to capture sound, but after watching enough captures, you got pretty good at reading lips.

"These three…" Tai tapped another capture going. The young man moved across a room to lean straight-armed on a worktable, staring into a data port. "That might be Hiro Ikeda Hayek. Theo," he added, in case she had forgotten Theo's register name. "The match is only 60%."

Velocity enlarged and ran the three captures of Theo. Neither Rida nor the dagan had found any captures of Hiro Ikeda Hayek on the nexus, so she only had a single still image to work with, one from his pirated medical files. "Did you ask Brontë? She'd know him."

"She'd just tell us more lies. Anyway, she's asleep. Or at least not answering her com."

Velocity linked to the dagan: *Wake Brontë. Get her up here.* Out loud, she said, "What about the other Ikans? Or Anja? David?"

The dagan spoke through her link: *Neither David Ikeda Ito nor Anja Ikeda Nowak appear anywhere in any image file captured by the insect drones.*

Velocity suppressed a surge of irritation she knew was irrational. "Route your speech through the com, please. What about the Ikans?"

The dagan's voice came from the navigation speaker: "The three male Ikans were not shipped to this station. All three have invoices on file."

Tai sat straighter. "Invoices—they were sold?"

"All to labor agents."

Tai cursed, using words from his childhood on Sarat, as he did only when he was dangerously furious. "Filthy pissing zayim. Naotan *scum.*"

"Do the invoices specify which agents?" Velocity asked. The dagan said they did, and that it had bookmarked that data. Velocity mulled this over. Why just sell the males? Trying to think this through, she felt a wave of exhaustion go through her, making the ache in her bones throb.

"The files on the Ikan16s, and on the Calypso Project in general, contain a great deal of data," the dagan said, "but in summary, it appears that the Atlas Society has decided Calypso males are maladaptive. Their conclusion is that Calypso males are more prone to violence, including violence toward themselves and the commonwealth, than their female counterparts. Their analysts advise limiting the further creation of Calypso males, and further advise that any Calypso males already created be channeled into military or security forces, or to settlement planets."

"Oh, well, that's charming," Velocity muttered. She rubbed at the old break in her hand.

"The files on the Calypso Project confirm that Hiro Ikeda Hayek—Theo—is a Calypso male. This may be why he is being kept alive."

"Because this Isra wants a violent child running her Combine?" Velocity shook her head.

"Brontë seems to believe that environment outweighs genetics when it comes to the Calypso subjects," the dagan said. "She may well have gotten this opinion from her mother."

"Or maybe Ikeda-Verde Combine does want a Calypso in charge," Tai said. "Maybe violent deviant is exactly what they're working towards."

"Speaking of Brontë," Velocity said, "do I need to go down there and drag her out of that bunk myself?"

The dagan said nothing. Tai turned in his seat, looking toward the navigator speaker, his eyes narrowing in a frown. "Dagan?" Velocity said. "Where is Brontë?"

"Brontë Ikeda is not currently aboard ship, Captain," the dagan said.

Silence filled the com. Velocity could hear her heart thumping. "Explain."

"Brontë Ikeda is not aboard the *Susan Calvin*," the dagan repeated. Velocity set her teeth, drawing a deep breath. She knew the dagan well enough to know that when it retreated into mech-speak, that the retreat was deliberate. She was still shaping her next query into something too specific to be dodged when the dagan added, "She left the ship twenty-two minutes ago."

Velocity worked her jaw muscles. Then she said, carefully, precisely, "Did you and Brontë discuss where she might go after she left the ship?"

"Yes, Captain."

"Tell me where she said she might go."

"According to what she told me, her plan is to approach her mother, Isra Ikeda Lopaka, and enlist her aid in recovering Rida."

And you didn't stop her? Velocity bit these words off. She considered reaching out to Brontë via the Pirian netbot. Instead, she said, "Are you able to locate Brontë via the station feeds?"

"Yes, Captain. She is on Level B, heading upspin."

"Keep her in sight." Velocity headed for the hatch. "Tai, keep trying to establish contact with Rida and Sabra. I'll be in touch."

"Can't you just order her back?" Tai said, touching his ear. Brontë had a netbot as well, he meant.

"Like she would listen?" Velocity said, and dropped down the ladder toward the umbilical three rungs at a time.

Chapter 22

Franklin Station, Freiheit, Republic Space

Adder was in the gym scrub, cleaning up after her session, when Nina appeared, her small round face bright with excitement. Unhurriedly, Adder dumped her sweat-soaked gear in the laundry chute and opened the sluice. Ducking her head under the spill of icy water, she scrubbed sweat from her hair. The night before, she'd gotten an Ikhen54 to crop it close to the skull, so at least she didn't have to fret about styling it. Straightening, she pointed to the stack of towels.

The kitchen girl handed her one. "I'm meeting your Brontë," she said, low under the torrent of water gushing from the sluice. "Interested?"

"Can I dress first?" Adder asked mildly.

Fifteen minutes later, they boarded a cargo lift. Its deck was gummed with filth, and it rumbled slowly through the levels. They were the only passengers. Adder didn't know whether that was due to the time, three hours before third shift began, or whether Nina had intentionally chosen a little-used lift. The kitchen girl kept up a steady chatter of trivialities, which made Adder think the lift might have security feeds. Many areas frequented by bonded workers did. The lift drifted out to Level B, where they exited into a service corridor. Here, despite the hour, bonded workers streamed past, hauling groceries, crates of wine, bundles of fresh-laundered linen, repair kits and toolkits, deck scrubbers, baskets filled with seedling flowers, and an entire aquarium filled with bright clear water and glimmering multicolored tropical fish.

Nina darted through these workers, moving at a trot. Adder, who had longer legs and was in better shape, kept up easily. Abruptly, the kitchen girl veered down a dim side corridor, ducked under a *Closed for Maintenance* ribbon, and scooted into another, very short, corridor. A short distance down it, Nina stopped and settled to her heels, peering through a hatchway. After a pause, she stood straight and sauntered out.

Adder followed her, out into a public corridor, though not a main one. This was a feeder corridor, leading from living quarters and storage compartments to a main concourse—in this case, Seisen Ichiba Market. Nina stopped well before the big hatchway that opened onto the market, however, and settled into a recessed alcove, one that led to another feeder corridor. Adder stepped in beside her. "Why are we stopping here?"

"This Brontë," Nina said, watching up the corridor, "she's supposed to be a hostage. But she sent me this post, says meet her here. Like she's free as any gutter pup."

Adder paused, studying as much of Nina's face as she could. "It was you said she was a hostage on this ship. Now you think she isn't?"

Nina grunted. "What's your Theo want with her?"

"He's heir to the Primary Seat. She's his heir."

"Is that the story he fed you? Or is that the one you're feeding me?" Nina shook her head. "This is their game. But it's us who pay."

Adder watched her, remembering that discussion with Theo. *Sharp. But I don't know about her loyalty.* "What's your point?" she asked softly.

"I don't have a point," Nina said. "I'm bonded labor. I do what I'm told."

"Listen—"

"Look there. Is that your Brontë?"

𝒵 ✝ ⅄ 𝓡

Growing up in Ikeda House, her every step dogged by at least one IVC Security officer, and an entire team of them if she went outside the House, Brontë hadn't learned until they reached the Drift what it was like to be on her own. Out on Hell in a Bucket, after Sabra dyed her hair that jarring orange color and dressed her in ragged bonded labor clothing, Brontë found herself invisible. She could run the corridors and concourses of the station like any other grimy local child, she could sit for hours against a wall, she could use public data kiosks and vendors, and no one—except now and then some of the grimy local children—even noticed she was there. No one asked if she needed help. No one worried about her. It was a freedom she had never known.

At first, Sabra had wanted to keep watch over her: to continue to act as her Security. But beyond the simple truth that one Security officer couldn't stand four watches in a row, day after day after day, what they needed to do on that station required the two of them to work solo, at least sometimes. If Sabra couldn't keep watch over her all the time, Brontë pointed out, then she needed to learn how to keep watch over herself. It only took five or six hard arguments with Sabra to convince her of the logic of this.

Time well spent, Brontë thought, making her way along a concourse on Franklin Station, a very different place from that Free Trade station out in the Drift, but governed by the same tacit rules. Specifically, a scuffed-up child dressed like bonded labor, who kept her head down, drew no attention at all. This concourse, on level B, had lower gravity than those nearer the docks. It had better décor also, and better outlets—négociants, couturiers, grocers whose shops were faced in elegant polished marble. She was almost too scabby to be walking loose on this level, and when she reached the rendezvous spot, near a cordwainer's called Aubin's, she took herself down the narrow service corridor to wait.

Once there, sitting on her heels against the corridor wall, she pulled her handheld from the cargo pocket of her trousers—one benefit to bonded labor clothing, all these pockets. While her clothing in Ikeda House had been of better quality, and much more comfortable to wear, it had few useful pockets. Loading her dropbox on the handheld, she slid to new messages. Nothing.

The scuff of cloth slippers on the deck made her muscles twitch. She looked up to see Nina trotting toward her from an access corridor, both taller and more compact that she had seemed in the captures. "Elena Ikeda," she said, drawing near. She was grinning.

As Brontë opened her mouth to protest this use of her register name—which no one except her family and Legal was supposed to know—another kid, about Nina's size and dressed, like her, in a kitchen girl's off-white, long sleeved jacket, emerged from the access corridor. Brontë scrambled to her feet. "Adder!"

Nina hissed for quiet, but Brontë pushed past her to fling arms around Adder. Under her embrace, she felt the cadet tense with surprise, or maybe alarm. She hugged harder, burying her face in Adder's shoulder, only just admitting to herself now how sure she had been that the Ikhan16 was dead—and that it was her fault. "Hey," Adder said softly. "Hey, now."

Brontë stood straight, swiping at the damp in her eyes. "Are you all right? Where's Wolf?"

Adder shook her head. "Theo's here. But I haven't seen anyone else."

"Theo. Take me to him."

Adder hesitated, glancing past her to Nina. "I can get the pair of you back into the habitat," Nina said authoritatively. "You'll have to get her past Theo's Security."

"Your mother has Theo under heavy guard," Adder explained. "Anja is dead, but there's still Torres."

"Is that what Isra told Theo?" Brontë shook her head. "That Torres is behind the coup? And he believes that?"

Adder hesitated, her eyes narrowing. "Torres is here on the station," she said slowly. "She's asked for a meeting with your mother. She's offered to trade you for Theo, specifically. If she and Anja weren't behind the coup, if they're not trying to take the Seat, why does Torres want Theo?"

"Torres doesn't have support in the House," Brontë argued. "Anja didn't have anywhere near enough support, but Torres has none. There's no way Theo believes this idiot story. Also, Torres doesn't *have* me. How can she offer to trade me if she doesn't have me?"

Adder glanced at Nina, who stepped forward. "Torres and Dr. Ikeda have been talking, via the link. She's got that Security Captain, that one that heads your crew?"

"Sabra," Brontë said.

Nina nodded. "Captain Anador. Could she have Captain Anador and not you? Torres doesn't say this, but she's trying to make your mother think it. Let's meet, she tells your mother. Let's talk about what we'll trade."

"Maybe it's a ploy," Adder said. "Get close enough to your mother, she can shoot her?"

"Why would she want to shoot Isra? She's nowhere in the line."

"Whatever," Nina said. "Dr. Ikeda thinks Theo is in danger. The Security squad she's got on him isn't letting anyone through. They clearly won't let *you* through."

Because Brontë was next in line of inheritance at this point, Nina meant. No way to deny the truth of this, but— "Get me to his Security gate," Brontë said. "I'll take it from there."

Adder and Nina exchanged looks, and very faintly Adder nodded. "Right, miss," Nina said. "This way then."

ᛝ ᛏ ᛢ ᛨ

The signal the dagan was feeding her muddied some as Velocity entered the station lift. She triangulated, and then brought up a second screen and searched for feeds near Brontë's last location. No luck. *Do it the hard way.* Velocity located the schematic for Level B, matched it to location, then plotted her way to a nearby shop: Ito's Fittery, at the heart of Seisen Ichiba Market.

Exiting the lift into the market, Velocity paused, hoping the signal would clarify. It did, a bit, showing Brontë's current location as downspin, thirty meters, port. She headed that way, doing her best to remain inconspicuous. This was not as easy, since the crowds of shoppers on this level were very different from those on Market Concourse D. Seisen Ichiba Market was clearly aimed at upscale tourists, as well as Combine Board seat holders and their families. Even the bonded workers moving among the sparse crowds were high status: secretaries, physicians, tutors. She moved to the side of the main traffic stream and checked Brontë's location again. Downspin, six plus meters. Increasing her own speed, Velocity scanned the crowds, looking for orange hair.

A few minutes later, she caught sight of not Brontë, but Nina. The kitchen girl was across and down the concourse, at ten meters, moving at a trot. It took a moment for Velocity to realize that one of the two children with her was Brontë. The bright orange hair was gone. Brontë had shaved her head. In her ragged gear, she looked like a bootboy held by some not-prosperous household. Trying to move faster without actually running herself, Velocity angled toward the children.

Before she could reach them, out of nowhere Security surrounded her. She jerked to a halt impatiently, thinking it was Station Security—she was, after all, behaving suspiciously on a market concourse. Only after she focused on the man in front of her did she recognize Captain Morel, and the Ikeda House uniform he wore. Even more impatiently, she looked past him, to see that another Ikeda Security team had surrounded the three children. Biting down on a curse, she looked back at Morel. "Dr. Ikeda wants a moment," he said.

"What?" She looked past him again. Brontë and the other two

children had vanished, along with the Security around them. Down the corridor beside them, probably. Velocity scowled at Morel. "Later," she said. "I'm in a hurry."

Morel motioned at the Security behind her, and two stepped up close, not quite taking hold of her. One had his hand on the restraints clipped to his belt. Exasperated, bitterness rank in her throat, Velocity moved back from Morel, raising her hands. "Fine. Let's go talk to Dr. Ikeda."

The squad of Security formed up around her. Captain Morel fell in beside her, and they headed spinward along the concourse. "Does *Dr.* Ikeda have something new to say to me?" Velocity asked, putting sarcastic emphasis on the title.

"I'm sure Dr. Ikeda will make that clear," Captain Morel said.

"You just follow orders?" Velocity said. Morel did not reply. All around them, shoppers on the concourse stepped from their path, moved aside, gathered behind them to put their heads together and whisper in speculation. "Here's something you maybe should consider," Velocity said, tipping her head toward Morel as those gossiping shoppers were tipping theirs toward one another. "Maybe you're in the wrong Navy."

Morel moved away from her slightly, shooting her an angry glance.

"Just something to think about," Velocity said with a shrug. "I've been talking to Captain Anador—you're acquainted with Captain Anador?"

"Shut it."

"Raised up in Ikeda House from birth, she tells me. Loyal as, well, loyal as a *dog*, I suppose would be how we might put it. Obedient, intelligent, worked with every waking beat of her heart to fulfill her orders—protecting the heir to Ikeda House's Primary Seat—which is…who is that heir, remind me, Captain Morel?"

"Shut it or I'll shut it for you."

Velocity shook her head. "Where's Captain Anador now, that's my question. And what is your bond holder doing about it?"

Morel wheeled on her. Velocity stepped back, raising both hands and widening her eyes in mock surrender. All around her, Security twitched with uneasy tension. And, all around them on the concourse, Franklin's citizenry watched avidly. "Move," Morel growled.

The IVC Security behind Velocity shoved at her. She started walking. Behind her and around her, the concourse crackled with furious whispers. Before Velocity could make another subversive comment, the dagan spoke through her uplink: *I've lost my connection to Brontë.*

Ikeda House Security just took her into custody. Her and Nina. Have you re-established the wormhole through the Ikeda House security wall? They're probably on the other side of that.

Still working to establish that breach.

What about Torres? Are you through the shieldwall there?

Soon.

Velocity breathed. Her heart was thumping hard. They were almost to the lift. Almost inside the habitat shieldwalls. *I am also in Ikeda House custody. I might need your help.*

I see.

Velocity pressed the point: *How much direct aid can you give us in this action?*

Though she knew the dagan didn't ever actually have to pause, she felt a pause. Then it said: *I'm restricted from committing acts of war unless the need is exigent.*

Acts of war. Velocity blinked. What an...interesting comment. They reached the lift; the Security manhandled her inside. Hurriedly, she sent: *Ikeda-Verde Combine is a civil consortium. It is not part of the Republic government. Acts against it can't be acts of war.*

Technically correct, the dagan agreed. *And not at all how the Republic World Parliament, or the Republic law courts, would view such an infiltration.*

Velocity had no time to think—the lift was in motion, heading toward Ikeda House. Once inside their habitat, their shieldwall would block transmission to and from her uplink. *Define exigent.*

Likely to lead to a path which would adversely impact the Pirian fleet or peoples.

Velocity twitched. This had not been the answer she had been expecting. Though, when she thought, it should have been. *Deciding who will have charge of one of the most powerful Combines in the Republic—a Combine that has major influence over the Parliament of Sovereign Worlds—is that an exigent circumstance?*

I can act as an advisor over military, technological, and strategical matters.

While Velocity was still composing a reply, the lift passed inside the Ikeda Habitat shieldwalls. Her connection dropped. She tried twice to reconnect, but whatever new wormhole the dagan was building to get through the walls once again, it clearly wasn't operational yet.

The lift opened on the koban. Here, Captain Morel directed an exhaustive search of Velocity, finding the Vyai she had tucked in the holster under the qipao, and her boot knife, but not the Sima MdF folded into her belt, which to be fair was freakishly tiny for a plasma weapon. "Sit," Morel ordered when the search was done. "Wait. And keep that mouth shut."

Velocity sat on the bench he had pointed to, obediently. Captain Morel left through the service hatch into the house. The rest of the Security quarter stayed to guard her, along with the two who had already been on duty. Velocity felt half amused and half alarmed—nine Security. Apparently she was a dangerous item. Keeping as innocent an expression as possible on her face, she tried to raise the dagan once again. Nothing.

Captain Morel reappeared in the service hatch and pointed at her. "Move."

Chapter 23

Franklin Station, Freiheit, Republic Space

Captain Morel led Velocity, not to the garden terrace where she had met with Isra Ikeda previously, as she had been expecting, but up one level, through a long corridor to a small atelier. This atelier also opened on the garden, though it did so via a veranda instead of a terrace. Isra was seated in an upholstered and embroidered chair behind an inlaid worktable. She nodded Velocity toward a sofa. "Captain Morel," she said. "Please see we're not disturbed."

"Doctor," he said: not in acknowledgement—registering his objection.

"You're dismissed, Captain." Isra pointed toward the door. "Miss Taveri is not about to pull that Sima on me. At least, not until she hears what I have to say."

Morel looked alarmed at the mention of the plasma weapon, and as if he wanted to haul Velocity back to the koban; but he did as he was told, shutting the hatch behind him. Velocity remained just inside the hatch, one hand hovering near the Sima. "You've got an inskull uplink," she said, only half believing this. She'd never met another Combine citizen with such an implant. But the quick saccadic stutter of Isra Ikeda's eyes was unmistakable: she was accessing data. And the stall in the koban made sense now. Someone had run a scan.

Sitting back in the chair, Isra tucked her slippered feet under her.

"Enough theatrics. Let's speak openly."

"Theatrics. Like having your Security drag me off the concourse?"

Ikeda smiled briefly. Sitting upright in the chair, she tapped on the wallboard behind her. A stilled image from a capture shone huge in this small room: Rida, on his knees, his head bent, blood bright on his face, one of Torres Ikeda's Security standing behind him, stick gripped in her fist. "You have my child. My House member has your crewman. We both have much to lose. I have considered the offer you proposed, and I'm ready with a counteroffer."

Velocity worked to keep her face blank, though she knew it was a futile gesture. This was almost certainly a smart room, and Isra Ikeda had an uplink. She tried to bring up, in her memory, an exact image of the Security officers who had surrounded Brontë back on the concourse—they been wearing Ikeda House uniforms. Had they been from Torres Ikeda's Security? She reached to connect through her uplink and bit her tongue in frustration when the connection failed.

Isra was speaking: "You'll surrender Brontë to me within the next two hours, and I won't have you arrested for treason, terrorism, and harboring fugitives. Further, I will see that your crewman is returned to you alive."

She only knew a few of Isra's Security officers well enough to pick them out by face, and even fewer of those dedicated to Torres. The dagan would know more.

"I could, obviously," Isra continued, "simply have Station Security place you into custody. You are holding a minor child of our line, and you have refused to return her to me. That's an arrestable offense, and one which would certainly result in your conviction. Once you were convicted, your assets would then accrue to your creditors, with anything remaining going to the state. As primary stockholder of this station, I'd get most of your cargo. Well before that, I'd get custody of Brontë."

"That sounds effective," Velocity said, the best she could manage in her distracted state. "Why haven't you done it?" Isra was frowning.

She had probably only just noticed the oddness of Velocity's physiological reactions. "Treason," Velocity said, hoping to divert her. "Or is it terrorism? I haven't really kept up with Republic law. Exactly which one would altering the human germline be considered here in the Republic these days?" She studied Ikeda's expression, and added, "Also, I have evidence. Have you?"

Abruptly, her uplink came live—the dagan, achieving the wormhole at last. *Isra Ikeda has her own uplink,* the dagan said. *And that's a smart room.*

So glad you've caught up, Velocity sent back dryly, relief cascading through her. *Do you have access to Torres yet?*

Very nearly.

Brontë is missing. Find her last location, find a capture. Who took her? Was it Torres?

Eyes narrowed, Isra Ikeda had sat straighter in her chair. Seizing on the first distraction she could think of, Velocity said, "Why Brontë?" When this didn't affect Isra, she rushed on, "You know I come from the Combines. I know how succession works. For Brontë to be in the line of succession, one of her parents also had to be in that line. You were that parent, until you recused yourself from the line. And yet you didn't leave the Combine, and you still, obviously, have ambitions toward power. Why not just stay in the line of succession yourself?"

"Why did you leave Dresden?"

Velocity snorted. "That's your claim? You were afraid for your life?"

"Is that why you ran?" Ikeda asked. "You were a coward?"

Velocity folded her arms theatrically, turning away and going out onto the veranda. The bonded labor gardeners were working in the fig orchard today, pruning and weeding. *It was near Seisen Ichiba Market,* she sent to the dagan. *Was it Ikeda Alonzo Security?*

I have it. Ikeda Alonzo House Security, confirmed. They took her off the concourse, along with Nina, and another child who I surmise is an Ikan16.

Took them where?

*I have traced them through a Security lift to the Ikeda Alonzo shieldwall.
I have not yet achieved a new tunnel through the Ikeda Alonzo walls.*

Velocity chewed the edge of her tongue. *Keep at that. And access
Isra's inskull.*

Behind her, Isra spoke again: "You left Dresden even though you
were the heir presumptive to the Primary Seat on the Taveri House
Board because you understood that leaving was the most strategic way
to manage your assets. Including," Isra added, "your own potential
power and influence."

Velocity placed her hands flat on the stone balustrade of the
veranda. "Managing power by surrendering power. That sounds
very Pirian, Isra. Who have you been talking to out there on those
settlement planets?"

"How much power does your sister have now?"

A flash of rage whitened her vision. Velocity kept her back to the
Ikeda holder until it faded. Not that it mattered, not in a smart room.

"Brontë wormed her way into my private data banks very young,"
Isra said. "I think she was nine the first time I caught her. Later, she
got crafty enough I sometimes missed her infiltrations."

Velocity stepped down from the veranda. "Brontë is your tool.
Does she know that? Your catspaw, through which you intend to rule
the Combine."

"You're missing the point, Tallis. A common failing of yours,
I suspect." Ikeda minimized the image of Rida on the wallboard,
replacing it with a g-set chart. "Interestingly, among all the other files
in my bank she wormed her way into, Brontë never accessed her own
g-set. Almost a deliberate blindness, there. Was it the same for you?"

"I didn't have to break into my father's bank," Velocity said flatly.
"He didn't lie to us."

"I know you're not that naive." Ikeda tapped the screen. "Your g-set.
And your sister's, of course. Both heavily edited, at your father's behest."

Velocity knew this was a lie. More than once, her father had told
them how he and their mother had agreed against even somatic genetic

editing for their children. He never would have agreed to germline editing. When she shook her head, though, Ikeda tapped the screen a second time. "Data doesn't lie, Tallis."

"Liars can fake data," Velocity said, her throat dry.

"Your father was a member of the Atlas Society. Did he tell you that?"

Velocity shook her head again. "He wasn't."

"He knew the risks, as we all do. He knew the dangers you would face. He might have pretended to accept your mother's purist arguments, but when it came to creating children, he was a realist. As we all are, in the Society. You are a Calypso child, as surely as my own child." Ikeda paused. "Did you ever wonder why your mother died so young?"

Velocity turned to face her. Her throat was still dry, and her skin felt tight. She shook her head again. "You've threatened me. You've killed your own people. You subjected your own child to experimental genetic engineering. Why would I believe anything you say?"

Isra was motionless, all except for the saccadic flicker of her eyes. Velocity turned back to the veranda. Staring out over the garden, bright with artificial sun and multi-colored flowers and fruits, she fought to breathe evenly. Adaiya, to be this angry. Also, not useful strategically. It occurred to her that this was strategy on Isra's point—that the Ikeda was making her angry as a tactic. Down in the tiny sparkling fishpond, two bonded labor boys waded and splashed, clearing out an excess of lily pads and flinging weeds at one another while they did so. She wondered why she had never questioned her father's account of her mother's death. *Because he wasn't lying*, she answered herself. *Why would you believe this **gadro** over him?*

"Tallis," Isra said. The data port was extruding a hardcopy. Isra tore it free and held it out, not taking her attention from her screen. Stepping down from the veranda, Velocity went to take it from her. It was legal copy, over-written argle-bargle like all legal copy everywhere. Squinting, Velocity sorted through the stock phrases and repetition, hunting out the meat. A sudden icy shock shot through her chest, her autonomic system understanding well before she did. Lifting her head, she met Ikeda's cool gaze. "You bought my ship."

"I bought the liens on your ship," Ikeda corrected, and flicked her fingers. "It amounts to the same thing, I agree." Velocity tightened her grip on the hardcopy; her fingers felt strengthless. "Now. First, you will surrender to me title of your crew. Also, you personally will sign a thirty-year labor contract with me. This contract will have a non-disclosure clause, for obvious reasons. You'll do all this before you leave this room. These conditions having been met, I will give you my word that I will recover the member of your crew held by Torres, and that having recovered him, I will allow your crew to remain with you for the first three years of your contract, subject to certain conditions. We'll subsequently renew that clause yearly, if our arrangement proves acceptable."

Velocity stared at her, still gripping the hardcopy tightly. Isra waited. After a moment, Velocity took a breath, and said, "Or?"

"Or I call in the liens on your ship. Take possession of the *Susan Calvin* and its cargo. If I do that, you're liable for all legal fees attached to such an action, as well as all the interest on the liens to date, which—and I have checked the valuation of your ship as of two hours ago—comes to several thousand RD higher than your ship is worth. If I call in the liens and take possession of the ship, you will owe me the difference. I have not yet accessed the list of the cargo in your hold. Is it sufficient to make up that difference?" This was the real threat, Velocity knew. Her skin burned with anger. "Yes?" Ikeda said. "Maybe? Well. One can hope."

"Or," Velocity said.

Ikeda lifted her eyebrows. "Did you think I would give you some other option? A way out? Why would I do that?"

Velocity swallowed, fighting panic. "Or: you return my crew. And you give me a trade license, and a sizable finder's fee. *And* you clear all these liens, immediately," she ripped the hardcopy viciously in half, "and my sergeant at arms doesn't gut your child like a fucking *trout* and toss her out our airlock." Ikeda went pale. Anger or fear: Velocity didn't know which. Maybe both. Her pupils were so wide the irises had almost vanished. "You know I have an uplink," Velocity said. "You know I just sent the order."

Ikeda shook her head. "You can't get a signal through our security."

"I have Pirian crew, you silk. They went through your code like rum through a deckhand." Velocity crushed the torn hardcopy into a ball and threw it at Ikeda, who flinched. "If I don't send the countermand in the next five minutes, you can start hatching a new heir."

In her head, the dagan said, *I'll remind you Brontë isn't on the ship. Also, I wouldn't kill her if she was.*

Oh, shut up. Don't you have an uplink to hack?

The silence in the atelier was total. Velocity could hear the laughter of garden boys, far off in the fish pond, perfect and distant. She could hear the clear vowels of their speech, and the splash of the weeds being hauled from the water. Somewhere further off, she heard the bright crack and thud of someone chopping through wood. It skipped, syncopated, with the thud of her own heart, as she and Isra stared at one another.

Captain, the dagan sent abruptly, and at almost the same moment, Isra Ikeda's eyes widened. She stood up out of the chair, her already pale skin going grey-white. Through the uplink, the dagan continued: *Override message just sent to Isra Ikeda Lopaka, provenance Torres Ikeda Alonzo 99% certainty. Message follows.*

What followed was a short capture, Brontë in restraints, on her knees in the midst of three tall, grim-faced Security officers. All were armed with Lopaka short rifles, and the one with his grip on the child's neck had his rifle drawn, though not actually pointed at Brontë. The child was not crying, but her expression was rigid, her mouth thin and hard. Her face was bruised around the mouth, and her nose was bleeding. She was clearly barely holding it together.

After a moment, Torres Ikeda Alonzo stepped into the capture. Looking directly into the feed, she said, "You are holding Hiro Ikeda Hayek. Release him to me, and I will return your child to you. Otherwise, I will do to her what you did to my wife. You have one hour."

The capture froze, stuttered, and began repeating. *End it,* Velocity sent, and the dagan broke the transmission. Isra was still standing, her eyes focused on nothing—focused on the capture, Velocity was sure. But while she watched, that gaze sharpened. "Captain Morel," Isra snapped.

"Wait," Velocity said. *Rida,* was what she was thinking. And, *Bad things happen in war.* Captain Morel had come through the atelier hatch almost before Isra had finished speaking. Velocity reached a hand out, as if she could stop him, and repeated, to Isra, "Wait. Hold on."

Isra ignored her. "Two full squads. Full armor, fully armed. Soonest."

"Yes, sir." Morel saluted and was gone.

"Doctor," Velocity said. "Hear me. One minute."

Isra swiped a hand, flat bladed at her, viciously impatient, and then drew herself up. "Fifteen seconds. Speak."

"If you run an invasion, Torres will kill Brontë. If you lose, she'll kill Theo. I'm a troubleshooter. Let me negotiate for you." Nine seconds, by her uplink, but she quit there.

Isra slashed her hand again, but paused and stood still, one long moment. Then she focused on Velocity. "Fine," she said. "Come along."

Chapter 24

Franklin Station, Freiheit, Republic Space

Brontë sat on the edge of the infirmary bunk, dizzy from whatever had been in the interrogation patch—she had peeled it off as soon as they had dumped her here, but the drugs were still thick in her blood. The two Ikeda Alonzo Security officers guarding her loitered near the hatchway, their heads bent together, talking tensely. Sabra would have torn strips off any Security under her command so lax on duty.

Moving with care, Brontë slid to her feet. Neither Security even glanced her way. When she padded toward the facility, just to her right, they did look up, but made no move to stop her. Inside, she washed her face, grimacing at the blood that had dried on her upper lip and chin, and at the dull pain of her bruises. She also drank a handful of water and examined her face in the mirror over the sink. Her pupils were wide. Not excessively wide. She repeated primes aloud, and had no trouble remembering them. Mentally alert enough, then. She flexed her jaw and spoke under her breath: "Are you there?"

Here. At least for now.

"Where's Adder? Is she all right?"

The Ikan16 is unharmed. She is restrained in a compartment 20 meters to your port.

"Sabra?" she muttered.

Another compartment, also restrained.

Mulling this over, Brontë bared her teeth at her reflection in the mirror. They were rimmed with blood. Repulsed, she sucked up another handful of water, swishing it through her teeth and spitting. Rust-red. Ick. "You can also speak to Sabra, yes?"

What do you have in mind? the dagan asked cautiously.

She was thinking of her mother, calling her *Little Mach.* Of the fond approval that always came into her voice when she said those words. She went to stand in the facility hatchway, watching the Security officers. "Torres has always been very…direct. Direct in her politics. Direct in what she says."

Direct in her tactics?

"An attack from her flank," Brontë said, "especially from someone like me, someone she doesn't consider a real threat, might succeed."

I will point out you are both unarmed and injured.

"Details."

The Ikeda Alonzo Security were huddled in conference near the infirmary entrance, gesturing and expostulating. Exaggerating her own weakness, Brontë hobbled toward them. They barely glanced at her, even when she drew close enough to be a threat. Which meant they didn't consider her a threat. Hiding her annoyance, Brontë spoke directly to the elder of the two, Officer Harawira according to her uniform tag. "You know I'm Elena Ikeda Verde."

Harawira did not react to this. Both she and the other officer, Ngata, had been with Brontë during her interrogation, and also when Torres sent that message to Isra. Remembering that message now, Brontë felt temper burn under her skin. She had been under the influence of the interrogation patch when Torres threatened to kill her—a threat aimed at her mother, really, she knew that even then—and the threat had not frightened her. Instead it had made her angry. Now, in memory, it made her even angrier. More than anything at this moment, she wanted to have her hands on Torres—not to kill her, but to hurt her. To hit her, to batter her, to make her *pay.*

Controlling this anger, she said to Harawira, "You know that I am the heir to the Primary Seat on the Ikeda House board. If you did not know that before, this is your formal notice of that fact." Harawira scowled, but Ngata was listening. Brontë spoke to her: "You took an oath to protect the House, the Combine, and its heirs. If you obey Torres, you are betraying that oath."

Ngata shook her head. "She's right."

"Shut up," Harawira snapped. "We have orders."

"Illegal orders," Ngata argued. "We're not even Ikeda Alonzo Security, not really. Anja had our contract. Why are we breaking our oath for some kotoran?"

Harawira scowled at Brontë, and hauled Ngata out into the corridor and downspin several meters, where they continued the argument in low hissing whispers. Sucking at her bruised lip, Brontë moved to stand in the hatchway. She looked up and down the corridor. Twenty meters to port would be…that door? Or that one. "Is Adder under guard?" she muttered in a bare whisper.

Stand by, the dagan said.

"What?"

Stand by, he repeated.

Down the corridor, the argument between Harawira and Ngata grew more heated. They were only a few steps from the hatchway that she had marked as possibly leading to the compartment holding Adder. *Little Bee*, the dagan said. *Your mother, Captain Wrachant, and a quarter squad of Ikeda House Security are on their way to your location.*

Brontë felt her muscles twitch. "What?"

You are to follow the Captain's lead. Do not act on your own.

"What's their plan? Are they going to negotiate?"

Follow orders.

The anger that was hot in her chest, hot at the back of her throat, blazed up hotter, blinding her briefly. When she answered, she spoke too loudly: "Tell me the plan!"

Harawira swung toward her. She stilled, clenching her fists. The

Security came toward her. "What was that?"

Brontë straightened her spine. "This is not a matter for debate," she said, in her mother's level, imperious voice. "You are sworn to my House and my Combine. You will take my orders." With barely a pause, she jerked her chin at the hatchway beyond Ngata. "Release my Security officers. Both of them."

Mzala, the dagan said in her ear. *This is not your role.*

"You have your orders," Brontë snapped at Harawira, who started to move toward the compartment which almost certainly held Adder—and then froze, and touched two fingers to the com button in her ear.

𝕃 ✝ 𝕩 𝕩

Right, the dagan said in her ear. *Time to go.*

Sabra lifted her head dubiously. Not only was she in restraints, the compartment was locked. One fish at a time, she told herself, and used the bulkhead to get to her feet. Once there she felt steady enough. The officer on watch was very junior, a young pup named Eddie Zhou. Eddie had duty here in her compartment most of the time, and from the start he'd been a talker, mostly about his family on Waikato and how he missed them, but also House gossip as well. It was from Eddie that she had learned about Anja's death, and how almost everyone among the Security thought someone among the ship's Security had done it.

He was young and badly trained, Eddie was, but he had potential. His real crime was his inability to classify her as an enemy. Sabra felt a twinge of guilt over what she was about to do. She quashed it firmly. "Eddie," she said, and he looked up from his handheld, his eyes widening with naive inquiry. "Come look at this," Sabra said, holding her palm out to him and nodding down at it.

Like the innocent he was, Eddie came traipsing over, his head bent to examine her open hand. She smacked it up into his face, knocking him backwards and hooking her heel around his legs at the same time, scything him off his feet. Using her open palm, now flat on his face, she drove his head down hard against the deck. The breath slammed out of him; the blow to his head dazed him. While he was still stunned, Sabra frisked him swiftly, found the key to her restraints, and had them off in seconds. She tucked the restraint key in her pocket.

"Hey," Eddie protested feebly. She wrapped the restraints around his wrists and sealed them. "Hey!"

"Quiet," she told him. "I don't want to hurt you." His eyes widened—shock now, not naiveté. He opened his mouth to protest again, and with a sigh she banged his head against the deck a little harder this time. She really didn't want to hurt him.

Leaving him dopey and still protesting on the deck, she started for the hatchway. "Is it locked?" she said, only barely aloud—the dagan had started talking to her about an hour ago, and she had learned quickly an inaudible mutter was enough.

One moment, the dagan said. And scarcely fifteen or twenty second later, Sabra heard the ka-thunk of the hatch lock sliding back. When she hauled at the grip, the hatch opened easily. "What about Security?" she muttered.

I've moved them elsewhere.

"Well, aren't you handy." Outside the hatch she looked both ways along the corridor. The dagan winked a light to her port, so she went that way. All along the corridors, the dagan flashed lights, guiding her at intersections and through hatchways, until they reached a hatch midway along a corridor. *Here*, the dagan said, and the lock thunked open. When Sabra opened the hatch she found Adder inside, alone, in restraints.

"Captain!" Adder struggled to her feet. "They've got Brontë! It's Torres; she thinks Dr. Ikeda killed her wife, she says she's going to kill Brontë *and* Mr. Theo!"

Sabra pulled out the restraint key and freed the cadet. "Where's Miss Brontë?"

"What?" Adder stared at her. "I don't—"

Sabra chopped down a hand to silence her; in her ear, the dagan said, *They are in the conference hall. We will need to hurry now.*

"They?" Sabra muttered, but wheeled and followed the trail of blinking lights at a swift trot.

$$\text{𝓩 ✝ 𝔁 𝓢}$$

The block of suites held by Torres Ikeda Alonzo had a koban at its gate, but the Security who staffed it were not as skilled in their ability to run searches as Isra's Security—or perhaps not as motivated. They didn't find Velocity's boot knife, never mind her Sima. Isra was as calm and unreadable as always; Theo more pale than usual, his young mouth set hard. "They can't come with you," the Ikeda Alonzo Captain said, past Isra at her quarter squad of Security.

"I will not enter the House of someone engaged in an active hostile takeover without my own dedicated Security," Isra said.

The Ikeda Alonzo Captain—Russell, by his name patch—stepped away, lowering his voice, and consulted someone via his earbud. After a moment, he returned. "You may bring two," he said.

He and Isra negotiated, settling at length on four. The other two were set to wait outside the gate. All three of the Ikeda Alonzo Security from the koban escorted them to the negotiation, leaving no one in the koban. Good thing their plan didn't involve a second wave assaulting the block, Velocity thought, only she must have sent it as well, because the dagan answered: *I'm holding that as our fallback position.*

And who will you use for this secondary assault force? Tai?

Isra's remaining Security. I can also probably hire a mercenary or two off the docks.

Ah. A last-ditch option, then.

On the other hand, the dagan said, *leaving no one on watch at the gate reveals much about Torres' relative strength. Brontë thought she might have hired more security, to supplement those she brought off the ship. That does not seem to be the case.*

Someone may have restricted Torres' access to her credit line.

Someone, the dagan mused. *Isra?*

It's what I would have done. The station will have extended her some credit, but that's bound to have been short, given the situation. She has probably long since reached its limit.

The conference room was small, being a rented commercial space. Its chairs and single oval table had been moved aside, lined up against the spinward wall. Facing them as they entered were Torres Ikeda Alonzo and four more Security, three ranged behind her and one holding Brontë on her knees, with the barrel of a Lopaka short rifle, an HJ16, slanted down toward the nape of her neck. "Stop there," Torres ordered.

Isra did. Velocity moved up to stand beside her. Captain Morel stood to Isra's other side. Russell flanked Morel, and the other Ikeda Alonzo Security who had accompanied them stood pointedly behind Theo and Isra. A little insulting, that, Velocity thought. Almost as if no one here considered her dangerous.

Torres looked exhausted and grim, her skin gone grey. Dark skin sagged under her eyes. "Isra," she said. "My dear aunt."

"We are here to negotiate," Isra said, pointedly adding no kinship term.

"My dear aunt," Torres repeated. "Neither of us are children. There is no negotiation. There is only these two dead, or me dead. I do not choose my own death."

Velocity stepped forward. "May I venture a guess," she said, "that you chose very little about this situation, Kas Ikeda Alonzo?"

Torres froze, her bruised gaze fixing on Velocity. Then she looked back at Isra. "Why have you brought this person?"

Isra opened a graceful palm, tipping it toward Velocity. "Our negotiator."

"Forgive me," Velocity said. "I've heard a great deal about you and Anja. It strikes me that someone—who, precisely, is beyond my competence—someone led Anja to believe the Primary Seat was within her reach. Then she convinced you. Or at least convinced you not to object."

The lines around Torres's mouth deepened.

"You don't want the Primary Seat. Dr. Ikeda doesn't want her nephew or her daughter killed. She also doesn't *want* to kill you." This last wasn't 100% true, but it was true enough to pass if this was a smart room—which likely it was not. Smart room tech was pricey.

"My aunt doesn't want me dead," Torres said, her words unsteady. "That's what she told you."

Velocity paused, never a good move in a negotiation. But Isra had told her no such thing, obviously. To hide her uncertainty, she spoke with more confidence than she felt: "Would Dr. Ikeda have hired a negotiator unless she hoped for a favorable outcome for everyone?"

Torres laughed savagely. She shoved aside the Security who was holding Brontë and seized the child herself, gripping her by the shoulder and one ear. Shaking her hard, she shouted at Velocity, or maybe at Ikeda, "Do you think Anja didn't tell me? She told me *everything!*"

Russell and Morel both tensed. Isra made a small motion, her hand held flat and level at her side, pushing downward in a small curve, and they went still again. Velocity did not think Torres, in her overwrought state, had seen this swift exchange, but she knew every Security officer in the room, on *both* sides of the room, had seen it.

Torres was breathing in ragged gasps. Her skin was flushed. "I know what you did," she told Isra, and shook Brontë again. "I know why you had to start the coup before you were ready."

"What is it you think you know?" Isra's voice was cool, almost idle, in contrast to Torres' raw, strangled words.

"Anja forced your hand. When she told you what we had learned—when she told you—" Torres shut up, with a sound almost like a sob. She shook her head. "I knew it was a mistake. I warned her. I knew you'd stop at nothing to shut her up."

"So you staged the hostile takeover," Isra said.

Torres' eyes widened. "What?"

"In self-defense, I'm sure you'll claim. Killing us, your aunts, your cousins, your uncles, to save your own life." Isra made a disgusted sound with her tongue.

"What are you talking about?" Torres demanded. "We didn't start the coup! That was you!"

"Please. My own child," Isra moved her chin at Brontë, "nearly died in the takeover. Would have died, if not for the heroism of her Security officer—the same Security officer you recently took prisoner, and have subjected to intensive interrogation. Yes?"

"Nearly died? Anja *is* dead! You killed her! You killed them all!"

"You know that isn't true. How would I have gained access to your ship, or your Security? Anja killed herself, when she realized how terribly she had failed. Your attempt to shift responsibility for her mistakes will only end in more needless death."

Velocity shot Isra a sidelong glance. She was no longer talking to Torres. She had not been for some time. Maybe since entering this room. Torres stared at Isra, her mouth open. She seemed, oddly enough, shocked.

With a certain amount of hopelessness, Velocity tried to seize control of the room: "We have an offer, Torres. Torres? Listen now. You release Elena. Release Elena, and recuse yourself from the line of inheritance. Isra will provide you with sufficient funding—we can negotiate the exact amount—as well as funding to buy transport out to a settlement planet. Neither party will make any attempt to contact the other in the future. We can all walk out of here."

Torres shook her head. She wet her lips, and then wet them again. "An offer," she muttered.

"A place to start," Velocity said. "Now you give us a counteroffer."

"A counteroffer." Torres gave an ugly, broken laugh. "Here's my counteroffer. I kill this brat, you kill me, my Security kills you, and Ikeda House can sink in its own rot. How's that?"

Isra drew a breath. Velocity tried to find something else to say, but before she could speak, Isra did: "Utu."

Brontë's eyes widened. Morel stepped forward easily, bringing up his TAC-20, and the dagan spoke in Velocity's ear: *Get Theo down.*

Velocity moved as she'd been trained to move, sliding down and sidelong, her straightened leg cutting across the back of Theo's knees. She caught him as he fell, rolled with him, pinned him to the deck. The room boiled; plasma weapons cracked and flashed. Sabra— where had Sabra come from? Why was Sabra here?—Sabra wrestled with Torres. Brontë fought the Ikeda Alonzo Security officer who had grabbed her. More plasma fire. Brontë's officer sprawled, her throat and jaw burned away, her eyes bulging with shock, and Adder tackled Brontë, pinning her to the deck.

Then nothing. Then silence. Velocity found she was gulping air as though she had been running. Into the sudden silence in the room, Morel shouted, *"Report!"*

No one replied. Then Sabra stood up, swiped at the blood on her face, and said, "Torres Ikeda Alonzo is cleared."

Adder stood as well, helping Brontë to her feet. "Elena Ikeda Verde is uninjured."

Morel looked wildly around. Isra, already on her feet as well, came over to Velocity and Theo. "All right here also," she said, already turning away. Her Security was taking weapons away from the few survivors of Torres' Security. "Go with my people," she told them. "And don't worry. We'll work this out."

As the Security were led away—Morel, Sabra, and Adder all stayed, Velocity noted—Isra made her way to Brontë, who gathered herself, standing straighter. "You did very well," Isra told her. Brontë, bruised about the face, head shaved, stared stonily back. Isra smiled and patted her shoulder. "Don't worry," she repeated. "We'll work it out."

"Dr. Ikeda," Velocity said, from where she stood by Theo. She didn't know who was more shaky, she or the young Primary Seat holder, but he was obviously trying harder to hide it. When Isra turned, Velocity locked her hands behind her back and lifted her chin. "Did you ever intend to negotiate?"

Isra smiled at her the way she had smiled at Brontë. "Negotiation would have been the better path," she said. "However, Torres was never going to take it."

Velocity clenched her fists behind her back. *This is why I hate the Combines*, she thought. *This.* Aloud, she said, speaking as evenly as she could, "One of my crewmen is still chained up somewhere in this block."

"Well, by all means," Isra said, "let's go set him free." She held out her hand toward the open hatchway, past the pile of bodies, past the swamps of blood.

Chapter 25

The *Susan Calvin*, En Route to Kaguya Hub, Republic Space (Two Months Later)

fterwatch Third, and the small familiar sounds of her ship hummed like a lullaby. Here in the Exchange, water rushed through covered streams, aerators bubbled in hatchery tanks, bees and other insects bumbled their busy routes among vines and plants and trees. Tethered by one ankle to a strut among the poppies, Velocity tracked a lacewing as it drifted on the air current from the vents, sailing toward the blueberries. Three jumps and more than ninety watches since they'd left Franklin Station, and she still had no idea how she'd let Isra talk her into this.

It had taken most of three watches, back there in the Ikeda Habitat on Franklin Station, to hammer out a deal all of them could live with. The first part had been simple: Velocity would take Brontë on board the *Susan Calvin*, along with Adder as Brontë's Security. Sabra would remain in Ikeda House, as Theo's Security—also as a hostage to Brontë's future behavior, although no one was saying *that* out loud.

Theo had wanted not just Sabra, but the three Ikan16s still on the station—Adder, Maggie, and Nora. Brontë had fought him over this: Sabra had been her dedicated Security since infancy and, nominally at least, she held the contracts of all the Ikan cadets. In the end, though, Isra had given Theo Sabra and two of the cadets, Maggie and

Nora. From what Velocity could tell, no one was happy about this compromise, least of all Adder.

Velocity herself wasn't entirely happy either. Brontë was second in line to the Primary Seat of one of the most powerful Combines in the Republic, even if she hadn't yet passed her qualifiers, and even if she was an heir in hiding. David Ikeda Ito, along with his daughter, had turned out to be not as dead as most had believed. To be specific, he had been in hiding among the Security on Anja's ship, and it had almost certainly been him or one of his agents who had killed Anja, though no one was admitting this.

This being the case, Isra had—not unreasonably—put strictures on where Velocity was allowed to take Brontë. For instance, Velocity was to limit their travel to the settlement planets, and specifically the settlement planets where Ikeda House had agencies large enough to command a Security regiment. To coax Velocity into accepting this constraint, Isra had granted her a five-year trade license, good for all stations where Ikeda-Verde Combine had an agency. "You may also, of course, continue your primary trade of troubleshooting," Isra had added, as if granting some favor.

Along with this, Isra was funding generous quarterly stipends to both Velocity and Brontë for as long as this arrangement lasted. In exchange, Velocity would oversee Brontë's education, and submit quarterly reports covering that and Brontë's health to Isra. In addition, Isra had supplied enough additional funding that Velocity had been able to fill her hold with trade goods, mostly wine, spices, chocolates, fine arts, and local agricultural products—seeds and cuttings for fruit trees not yet common in the settlement planets.

By any reasonable account, this was a workable arrangement. Trade profits would be higher on the Republic side of the Drift, while having a trade license would mean their bribes would be lower.

A fine plan. And not what they were doing. Instead of heading for the settlement planets, the *Susan Calvin* would set course across the Drift into Pirian space. This was Brontë's idea, though Velocity suspected the dagan had inveigled her into proposing the plan. (Brontë said not.) Brontë said she wanted to know more about Pirians. She said that if she was going to lead Ikeda-Verde Combine as it should be led, she needed to know about Pirian ships, their society, their wizards, and most vitally, their science.

All through the negotiations on Franklin Station, one point that had become clearer and clearer to Velocity had been how carefully Isra had worked to have a knife she could hold to each person's throat. Sabra was one knife she held to Brontë's throat; another was the genetic work that had been done on the child's germline. This genetic work was also the threat Isra meant to use with Theo, Velocity knew, though she had wondered, looking down the long conference table into Theo's impenetrable dark eyes, whether Isra would find the young man she had chosen as her puppet all that easy to control.

She knew that Isra counted on controlling Velocity in a number of ways—one being the liens that remained on the *Susan Calvin*. The fee which Ikeda House had paid for her services had been enough to clear just over forty percent of the debt against her ship. Velocity knew from experience how little good that would do, in the long run, even with the trade license and stipend.

The other leash Isra had on her was her claim that Velocity was another product of the Atlas Society's Calypso Project; and that her father had murdered her mother to cover up his involvement in that project, or else to cover up the fact that she and Alice were children of that project. Velocity had deliberately not taken Isra's bait and asked her what, exactly, she had meant by her hints.

Now, though, she thought again of all the times her father had told her and Alice the story of how their mother made him promise not to have their genome meddled with, even on the somatic level; how they had never been upgraded, not even for simple fixes like stronger bones or a better immune system; how their mother had made him promise, on her deathbed. What an odd request that was for anyone to make, when you thought about it. Also, wasn't it odd how often and how *vehemently* he had told them the story?

She also thought of Brontë, explaining angrily how the Atlas Society—how her own mother—had built a defect into her g-set, or at least not cared enough to keep it out. "It was more important to them to make me a genetic monster than to give me resistance to low-pressure sickness."

Every time Brontë told her this story, Velocity thought of how her own bones ached under gravity, or in the cold. She had always blamed this on the injuries she had suffered as a child, the broken bone in her hand, the green-stick fracture in her wrist. But all her bones hurt, her joints, her spine. Had her father, had those who had built her... had they made compromises, as Brontë's creators had? Allowed in undesirable traits so that they could include other traits, ones they thought more vital?

What traits would have been so important that her father would have allowed in a possibly debilitating bone disease? Velocity shook her head, rejecting this argument. Not her father. He would never have done that. He would never have done anything like that. Not to her. Not to Alice.

On the other hand, Velocity knew well that if any House was using this technology, all the Houses would have to use it. And she knew her father would have understood that as well. He was not a fool. *Which*, Velocity argued fiercely with herself, *doesn't mean he'd use his own children in the battle.*

Drifting in the Exchange, she covered her eyes with both hands, sick of arguing in circles. None of this speculation mattered. It was a question too vital to leave unanswered. She didn't have the scientific knowledge or equipment to analyze her own genome. But she knew a Pirian genetic engineer would have both. When they got out to Pirian space, if they got out to Pirian space, she would have her g-set run. Whatever Isra did or didn't have on her, she needed the facts.

Brontë, on the other hand—Velocity knew she had never considered whether her mother had told her the truth about her g-set.

She had simply accepted everything in those files, just she accepted the Combine society's judgment about what was in the files: that having been edited this way made her an aberration. A monster.

"That's not true," the dagan had told the child. This conversation had taken place while the ship had been heading out from Franklin Station at a quarter push, accelerating toward their first jump. Unable to sleep, the Combine child had left the cabin she now shared with Adder, and come down to the pit to do Indaiyi with the dagan—her perfect teacher, who never tired, was never grumpy, who never slept and was always patient. Her perfect parent. "Modifying zygotes on the germline level, if properly done, does not create aberrations. Quite the opposite."

"That's not what Republic science says." Brontë huddled in a knot on the deck of the pit.

"Your mother disagreed with the conclusions of that science," the dagan said peacefully. "Others from your Republic did as well. Perhaps you should wait to see what our science has to say and draw your own conclusions."

Despite all they had to gain, Velocity was still hesitant about crossing into Pirian space. Rida was sure they could keep Isra convinced that they were still on the Republic side of the Drift. But if Isra didn't have a web of spies lacing through the stations where IVC held agencies, Velocity would eat that precious trade license. Also, there was the sheer distance involved. Although she had previously taken the *Susan Calvin* as far into the Drift as Syaitan Station, Pirian-held space was several jumps further on than that—perhaps fifteen jumps further on, perhaps further. Everyone you talked to on the Free Trade stations had a different story to tell.

It was Rida that had convinced her. Well, Rida and Tai. Though physically Rida had recovered almost entirely from what had been done to him by Ikeda Alonzo Security, his recovery otherwise had been slower. "He doesn't blame you," Tai told Velocity, "he's just remembering things, about that school. Things he thought he'd forgotten."

Brooding, Velocity drifted weightless among the poppies and bees and lacewings, watching the screens via her uplink—one running an informational about the recent coup at Taveri-Bowers Combine (touched off by the rumor that a long-lost heir to the Taveri Primary Seat was returning), and the other showing Rida and Tai in their cabin, Tai with his arms wrapped tightly around Rida. Rida didn't have to blame her. Velocity blamed herself plenty. She had dragged him to the Core, she had sent him out into the station, she had let him fall into the hands of Torres, when she knew, better than anyone, what those who ran the Combines were capable of. If Rida needed to get out of the Republic in order to heal, out of the reach of the Combines, even if that meant leaping into the great unknown of Pirian-held territory, well, that was what they would do.

And, in any case, the dagan was also right. A Pirian education for Brontë Ikeda Verde, who might well one day inherit the Primary Seat of Ikeda House, could prove an excellent tactic.

Captain?

Velocity shut her eyes, repressing a surge of temper. The dagan had long since stopped pretending it was just a mechanical tool that could be switched on or off like the coffee machine, or be given commands like that machine either. Now it felt free to speak at any hour of any watch, either via her uplink or through the ship's systems. Velocity was still trying to decide how she felt about this—or rather, not how she felt, which was clear (edgy and occasionally even, as now, angry) but rather whether that response was rational.

Brontë argued the dagan was more than a mechanical, that it was a living being, even if it was a created one. *I'm created*, Brontë said, *does that make me not real?* Rida said she might be right. Velocity did her best not to dismiss these arguments out of hand. She was even reading the data files Rida collected for her, though this was mostly to indulge him. She didn't think artificial life was possible, for one thing. Second, even if artificial beings could exist, the Pirians, of all people, would not build or sell artificial beings as if they were property. That would be *entirely* adaiya.

However, if the dagan was just a tool, on the same level as a very smart toaster, then her anger was irrational. Who cared if your toaster listened in on your conversations with your bunkmate, or spied on you while you brooded among the poppies? She rubbed the spot over her eye, the little bump of scar left behind at the uplink injection site. *Did you need something?* she asked the dagan.

I thought you'd like to know—Brontë's in the galley.

It was the pit of Afterwatch. Everyone, and especially the children, should have been sleeping. But Brontë, like Rida, wasn't sleeping well. Nightmares were the least of it. Sighing, Velocity rolled into a ball and launched herself toward the Exchange lock. *Is she into the rum again?*

Just tea and honey so far.

Did you offer her a patch?

Medicating trauma is a short-term solution.

Velocity made a face. She swung down into the Exchange decom, sealed its hatch, and started up the cycle. Antifungal spray jetted out from its hundreds of valves. Velocity scrubbed it into her hair and all over her, and then did the same with the hot rinse that followed. *How far to jump?*

Just under nine hours.

A hot blast dried her, mostly. On the other side of decom, she finished drying with her shirt, pulled it on, and pulled on her leather leggings. Then she kicked up to the trail toward the galley. There, she found Brontë wedged into the booth, clutching a fiche of tea. Velocity brewed herself coffee, added a shot of brandy, and drifted over to the booth. "Can't sleep?"

Brontë didn't look up. "Don't act like Uri isn't telling you every single thing that happens," she said sullenly.

Uri. This was the dagan. Brontë had not only decided the dagan was a living being, she said it needed it a name and a gender. The dagan had ingenuously encouraged her in this deck rot. Between the two of them, they had chosen the name Uri for it. For *him*, as Brontë insisted.

"Well," Velocity said.

"Well, *what?*"

"Well, not every single thing."

"You're not even remotely funny."

"Is there anything I can help with?" Velocity said. Brontë lowered her head further, burying her face against her wrists. "Are you worried about Wolf and the rest?"

"No," Brontë said, her voice muffled. "Rida's got good data. We'll recover them."

Using their contract numbers, Rida had traced the three missing male Ikan16s through their labor agents, tracking them to Cholon Mining in the asteroid field off Strasbourg. Strasbourg was a settlement planet eight jumps from the Drift. Ikeda-Verde Combine had an agency on Strasbourg's main station, and Brontë had already, with Rida's help, sent a dispatch to this agency, with orders to locate the Ikans and buy out their contracts. The *Calvin* was on its way to Strasbourg now.

Velocity hooked an ankle around the booth brace and pulled herself down to the bench cater-cornered to Brontë. "What, then? Second thoughts about going out among the savage Pirians?"

The child did not react to this. Instead, she buried her chin further in her folded arms. The clarity of the bones under the skin of her wrists made Velocity notice how clearly all of her bones were showing: the bones of her face, those in her wrists, the knobby bones in her jaw and at her collar. She muttered something, too low and muffled to hear. "What?" Velocity said.

Lifting her mouth clear of her arms, Brontë enunciated: "This is exactly what she planned. Exactly what she wanted—me out here, in exile, Theo in the Primary Seat, and her behind him, pulling all the strings."

"Ah."

The child lifted her head slightly, scowling. "What's that supposed to mean?"

Velocity hesitated, and then said it anyway: "This message you received on Bastiat—the one you were sure Adder didn't send." Brontë went pale, lowering her eyes. "You thought it couldn't be from David, because he was dead. Only he's not dead. Do you still think he sent it?"

The child kept still, rigid with—was that anger or fear? Maybe both. Velocity breathed in the slow rhythms the dagan had taught her. The dagan had taught her that, too: how silence could be an effective weapon.

"I'm not an idiot," Brontë said, eventually. "I know who sent it." Velocity said nothing. "It doesn't mean she wanted me dead. That's not—" Brontë shut up, and then buried her mouth against her wrists again. This, Velocity finally understood, was at the root of the child's misery. This was why she was siphoning off rum, and not sleeping, and spending literally hours on the rowing machine. She had known, maybe all along, that the message came from her mother; and she had spent months trying to believe some explanation other than that her mother had set her up to be killed. "It doesn't have to mean that," she muttered.

"She sent you out to exile on this planet, Durbin. You didn't turn up there—instead, she started seeing funds being processed on Bastiat. Funds that looked like you were returning to the Core. Or worse, heading somewhere, to some planet or station, where she couldn't reach you."

"Moving out of her control," Brontë muttered. Velocity decided, again, that silence was the best tactic here. She let the child brood. "Worse than that," Brontë said eventually, "maybe she thought it wasn't me using the funds. She knew David wasn't dead. Maybe she thought I was his hostage. She sent the message about Theo being dead, thinking he would intercept it, not to draw me in, but to draw him in."

Velocity said nothing.

"Maybe David did intercept the message. Maybe he made sure Anja intercepted it too." Brontë brooded some more. "Maybe that's what my mother wanted. And maybe it didn't matter to her whether he brought me in as a hostage, or whether he had already killed me, or whether she was putting me at risk by telling him I was now heir to the Primary Seat. Maybe she thought it was worth the gamble."

"Those are interesting theories," Velocity said. "I don't hear evidence, though."

"I think my mother," Brontë stressed the word darkly, "has more eggs in her basket than me and Theo. I think she has lots of us, and lots of baskets. She does, and the Atlas Society does. They're testing prototypes. Their experimental prototypes. That's how engineering works, isn't it? You test your prototypes to failure."

Velocity hesitated, thinking of staying silent once again. Then she repeated, "Theories need to fit evidence. Does this one fit the evidence you have?"

"This is a Society that works in terms of centuries. Over hundreds of years. They're testing Theo there in the Primary Seat, and me out here among the savages. If we fail, they run another set." Brontë grimaced. "Who even knows if we're the first set they've tested, for that matter?"

Unbidden, from nowhere, Velocity found herself thinking of the night she had left her father's habitat. She remembered how she had dressed in the dark, and used the code she had stolen from her father's files to slip through the gates; how she had ridden the express lift out to the dock and met up with the ship's officer she'd been chatting up for half a month, in tea shops and via the nexus, who had sold her passage on her ship under an alias; how she had climbed aboard the ship and into the officer's bunk. How she had never once looked back, how never once had she even thought about her sister Alice.

She had spent no time thinking of how her actions would look to Alice, or what motives her sister might attribute to her—her sister, whose rooms she had shared, whose life she had shared, whose genes she had shared, for all the hours of her life up to that moment. Alice, who she had not once considered taking with her. Alice, who she had left to die in her place.

"Well?" Brontë demanded.

Through her uplink, the dagan mentioned to Velocity: *It's not the job of a teacher to supply answers. It's the job of a teacher to supply questions.*

Typical Pirian yap. Velocity sent a reply: *What if the teacher really is an idiot, though?*

Any teacher who is afraid to be an idiot, the dagan said primly, *will never teach anything worth learning.*

Aloud, to Brontë, Velocity said: "Drawing conclusions before you have sufficient evidence never works out well in the end."

Brontë snorted. "Here I am, in exile, dancing at the end of her strings. What other evidence do I need?"

"That assumes I'm working for your mother."

"For someone who isn't working for her, you're taking buckets of her money."

"Your mother took a salary from your Combine. From IVC. A substantial one. Was she working for them?"

"Are you saying she wasn't?" Brontë snorted again. "You know nothing about Combines."

"Do you think you're ready to hold the Primary Seat?"

The child scowled. "What does that have to do with anything?"

"Anja forced your mother to move far too soon. Theo himself isn't ready. He's a smart kid, and he's ruthless. With your mother's help, he might be able to hold that Seat. But he isn't ready, and she has to know you aren't either."

"My mother's help," Brontë said, as if thinking this through for the first time, "or Uncle David's."

"Your mother has worked for years to run that Combine. That doesn't mean you have to let her run you. Also," Velocity hesitated, but only fractionally, "you should consider whether you want the Primary Seat at all."

Captain, the dagan said, and there was no mistaking the urgency in its tone.

"I don't know who to trust anymore," Brontë muttered.

"Trust no one," Velocity said. "Believe nothing."

"Oh, ha ha ha."

Velocity smiled, memories of her father once again rising unbidden to her mind. If he had done as Isra said, edited her and Alice under instructions from the Atlas Society, in order to make them better candidates for the Taveri House Primary Seat, more ruthless, more lethal, it hadn't achieved his desired results, not so far as Velocity could see. Were they one of those failed sets Brontë was brooding over? Was the next generation of Calypso heirs growing up even now in Taveri House?

Brontë was frowning at her. She made her smile brighter and sharper. "Sorry, mzala. No shortcuts in life. You learn who to trust the same way you learn all the rest, by getting it wrong ten thousand times." The brandy in the mix of coffee was hot in her belly. "If you get lucky, the learning process won't be fatal."

This is not useful, the dagan said severely.

Not useful to you, maybe. People aren't puppets for your Pirian wizards to play with. Especially, Velocity added, *people on **my ship** are not your puppets.* "Your mother might have aimed you at that Seat. The dagan might be subverting you for its own reasons. But in the end, the path you choose is up to you."

Brontë frowned. "The dagan is subverting me?"

"Oh, not just you. It's a Pirian tool, remember? Its foremost directive is subversion."

Education is not subversion.

I know I'm an idiot, Velocity told it, *but I do eventually learn.*

Brontë studied her. "You know that, and you still keep him on your ship?"

"Well, I can't sell him," Velocity said piously. "He's an intelligent lifeform. That would be slavery."

Unamused, Brontë said, "You could abandon him, on some station. Like you were going to do with Sabra and me."

"I could. Maybe I still will. We'll have to see how much he annoys me."

Your sense of humor is truly adaiya, the dagan commented.

Just like me, Velocity agreed.

Brontë laced her fingers around her empty fiche. "Would you really do that?"

"Do you mean, would I really have left you and Sabra on that station?" Velocity kicked loose from the booth and snagged the child's fiche to put it in the sterilizer with her own. "If you don't plan to sleep, there's laundry needs doing."

Brontë's eyes widened in alarm. "That's—Rida is up for laundry this spin! I'm not, that's not, I'm not due for laundry duty for another twenty watches!"

"Work or sleep," Velocity said cheerily. "No skin off my neck which."

"You're not sleeping either," Brontë pointed out, and Velocity laughed. "So you have to do laundry too. That's only fair."

"This is a ship, not a democracy," Velocity told her, but when Brontë headed toward the laundry, she went too.

Acknowledgments

I want to thank everyone who helped me get this book right, including my writing group, and my excellent editor, Athena Andreadis, who fights on the front lines to make the science fiction world a better place. I'd also like to thank Kay Holt, for everything she has taught me about writing science fiction and being human. Thanks also to my chair, Cammie Sublette, who has been nothing short of stellar in her support for the writers in our department, especially me. Finally, as always, I couldn't have done this without the support of Mark Burgh, and the best kid in the world, Cooper Burgh.

About the Author

Raised in New Orleans, Kelly Jennings is a member and co-founder of the Boston Mountain Writers Group. Her short fiction has appeared in many venues, including *The Magazine of Fantasy & Science Fiction*, and the anthology *The Other Half of The Sky*. The story she published in that anthology, "Velocity's Ghost," was given an honorable mention in *The Year's Best Science Fiction 2014*. Her first novel, *Broken Slate*, was published in 2011. She is a member of the Science Fiction Writers of America.

9 781936 460830